PENGUIN BOOKS

The Yorkshire Ladies' Football Club

The Yorkshire Ladies' Football Club

GRACIE HART

PENGUIN BOOKS

PENGUIN BOOKS

UK | USA | Canada | Ireland | Australia
India | New Zealand | South Africa

Penguin Books, Penguin Random House UK,
One Embassy Gardens, 8 Viaduct Gardens, London SW11 7BW

penguin.co.uk
global.penguinrandomhouse.com

Penguin Random House UK

First published 2026
001

Set in 14/17pt Garamond Premier Pro
Typeset by Falcon Oast Graphic Art Ltd
Printed in Great Britain by Clays Ltd, Elcograf S.p.A.

The authorized representative in the EEA is Penguin Random House Ireland,
Morrison Chambers, 32 Nassau Street, Dublin D02 YH68

A CIP catalogue record for this book is available from the British Library

ISBN: 978–1–405–98318–1

Penguin Random House is committed to a sustainable future for our business, our readers and our planet. This book is made from Forest Stewardship Council® certified paper

FSC www.fsc.org MIX Paper FSC® C018179

This book is dedicated to all lovers of the wonderful game of football. Especially our wonderful Lionesses and, most importantly, those female players who, despite prejudices, play for their love of the game. Nettie Honeyball paved the way, and my hope is that all women grow to love the game that the FA once stopped us from playing.

Also, a huge thank you and love to my husband, Ronnie, for all his advice. Those years of being a football widow have finally come to fruition.

I

Bradford, West Yorkshire 1916

'All these men going to war, it makes no sense,' Hattie Braithwaite said as she clutched tightly to her husband's sleeve and followed him and her brother through the throng of soldiers, all dressed in khaki, with their loved ones gathered on the station platform. 'Haven't we lost enough men without the likes of you and my brother being conscripted?'

'It started as war fever, my love, but now everyone is hesitant, what with the war dragging on. It was inevitable that we would be caught in the conscription when it came into being. Besides, it is only right that we go and do our bit for this country of ours. We need to show Kaiser Bill that we won't let him get away with thinking he owns Europe. Besides, my love, both me and Oliver will be back before you know it, the war can't go on for ever.'

Bruce Braithwaite pushed his way through the crowds towards the carriage which he knew his and Oliver's battalion would travel in to the coast, where after some brief training they would be sent to fight at the front lines. He hadn't wanted to be drawn into the war, but both he and his brother-in-law felt that it was their duty as they watched and debated the number of men and even boys that were enlisting for King and Country from the streets of Bradford. Both would have been more than happy staying and working in the woollen and cotton mills in the textile town that was home, but they knew that their country needed them and they both knew what they had to do. Even though that was to change, the Government was short of men to fight their war, and as for munitions to kill the enemy, the cotton mills would soon be commandeered for the making of arms. Nobody and nowhere was safe from the raging war, not even the busy mills of Bradford; war was more important than weaving.

Hattie hung on to her husband as all three pushed past women crying and men hugging their loved ones and swearing that they would return as soon as they could, while lifting their children to kiss them lovingly before boarding the train. The platform was awash with hats and khaki uniforms, with flags waving and Bradford's brass band playing rousing songs to see off in good cheer their brave young men. Hattie felt her stomach churn as Bruce and Oliver stopped outside the door of their carriage and turned. Most of the street's men were aboard the train, and they all yelled and whooped as Bruce held Hattie tight in his arms.

'You'll look after Father, won't you? I'll send you both money when I can. You should be all right. Woollen mills are not as affected as the cotton mills, and you'll get a job making munitions, if the worst comes to the worst. Joshua Swainbank, your new boss, has promised me he will look after you. And don't worry about Ollie and me, we will keep our heads down and show them just what we Yorkshire men can really do when riled.'

Bruce held his young wife close to him and kissed her as his sergeant walked the platform, urging his men to get into the waiting train. As it built up steam to leave the station, the platform filled with white clouds, and the women cried and said their last farewells to the ones they loved.

'I'll be all right now, stop those tears. I'll be back before you know it.' Bruce wiped tears from Hattie's eyes and kissed her tenderly before climbing into the train. She was his wife of just a week and it was breaking his heart to leave her.

'Don't worry about us, Sis. We will cover each other's back. We always do. I'll give Jim and Bob your love, if I get to see them,' said seventeen-year-old Ollie as he held his sister close and kissed her. 'You just look after yourself. It's an adventure for us two. I never thought I'd be going to France. All those mademoiselles just waiting for me. And don't worry, I'll make sure Bruce doesn't give them a second look.'

Hattie hugged her brother. 'Just you behave yourself and come home to me. And no bringing a French lady back with you. She won't understand a word you are saying, anyway.' Hattie tried to smile as she held her youngest brother at arm's length then kissed him on the cheek before he too got into the train in his khaki serge uniform, with his gun over his shoulder, his young face peering through the window as both he and Bruce looked out. Both were pretending not to be frightened of going to war and leaving the only place they had ever known. Hattie had already been on the platform the previous week. Doing the same thing, waving off to war her two older brothers, Jim and Bob, and she had cried and prayed that they would return home safely to their wives and families. However, today, it was her husband and her youngest brother, both more precious to her than life itself, and she hung her head as she watched the train pull out of the station and wept openly with other women as they wrapped their shawls around themselves in protection against the unusually cold late-September wind.

'Well, lass, let's hope they will be back before Christmas. I can't see it myself. They promised that last year but it didn't come to pass.' An elderly woman put her arm through Hattie's as they walked up the steep slope from the station and stood on the cobbled streets looking around them both. 'These mills are going to be short of their menfolk. They are going to be reliant on us women, although they always have been if the truth be told.' The old woman caught her breath and looked at Hattie. 'Your fella gone to fight then? I've just seen my son off. Thank the Lord he's a single man with no family other than me to miss him, if the worst happens.' She put her hands in her pockets and gazed with interest at Hattie.

'Yes, my husband and my youngest brother. My two older brothers went last week, and there's only my father and me left at home now. The house is going to be quiet.' Hattie sighed and tried to stop the tears.

'No bairns then? Be thankful for that. You wouldn't want children without a father, and there will be plenty of them if the Kaiser has his way.'

Hattie shook her head. 'No, we have only been married a week. We wondered if we should because of the war, but our wedding had been planned for six months and we couldn't let everybody down.'

'Just as long as he hasn't left you, you know . . .' The old woman looked at Hattie's belly and then she clearly decided she needed to get home as she looked with pity at the young, dark-haired lass who was broken-hearted.

'No, I don't think so. We were both careful, both of us know that me being with child right now would just bring more heartache.' Hattie blushed. Things like that were never talked about at home, and she decided the old woman had found out enough about her. Besides, she had to get home to make her father's supper.

'Just as well, it would only be another mouth to feed, and life is hard enough. I'm going to get myself home now, you take care and try not to worry about your fella. He will be all right.'

'Yes, you take care,' Hattie replied and put her best foot forward to walk home the fastest way, following the steep cobbled streets on her way to the back-to-back mill house that she and her brothers had been brought up in. Passing mills and industries that made Bradford the town it was, she walked past the grey, grimy, workers' small houses where large families lived together cheek by jowl. She watched a group of young lads playing football on a piece of derelict land and smiled. Her brothers used to always put her in goal until she had proved to them one day that she could dribble and pass the ball better than any of them, despite being a girl. Those days were gone, she thought, as she walked up the steep hill past the tall chimneys of Swainbank and Gregson woollen mill, where she would soon be starting work – the first full-time job in her life after looking after her father and brothers since the death of her mother. Please let the mill keep going, she prayed to herself as she passed a deadly quiet cotton mill, with its windows wide open but not a sound coming from within. The noise of the jennies usually filled the air both day and night, but not now. Cotton had to be imported, and because of the war, supplies had nearly come to a stop. Some of the cotton mills were soon to start a new chapter in their history with munition-making machinery. The army needed men and shells, and her home town was going to supply both, whether the locals liked it or not, she thought, as she unfastened her shawl and walked into the family home in near darkness as night fell.

'So you are back! About time!' Burt Gilbert said sharply from his seat in front of the dying fire. 'I suppose those fools have gone to war like lambs to the slaughter. They'd not have got me if I were their age.'

Hattie said nothing as she lit the oil lamp that was in the centre of the table and tapered the wick, making the light flicker and reach into each corner of the small, humble mill cottage that was squashed back-to-back on Bradford's steep hillside.

'Yes, they have gone along with most of the men from Bradford and hereabouts. Did you not think of lighting the lamp and building up the fire instead of sitting in the gloom?' Hattie asked her father, and just for once wished that he would show her a little sympathy and compassion instead of thinking of himself and his own needs.

'Why should I do it myself when I have a dog to do it for me? One that has trailed out all day.' Burt looked hard at his daughter.

'Well, you are going to have to look after yourself a bit more once I'm at work next week. Either that or go hungry and cold,' Hattie said as she got from the pantry what was left of the loaf of bread she had baked that morning before her husband and brother had taken half in sandwiches for their journey to the barracks.

'Your mother would never have talked to me like that. You are my daughter, you've got to look after me and show some respect,' Burt growled as Hattie buttered the bread and pulled the already-filled kettle onto the fire.

'Aye, and look where that got her, Father! Dead before she was thirty, and us lot left without her. All I'm saying is that I can't be here and at the mill, now I've got to work. Perhaps you could do just a little more for yourself,' Hattie said and felt sick to her stomach. She never spoke to her father that way, but how he could not realise how she was feeling was beyond her. Her heart was breaking. All those that she loved were now gone from her world, and she was left with the most selfish man in the whole of Yorkshire, she thought, as she spread the dripping from the previous night's roast onto the bread and handed it to her father.

'Is this the best you can do? Bread and dripping! No wonder my back aches and my heart and head pound. That's not enough to feed a rat, let alone a grown man.' Burt reached out and bit into the bread and dripping. Hattie watched him, a man in his late sixties with all his problems, who clearly felt bereft to be left with just his daughter. He often said she didn't take after her mother; that she had a mouth on her and was stubborn and determined, and had too much spirit running through her veins and always had ever since she had been born. Now, she was going to work in the mill, and he'd be left in the house alone to fend for himself. He watched her standing next to the window and pulling the curtains on the night. It was going to be hard living with him as he entered his old age, but needs must, Hattie thought, as she went upstairs and left him to the sounds of her bedroom floorboards creaking above his head.

Left by the fire, Burt wondered if he should think about making the widow Betty Booth an offer of marriage. After all, she lived in a nicer part of Bradford. Anything would be better than living with his sulky daughter, and Betty was a wealthy widow. She could bake and he knew she was more than fond of him. Burt pushed his empty plate to one side. Aye, that's what he would do. His lass would learn respect then, when he wasn't there to keep her company just as the roof over her head was in danger.

Hattie sat on her bed, the bed that the previous night she had shared with her husband, Bruce. She picked up the pillow where he had laid his head and breathed in the scent of him. Please let him return home safe and sound, and let her brothers also be kept safe out of harm's way as they fight the dreaded Hun. She hugged the pillow tightly, cried into the cotton cover and rocked her body in despair. Downstairs, she heard her father yelling at her. He was always yelling at her and demanding that something get done. Well, he was just going to have to yell. She needed a brief moment to herself, no matter what his needs were. She lay back on her bed and looked up at the ceiling, which was aged and cracked, like the rest of the mill house, but it was her home, where she had lived all her life. The dream of moving out and starting a new life with Bruce had been shattered with the start of the war. She closed her eyes and remembered the happy days when Bruce, Oliver and she played football behind the back-to-back terraces in the ginnel. Her mother used to despair of her, saying nobody would marry a tomboy. But even in those young years, there had always been something between Bruce and her, just a long gaze and a knowing that they were the best of friends. Those were good times, times when she had no worries and life was easy. She put her hands over her ears as her father yelled her name again, and then she raised herself from her bed. She would have to see what he wanted if she was to live in peace. She was in no position to fall out with her father, now that all her support was in foreign lands. She was on her own!

2

It was Sunday morning, and Joshua Swainbank sat at his office desk and gazed out over the dark, threatening, rain-clad skies that hung over Bradford. They matched his mood and the look of the city, he thought, as he picked up the letter from the British Government. He looked at it, sighed, and read it again as he leaned back in his chair and listened to the sound of the church bells. They could be sounding the death knell of his firm if he did not do what the Government was asking of him. It was either convert to weaving khaki serge and pattern webbing for the troops or close the mill's doors, probably this time for good. He had no option if he was to keep his workers in employment, and every one of them depended on him for putting food on the table and a roof over their heads, as much as he did himself. This was not a good time to be a woollen mill owner; no wonder his partner, Patrick Gregson, had left him high and dry with his unpaid bills to pay. On top of that, the love of his life, his wife, had died earlier that year in childbirth, with the baby girl dying a day later; so not only was his business on its knees, but his whole life was one of despair and loss. Joshua looked at the piece of paper again and re-read every word. It could be the making of the mill, or it could break him. Either way, his heart was aching, and his head was spinning from grief and deceit. However, he couldn't let the people of Bradford down; they were the salt of the earth, and so many of the men who worked for him had been called up to fight a war that nobody wanted. All going willingly, thinking that they would be back by Christmas and that it would be an adventure. Joshua thought differently, and was every day reminded of when, while fighting in South Africa in the Second Boer War, he had found himself stabbed in the thigh, leaving him with muscle damage that made him lame in his left leg. Perhaps a blessing, he thought, else he would only have been made to fight again for his country. Instead, he had been given orders to make reels of woollen serge material, to be dyed khaki, and for new machines to be allowed in the factory to make pattern webbing, to make the attachments for the uniforms. After that, the cloth and webbing would have to be passed over to Higher Mill in Thornton to be made into a recognisable uniform.

He looked at the paper that included the instructions for Higher Mill and what was expected of them once it was out of his hands, and realised that he had the easier task in hand. He already had the looms and most of the machinery to do the job, unlike the mill in Thornton. He quickly glanced again and read their instructions and what was needed from Higher Mill.

The supply of thick woollen khaki tunics and trousers. The tunic to be supplied with two breast pockets for personal items and the soldier's AB64 pay book, two smaller pockets for other items, and an internal pocket sewn under the right flap of the lower tunic where first field dressing was kept. Rifle patches, to be sewn above the breast pocket, shoulder straps to be fastened on with brass buttons, with enough space for a brass regimental shoulder title, plus a clear shoulder space for the rank insignia. And that was just the uniform, there was another list of things that the fighting man needed to have: belt, braces, cartridge pouches, bayonet frog, water carrier, haversack and valise straps.

The more he read, the more thankful he was that

they had chosen his mill to be the weaver and webbing maker. There were not many machinery alterations needed, and no need to change any of his workforce. Perhaps he should be grateful and not feel as if he had been thrown into the abyss of war. There might even be hope of making money and giving new life to his business. At least he would be paid regularly by the Government; they would want to keep the lads on the front line clothed and ready for action. He stood up and walked over to the balcony where he could look down on the workings of the mill and lit a cigar, breathing in slowly, enjoying the smell and taste of a fresh cigar from his contact in Havana, and thought that it would probably be the last one he would be smoking for a while. A war stopped any pleasures. The jennies were quiet, and the mill was silent, eerily silent, too silent for him. It was letting memories of past years run through his mind; memories of when his father and grandfather were in charge, and the mill had been in full operation. The air was filled with dust and woollen fibres, and women and men filled all floors, carrying baskets of wool and lip-reading above the noise of the chattering machines. It was a place of wonder when he was a boy, and he always remembered his father standing in the very same spot as he was standing now, with his hand on his shoulder and saying with a break in his voice, 'One day, son, this will be all yours, but it takes work and endurance to keep it going.' How true those words had been. He had been so naive back then and thought that he would make changes, make everything ten times better and make more money than his grandparents and parents had ever made. It wasn't until his father had died and he inherited it that he realised it was a race of endurance, and although they lived a seemingly opulent life compared to some in Bradford, his father had been in hock to the bank and the bank owned a good part of the mill. That was when Patrick Gregson, a business colleague, who he had not known that well, had come to his aid and offered to become a partner in the failing mill. A bad day for both the mill and himself. After Patrick initially poured money into the mill, he was hard to work with; he had no experience in weaving and wanted a regular income from his investment, which was just not forthcoming. He also had no respect for his workers and regularly took advantage of any young woman who caught his eye. The mill had started to get a bad reputation, and Joshua wished he had never set eyes on his extravagant, over-sexed partner. Joshua put his hands in his pockets and sighed.

In the past, he had made plenty of mistakes that he was not proud of, but now he had to make a decision that might make or break the mill. He would agree to the War Ministry taking control of what they produced. The mill was needed by the fighting troops to clothe them, and he needed the work from the Ministry to keep his factory going. There was no option, he thought, as he put the letter that had to be replied to on the top of the pile for his secretary to action the following day, and swore under his breath. He'd make his way home, but before he did, he would partake of a quick pint in The Diplomat which stood just across the other side of Sunbridge Road. After all, he had nothing to return home for any more, just a large empty house with a maid who would be enjoying her Sunday afternoon back at her home. The company of the nearby pub was calling him. At least there would be some friendly faces and some banter to partake in, he thought, as he put his bowler hat on and pulled on his coat. He locked his office door and walked down the many sets of well-trodden wooden steps to reach the bottom of the mill and the large, solid doors of the entrance.

Above his head hung block and tackle to hoist bales of wool into the heart of the mill and he looked up as he heard the chain jangle, locking the mill doors behind him, and walked out onto Sunbridge Road. He nodded at couples and dodged the horse and gigs and the occasional motorcar as he crossed the street to his favourite pub, standing tall and regal straight across from the mill. Its stonework was blackened by the smoke and pollution from the mills, as were all the buildings, but inside, he was always guaranteed a warm welcome. A few pints and then he would return home to Grafton Road, where he would try to forget his problems and relax before starting work again at six the following morning.

Joshua walked in through the doors of The Diplomat. It was one of the grander pubs in Bradford, but it was still a working man's pub, and most drinkers were local to the area.

'Are you still working on a Sunday, Mr Swainbank? Is it a case of no peace for the wicked? Usual, is it?' the landlord asked as Joshua placed his hat on top of a table and made eye contact with a group of local men that usually frequented the pub on a Sunday afternoon, mostly to commentate upon the previous day's football matches by the two local teams.

'Aye, that will be grand, George.' Josh watched as the landlord poured him a pint of best bitter, and then he sat down in his usual seat and listened to the conversation around him.

'That new goalie at City has bloody butterfingers, he can't save nowt,' an elderly fella in a flat cap said and shook his head. 'The team have gone to hell since they won the FA Cup in 1911. It went to their heads.'

'Well, you should be supporting Bradford Park Avenue. It's more your local, it's only over the way. You want nowt trailing up on Manningham Lane. Now, the new goalie there is as hot as mustard. Since Park Avenue changed over from playing the game of rugby, I'd rather spend my time there. It's proper football they play with a right good manager.'

'Well, neither are up to much, half their teams have gone to war, it's only subs that are playing now. The poor buggers, I hope they all come back.' Both men shook their heads and took a long sip of their pints.

'It's a right rum do, hardly any football and none of this and none of that. They'll be stopping our pints before long. Then what excuse can I give to my old woman for not wanting to walk the dog any more on a Sunday afternoon?' The older of the two men looked down at his rough-haired terrier tied to a piece of string.

'There's a new striker at City, Powell, or Howell, I can't remember his name. He doesn't let the grass grow under his feet. Put one good and proper in the back of the net yesterday. Nowt was going to stop it,' said Richard, the owner of the flat cap, and shook his head.

'He strikes with his left foot and takes advantage of bad defence.' A woman's voice from behind a high-backed chair entered into the conversation, and both men looked at the tall, strong-built woman who stood up with an empty pint tankard in her hand. 'He's called Fred Howell, and he's a damn good goal getter. Focuses and scores, never flinches, no matter who kicks his shins.' She went and stood at the bar and gave a wry smile to the barman. 'Another pint and I'll have a packet of Senior Service, if you care.' Mags Fleming looked at the surprise on the two older men's faces as they looked her up and down. 'He's my cousin from Bradley, but City haven't got him long, he's just enlisted.'

'That's a bad do, he is one of the best strikers I've ever seen. It'll be a sad loss. I hope he gets to come back in one piece when this war is done,' the man with the terrier said as he took in Mags, dressed in men's boots, a long black skirt, a tight waistcoat over a white blouse and lighting a cigarette as she stood at the bar.

'He lives and breathes for football. He should never have enlisted, but he didn't have a lot of choice. Now the goalie at Park Lane should have enlisted, because he can't save bloody anything.' Mag leaned against the bar and supped half her pint in one gulp. She glanced over at Joshua and nodded at him. He was a toff, she could tell, probably preferred cricket and rugby to football.

'Do you not like football, mister? You've not had a lot to say.' Mags looked at Joshua and breathed out the smoke from her cigarette, clouding the bar with tobacco-filled air.

'I don't have time for it. But I don't mind it. I've no alliance to either club, so I can't comment.' Joshua sipped his pint and looked at the woman, who was drinking and smoking as good as any man.

'That's your loss then, it's what makes a Saturday. Standing in those stands shouting for your team. Especially after a hard week working in the bloody mill for next to nowt in pay.' Mags knew full well that she could be talking to a mill owner, especially when the two men who had been full of football knowledge nudged one another.

'So you work in one of our mills? Which one?' Josh asked and watched as the two other men turned their backs on her.

'I did up to Friday. Fairbanks, up in Esholt, but they've just closed their doors. After nearly a hundred years, they have had to close, because of this bloody war. Lord knows how I'm going to make a living. I'm desperate for a job. I can turn my hand to most things. Although I won't lower myself as some women do when desperate.'

Josh looked in a little bit of amazement at the woman, who swore, drank and smoked. 'What did you do at Fairbanks? It's a woollen mill, am I correct?'

'Aye, it is. We spun wool for carpets, coarse and rough work, but the best wool for carpets for miles around.' Mags spoke with pride. Even if she hadn't got paid that well, she had been proud of her job. 'Do you have a mill? Are you looking for workers, because as I say, I could do with a job.' Mags swilled her drink back and looked at the quiet, well-dressed man. He wouldn't take her on; she was half-cut, and she could tell what he thought of her just by the look on his face.

'I am, as it happens, I own the woollen mill across the road, Swainbank and Gregson, and I'm about to take on some extra work for the War Ministry.' Joshua smiled as she nearly choked on the last drop of her beer.

'Munitions, all the mills are stopping weaving and making munitions. I'll not be working in one of those, I'd blow my blinking self up.' Mags rubbed her mouth on her sleeve and decided it was time she staggered home out of Bradford.

'No, woollen serge for our brave lads to fight in and webbing for their belts and pouches.' Josh looked at her and smiled; he couldn't help but like the straight-talking lass. 'Come and see me in the morning, and I can perhaps find you a job with us. Six thirty, don't be late, or else I'll be putting out an advertisement on our notice board.'

'Bloody hell. Oops, sorry, sorry, it's the beer. I mean, thank you, sir, I'll be there at six thirty, Mr Gregson, sir.' Mags changed her demeanour.

'Six thirty and it's Mr Swainbank, and yours is?' Josh watched as she picked up a battered black hat from her chair and wandered over to the pub's doors.

'Maggie Fleming, sir, and you won't regret taking me on, not for a second, sir. I know I'm worse for wear now, but I'm a bloody good worker,' Maggie replied and held a hiccup in as she made for the doorway.

'Six thirty, tomorrow morning, Miss Fleming, and don't be late.' Josh watched as she disappeared.

'You're a brave'en to take that one on. She drinks, smokes and swears as good as any fella,' said the barman.

'Well, let's hope she works as good as any fella, as I'm short of them because of this war.' Joshua decided he'd had his fill of drink and entertainment for that Sunday. He would return home to his plate of cold meats for his Sunday dinner and hope that he would not live to regret taking on Mags Fleming.

3

It was still dark when Hattie closed the front door of number 2 Gladstone Street behind her. She was glad to get out of the house and away from her father, who did nothing but complain from the moment he got up until the minute he went to bed. He'd be moaning this morning when he had to look after himself, Hattie thought, as she walked quickly down into the centre of Bradford to her new work. She'd left him with bread and jam, and the kettle was filled. All he had to do was put it on the hob to boil, but he'd still moan. She had even backed up the coal fire to make sure the house was warm when he finally awoke, and left a mutton hash to slowly cook in the side oven, ready for the evening meal. What more could she do, if she had to work, she thought, as she turned the corner into Sunbridge Road and took a deep breath in. She knew the mill well; her brother and husband had both worked there, and she had often visited with messages and taken a snack for their breaks. But this morning was different; she was to start work there and line up with the row of women in their shawls and clogs and the few men who had not yet enlisted or who were too old to fight. It was still dark along the streets, but one by one, candles had been lit in homes, as they prepared for work, and the gas lights of the mills started to blaze as the sleepy city of Bradford woke up to life. The row of workers just shrugged their shoulders and nodded their heads to acknowledge her as she took her place in the line. She had seen Joshua Swainbank the previous week, and she had been told she was to work on the second floor at the carding machines, cleaning and pulling all the wool fibres into order before they were taken upstairs to be spun. It was a hard job and a mucky one with the lanolin from the wool attaching itself to everything with grease. She had hoped to be on one of the looms, but with having no experience and the women guarding their jobs there, she had not been lucky. It was a matter of learning from the bottom and hopefully working her way up to be at least a spinner or, hopefully, a weaver. As long as she was getting paid, she wasn't going to complain, although both Bruce and Oliver said they would send money home, and she was sure they would be true to their word.

'Now then, Hattie, is it your first day? Have them two fellas of yours got away? Bradford is without half its men at the moment; whole streets have gone, all pals together.' Winnie Mathews smiled as she turned around and looked at the lass she had known all her life. 'Where have you got a job at then? Are you with me? I'm blinking hoping so, I could do with another pair of hands, and I know we will get on grand.'

'No, I don't think I am. I've to go to the carding department. Mr Swainbank doesn't want me near the jennies. He said he was really short of carders,' Hattie replied and sighed.

'He's short of everybody at the moment, especially in the warehouse. I don't know how they are going to be able to take delivery of raw wool from up the Dales. There are only two men in the warehouse, when there used to be at least ten.' Winnie nudged Hattie, looking over at the aloof Maggie. She whispered, 'I don't ken her. Do you think she's got a job, or is she hoping to find work? She's an odd'en, that's for certain. I've just seen her spit a mouthful of tobacco. I wouldn't want to fall out with her, that's for sure.'

'I don't know who she is. Probably new like me, from one of the mills that have closed down. I just hope this one keeps going. I need the money.' Hattie looked at Maggie and wondered who she was, and if she would be working with her.

'Aye, we all need the brass. My lad's not sent a penny back since he went and fought on the front. In fact, I haven't heard from him for a week or two, but no telegram boy has knocked on my door either, thank heavens. It'd break my heart if I lost my Sid.'

Hattie thought of those she loved as she moved forward in the line and just hoped that her brothers and husband would be safe. The mill's doors were open now, and people pushed forward to get into their work. A minute late, and they would have their pay docked.

'If you are in the carding department, you'll be working under Sara Turner. She's all right, but you need to go upstairs to the offices first, get your instructions and your pay number. You'll know where it is, don't you?' Winnie asked as they approached the open doors of the warehouse and the stairs to all the flights of the four-storey mill.

'I do, but her in front of us doesn't by the look of it. Folk keep pushing past her. I'll take her upstairs with me. She must be a new starter or asking for a job.' Hattie stood and watched as Winnie walked past and started to climb the wooden stairs to the weaving room level. The noise within the mill was already deafening, with machinery being started and people shouting above it all.

'Aye, you take the lass under your wing, although she looks as if she can probably look after herself. No doubt I'll see you sometime in the day if you bring the wool up to me. Hope all goes well,' Winnie said loudly before she made her way to her work.

Hattie hesitated for a minute, but it was no place to stand as people pushed past her, and the mill's warning whistle blew, telling workers that they should be at their work if they wanted to be paid.

'First day?' Hattie said loudly to the woman who had caught her and Winnie's attention and who stood just inside the warehouse looking around her.

'I think so. All I know is that I have to see the owner. He promised me a job in the pub yesterday. Which in itself is a bit of a miracle, because I was half-cut after having a pint too many and was full of nonsense about football. He must be bloody desperate if he thought of taking me on in the state I was in.' Maggie smiled and looked at the young, good-looking woman who was the only one who had shown her the time of day.

'That would be Joshua Swainbank. He's the owner, and aye, he is a bit desperate for workers. Things are not that good at the moment, but at least he's keeping the mill going, doing what it's supposed to be doing. I'm new today as well, but my brother and husband used to work here; one down here in the warehouse and the other in the carding room where I'm to work. I've got to go up to the offices first, so come with me.' Hattie tugged on Maggie's sleeve and pointed upstairs. 'His office is right at the top, he's got a viewing platform to look down upon the weavers, so he's always about.'

'Is he all right to work for? My last boss was a real sod. If he could dock your pay, he would, and he never gave you the time of day. It's a good job t'mill closed, he wasn't liked, but you still have to pay your bills,' Maggie said as she followed Hattie up the stairs and looked at each department as they climbed to the top. 'It's a big enough spot, in't it?'

'My brother and husband always said he was all right, better than his partner, who disappeared last year. He was a devil for trying it on with the women who worked here. But Mr Swainbank is a gentleman, else my Bruce wouldn't let me work here.' Hattie climbed the last set of stairs that led to the upstairs glass-enclosed offices and the metal walkway where the workers down below could be watched.

'He'd only have to touch me the once and I'd bloody hit him. I'm not having any of that, I can tell you,' Maggie said in a gruff voice and shook her head. 'Boss or no boss.'

'You'll be all right. Here you are, this is Mrs Mason's office, she's his secretary. She's more to be watched than him, according to my Bruce and my brother. She's a bit of a snob. And the accountant, Jim Dowbiggin, if he can dock you a penny he will, so keep them both sweet.' Hattie stopped outside the main office door and knocked as loudly as she could upon it, and watched as Mary Mason got up from her seat.

'I expected you at least five minutes ago. It is expected when you first start a job at Swainbank's that you make sure you receive your instructions at least ten minutes before your work starts,' Mary Mason said sharply, looking at Hattie and then going back behind her desk.

'I'm sorry, I didn't know. I don't think I could have got here any earlier as the factory doors weren't open when I arrived,' Hattie said in a quiet voice.

'Oh, that will be because we've lost another of the warehouse managers to this blasted war. I will have to have a word with whoever Mr Swainbank has decided to put in charge down there.'

'It's my husband that you have lost from the warehouse. He used to always open the doors in the morning, and yes, he's gone to fight for his country,' Hattie said quietly and then looked at Maggie, realising that she did not know her name.

Mary Mason looked at Maggie over the top of her glasses. 'And who are you, may I ask? I know nothing about you.'

'I'm Maggie Fleming. Mr Swainbank saw me in the pub and said I had to report to him this morning, and he would probably give me a job. Thank you,' Maggie added in a defiant voice.

'A woman in the pub, on a Sunday! Really, I don't know what the world is coming to. I hope that you are not one of those suffragettes; we don't encourage them here. I sometimes wonder what gets into Mr Swainbank's head, but anyway, just wait there and I'll see if he can see you now.' Mary Mason got up from behind her desk. 'I'll come back to you, Hattie, in a minute.'

Maggie shook her head and looked at Hattie.

She had every sympathy with the suffragettes, but thought it best not to give her opinion as Mary came back and announced that Mr Swainbank was ready to see her now. Mary walked her into the office where Joshua Swainbank sat behind his leather desk, with his accountant in the opposite corner, waiting for her.

Mary Mason looked at Hattie. 'She's a strange one, but Mr Swainbank seemed glad that she had shown her face. So who am I to comment? Now, to get back to you. You need your clock-in card. This must be placed in the time machine every morning and evening when you finish your work. You'll be docked a penny for every five minutes that you are late. You are to work in the carding department. No jewellery is allowed to be worn at work apart from your wedding ring. Sara Turner is your overseer; you must do as she instructs.' Mary Mason sighed. 'I don't know why I'm telling you all this, you'll know it better than I do, probably, seeing as your family have always worked here. Follow them and you'll not go far wrong. Now, get a move on. Sara will be waiting for you, and I'm sure you have heard that she's not got a lot of patience, although always fair.'

'Thank you.' Hattie picked up her list of rules and her clocking-in card and quickly glanced through

Joshua Swainbank's window. Maggie was standing in front of him as he interviewed her, and Hattie hoped that all would go well for her as she left the upstairs offices and rushed down the stairs to the wool carding floor.

The noise was intense as she walked across the wooden floor and felt the vibration through her body from the carding machines. All around her were machines with rollers and belts turning as the raw wool was fed into each machine to be made clear of any burrs or matter that should not be in the wool, and then detangled, cleaned and combed on large rollers with spokes on them to make a continuous flow of clean wool, called a silver. The air was filled with dust and wool fibres, and Hattie watched as the latter floated upwards towards the windows, like fairies bidding an escape from the industrial scene. Men were carrying bales of raw wool up from the warehouse and piling them up next to the carding machine, while other workers took baskets of silver that were ready for spinning into cloth to a pulley lift at the side of the mill to be taken up to the spinning gallery.

'Don't just stand there gawping, Hattie Braithwaite, you're not paid to do that. Come and start working at this carder,' Sara Turner, a large lady with a rosy face and greying hair, shouted at the top of her voice. 'I'll stay with you for an hour or two, and then I'll leave you to it. If you're anything like your brother, you'll soon get the hang of it.'

Hattie walked over to Sara and followed her to a carding machine, where Sara picked up an untreated fleece and fed it into the machine, hoping that she was doing everything correctly.

'You need to check the fleece before you feed it in, look for any leaves or twigs and pull them out, or the silver will not be worth anything,' Sara shouted above the noise as she passed Hattie a lanolin-filled fleece and watched her inspect it. 'Then feed it into that tray, and the rollers will pick it up and organise the clumps and fibres into the same length, carding it so it is ready to be taken upstairs. Mind you don't catch any of your clothes or fingers in the belts and pulleys. I don't want to be wiping bits of you off the floor or spoiling a bale of wool.'

Hattie just nodded her head and followed Sara's instructions. She could hardly hear her above the noise, and the heat of the mill was nearly unbearable as she concentrated on the job in hand.

'You'll get used to the noise and heat, but you'll

need to be a bit quicker at inspecting your fleece. It'll come with time.' Sara smiled and stepped back as she watched the new girl. 'If anything goes wrong with the carder, there's an emergency button here, but only use it if it is an emergency. Time's money, and money is what we all need at the moment, including the boss upstairs.' Sara patted the new girl on her back and stood and watched. She hopefully would have no problem with her, she had seen her visiting her brothers often enough, and he in turn would have told her the workings of the mill. All the mill needed now was some secure work, and then they would weather the storm that the war had dragged them into.

Hattie watched as the rollers took the fleece, combed it, straightened it and made a perfect continuous flow of fine wool that emerged from the other end of the machine to fall into a wicker basket to be taken to be spun. The machine had taken all the work out of hand carding between spiked combs that had taken hours back in the day. It was an amazing machine, but even after her first fleece, she knew she was going to go home tired and shattered each day. Life was going to be a lot harder now, both at home and at work. It was going to be all work and no play.

*

Maggie stood in the large warehouse on the bottom floor of the mill. She'd been given a job unloading the fleeces, despite telling Joshua Swainbank that she was a weaver in her previous job. She stood at the warehouse bay and looked at the two men with whom she had to work. They were sniggering and whispering as they watched a horse and cart pull up with a new delivery of woollen fleeces.

'Right, you bastards, are we going to unload this or are you going to gossip about me all day?' Maggie said and swore at them as she shouted at the cart driver to draw up a bit closer. She meant to start as she was going to carry on, and she was as good as any man, as they were soon to find out.

'You can't talk to us like that, you've only just started,' Bob replied, taken aback. No woman had ever called him that before.

'Then stop yacking about me and let's get some work done. I don't want to be down here in the warehouse, but that's where I've been placed. So put up with me or go and complain about me.' Maggie stood with her hands on her hips as the carter below called for the loading hook to be lowered.

'Right then, I think we all know where we stand. It's just that we have never had a woman working in the warehouse before,' Bob's mate said and looked her up and down. 'Haven't I seen you in the stands at Bradford City? I'm sure I've seen you at the match, now I think about it.'

'I'm Fred Howell's cousin, the new deadly striker there, not that it should make any difference to you. But I could get you a ticket for this weekend's game,' Mags winked.

'That would be grand, at the centre line? Bob, you come with me.'

'I'll see. Now come on, let's get this wagon unloaded, else there will be hell to pay. And let's at least see what you are made of, Maggie Fleming. I'll have no peace all day now he knows you are related to Fred Howell. Football mad, he is. That's all I need!' Bob moaned.

'Aye, a free ticket will be grand and take no notice of windbag Bob, he doesn't know a rugby ball from a football. Fred Howell's cousin, bloody hell, we are going to have some right good chats.' Len nodded his head and helped Bob with the winch.

Maggie smiled. She was going to fit in all right, that was until a weaving job became available, and then she would leave the warehouse and go where she truly belonged, weaving tweed and serge.

*

Every inch of Hattie's body ached as she made her way back home. She had walked to work in the dark, and she was returning in the falling dark as she turned the corner into Gladstone Street. At least supper was made, and the house should be warm and welcoming, she thought, her shawl falling from her shoulders as she opened the door. Instead, as she entered the dark hallway, she realised that the lamps weren't lit and the house felt cold and there was no smell of the stew she had prepared and put into the side oven.

'Father, I'm back. Did you not think of lighting the gas lights?' Hattie cried as she hung her shawl up and lit the gas light with the matches that were kept on the table in the hallway, and made her way into the kitchen.

There was a faint glow from the dying embers of the unattended fire, but no sign of her father.

'Dad? Dad, where are you?' Hattie shouted at the bottom of the stairs, but there was no answer. She returned to the kitchen table and lit the brass lamp, altering the wick as the flame jumped up, showing that the kitchen was empty.

She picked the lamp up and made her way up the stairs, checking the two bedrooms. Then returned downstairs to look into the small front room, reserved for best and visitors. But there was no sign of Burt. Returning to the kitchen, she reached for some dried kindling from the hearth and riddled the ashes of the fire with them until they took hold and started to burn, and then she carefully added lumps of coal from the unused coal scuttle until a good blaze started burning.

There was no sign of Burt, and it seemed he hadn't been in the house for some time. She opened the oven beside the fire and looked at the mutton hash she had prepared earlier that morning and had looked forward to eating. It was stone cold and the fire hadn't been tended to all day. Wherever Burt was, he had gone early.

'What is the old ungrateful devil up to?' she wondered as she sat with her head in her hands, wondering what else was going to be thrown at her. Nothing was right in her world, and she could see no end to her worries.

4

Joshua sat at his desk and looked at the letter that had come from the British Army Council. He sat back and sighed. It was partly good news, but he would have liked to have secured all the contracts that the Government had offered him. Still, the making of the serge for uniforms would be better than nothing. He shook his head and read that the webbing was to be made by The Mills Equipment Company in America, as they had come up with a design for woven cotton webbing that protected and helped the soldier carry his Lee–Enfield rifle. Keeping our American cousins sweet, Josh thought, as he put the letter down and decided how to go about telling his workers that they were going to be helping with the war effort.

'Well, Mrs Mason, it seems that we are to start making khaki serge for our lads on the front line, so I think we should make an announcement and tell the workers. It will give them a purpose and give them pride to be helping our menfolk on the front line.' Josh stood in front of his secretary and passed her the confirmatory letter.

'Oh, so we are not to make the webbing? The Yanks have got that, I see,' Mary Mason read and looked up at her boss.

'Good, it would mean us investing in new machinery and we haven't got the room, the skills or the money,' Josh's accountant said, and then went back to looking at his figures that he had been trying to balance.

'Aye, I must admit, I'm not going to lose sleep over that part. We will have enough work with making the cloth. It's been a while since we made serge, but it's similar to worsted, only two up and two down with its weave. All our machines can manage it and the weavers. Our lads are going to be dressed for the job if nothing else. It's the most durable material there is.' Josh stood and looked down upon the weaving machines below. 'Type me a notice, please, for every department, telling them from next week we are part of this country's war effort and that the cloth that we will be making is to be taken to Higher Mill at Thornton, to be made into uniforms. That we should be proud of ourselves. With a bit of luck, this work will save the mill and make jobs more secure. I shouldn't say it, but thank God for this bloody war.' Josh breathed out loudly.

'Aye, sir, don't say that. Think of what you are saying. All those lads that might never come home. It's already gone on longer than anybody expected. They were all told that they would be home by Christmas, and that was a year ago. All those lives already lost and still more to go.' Mary pulled her typewriter towards her and filled it with a sheet of blank paper.

'I shouldn't have said that, I know, but I'm just thankful we have secured the contract. Perhaps this will mean our luck is changing. We need it to, especially after that useless partner of mine left us in such dire straits.' Josh hung his head. He blamed himself for being taken in by the sharp-talking faker.

'Now, you must not blame yourself for Mr Gregson's weakness. We were all fooled, including that silly Madge Brunskill that he ran off with. I bet he's left her high and dry, once he had his way.' Mary Mason shook her head. 'Onwards and upwards, that's what I say.'

'Indeed, Mrs Mason, onwards and upwards. Let

us hope this contract is the making of us,' Josh replied and hoped that it would be, as his accountant gave him a telling look which he tried to ignore.

Word quickly spread around the mill that they were to make cloth for the uniforms of British soldiers fighting on the front line. A steady trickle of workers went and read the notices that were pinned up at the top of each stairs, and the overseers of the looms had been in meetings all morning with Joshua.

Hattie stood next to Sara Turner. It was nearly her dinnertime and she needed some fresh air, air that was free of the relentless smell and dust from the woollen fleeces. She was looking forward to her slice of bread and cheese that was wrapped up in grease-proof paper next to the carding machine and had been tempting her for the last hour.

'Will making army serge make any difference to us down here?' Hattie asked above the noise as Sara told her about what was on the poster.

'No, not a bit, it's them that will be dyeing it and the weavers upstairs. They'll have to alter how their looms work, but don't ask me how. My job is in here, carding. It's good news, though, it keeps us all in work and clothes our men. Serge is a rough material, but warm and durable. Mr Swainbank has done well to get that contract. He's a good man, just like his father.' Sara looked at the clock on the wall and then watched as Hattie fed another cleaned fleece into the carding tray and then watched as it made its way through rollers and brushes until it came out silky and pliable.

'It's your dinner time, go and get your food and then be back by one. I'll take over your machine until you are back,' Sara said over the noise of the machine and saw the thankful look on Hattie's face. 'Ready for your dinner, are you? It's hard work being at these machines.'

'It has been every day since I started here. I've gone home shattered; the work never stops.' Hattie faked a smile. 'But I'm grateful I've got a job, and now knowing I could be helping my Bruce and Ollie makes it all the more important.' She reached for her cheese and bread and let Sara take over from her as she decided to head downstairs and sit in one of the loading bays at the back of the mill. There, in the cobbled yard, there was a little peace, and most of the workers ate their lunch away from their work, given the chance. She needed five minutes to herself. Worries weighed heavily on her shoulders, and she hadn't heard from either her brother or husband since they had left, although she realised that she was being too optimistic and that they had not been gone long. But even more worrying was the disappearance of her father. It wasn't unusual for him to stay a night or two with his old cronies, but he had been gone longer this time. She had asked neighbours if they had seen him and even thought about going to report him missing to the local police. That was until she realised that nearly all the savings her husband and brother had put aside in the old biscuit tin on top of the fireplace had gone. Plus his best suit and tobacco jar. Her heart had missed a beat when she had gone to the tin that held the precious savings, only to find it empty. With tears streaming down her face and her stomach churning she had run upstairs into her father's bedroom only to find his clothes gone. He had obviously decided to move out and leave her high and dry, but to where? He would not walk out of the family home without a reason. He might be hard to live with, but he was her father, and she needed to know if he was all right and safe. And she needed to know if he was coming back, especially with the rent being due on Friday and her with no means to pay it.

She couldn't lie, she had enjoyed the peace of not having him moaning at her all the time, but now he had left her with money worries and with only herself to pay bills until hopefully her husband sent her some money. He had promised that once the army had started giving him his allotted pay of a shilling a day, five shillings would be sent to help with the rent. The first payment couldn't come quickly enough, as the rent alone was four shillings a week, and her landlord would not wait for ever. She would have to go and queue up at the Post Office and see if the Separation Allowance that Bruce had through the army pay panel had been sent to her. She would go on her Friday dinner break and hope that it would be there for her, she thought, as she bit into her cheese and bread and looked at a battered leather football left in the corner of the yard. One that the mill hands had played with in their spare time.

'You've had the same idea as me. A bit of peace, if you can call it that, with the sound of the machines inside this hellhole.' Maggie Fleming looked down upon the blonde-haired young woman she recognised from her first day as she sat down next to her on the loading bay and took her lunch out of a clean, spotted handkerchief. 'I'm blinking starving.

This growler has been tempting me all morning, but we have been that damn busy.' Maggie took up the pork pie, locally known as a growler, and bit into it. 'I could just have done with some of my mother's home-made pickled onions to go with it, but never mind, you can't have everything.' Maggie smiled with her mouth full of pork pie which made Hattie's mouth water.

Hattie finished her cheese and bread and smiled. 'Are you all right? They took you on then?'

'Yes, I'm in the warehouse, filling in for another idiot that joined up to fight this bloody war,' Maggie said and licked some pork jelly from her lips.

'I think you'll find that the idiot, as you call him, is or was my husband. You must have his job. It will be hard work, but the two lads in there will be all right to work with. Bob and Len were always all right with my Bruce. Len, especially, they used to go and watch the football together. Bob thinks he owns the warehouse and can be a little bolshie.' Hattie watched as Maggie sidled up nearer and smiled as she wiped her mouth clean with a large handkerchief.

'Aye, I've won him round by offering to get him a ticket to watch the match on Saturday. It will be the last one my cousin plays in for a while. He's going to fight instead of playing his beloved game. Poor City, they are losing all their players. They will be struggling to make a team soon.' Maggie sighed and then glanced at Hattie. 'Sorry, football is in the family. I'd play myself if only they let women play. I don't suppose you are interested in it? You look too feminine to enjoy kicking somebody's shins and tackling somebody's ankles for the control of a bag of wind.'

'Oh, no, you couldn't be more wrong. I used to love a kickabout with my brother and husband. In fact, they used to always tease me that I played better than them. I was only just looking across at that old, worn ball over there in the corner of the yard. I bet both of them had a kick of it in their spare time.'

'That's what we should do when we have a few minutes to ourselves. Not that we will have, now we are being asked to work and make cloth for the army. But it would do us both good. All work and no play makes life a bit boring.' Maggie put her hand on Hattie's leg and patted it. 'It would be good for both of us. We'd get to know each other even better.'

'Yes, I'd like that. We could meet here each lunchtime, if you want. Just for a kick around.' Hattie looked at Maggie's hand and hoped that she would move it.

'Right, we will do that. Perhaps there are others that might join us, just for a laugh. After all, we need something to laugh about. There's not much joy in the world.' Maggie moved her hand and put it around Hattie's shoulders, and gave her a quick squeeze. 'I'll look forward to seeing you tomorrow. I'll ask Len to join us if he can, although Bob will have something to say about that.'

'Yes, I'll look forward to that, although we don't get long for lunch, and I don't want to cause any bother, what with just starting here. I know they are good at this mill compared to some in Bradford.' Hattie stood up and smiled at her newfound friend. 'One o'clock and my name is Hattie.'

'Aye, one o'clock and my name is Maggie, or Mags. I'll look forward to seeing you,' Maggie replied and grinned as she walked back inside the mill, her black skirt swishing around her legs and her clogs clattering as she nearly ran back to her work.

Hattie breathed in and put her hands in her pockets. At least she had found a new friend by starting work at Swainbank's Mill, but she was a bit different from her usual female friends.

The day went so quickly, and after saying goodbye to her fellow mill workers, Hattie felt a cloud of darkness and loneliness wrap around her as she opened the door to her now-empty home. The house used to be filled with the sounds of her husband and brothers' voices, and she used to love this time of day when she would have their much-needed dinner on the table waiting for them. She even had to admit that she was missing the moaning of her father. She hung her shawl up on the coat rack in the hallway and reached to light the gas light, but nearly jumped out of her skin as she heard a noise in the kitchen.

'Hello, hello,' Hattie shouted and got hold of an umbrella to fight off her intruder as she let the light fill the hallway and plucked up courage as she walked with intrepidity into the dark kitchen.

'Well, light the bloody lamp and then you can see it's me, you simpleton. I've just been resting my eyes before you returned home. You should lock the door when there's nobody here, not that there's anything worth stealing in this hole,' Hattie's father growled as he stretched his legs and moaned at his daughter as she exhaled and put the umbrella down.

'I thought you were a burglar, sitting in the dark and not saying anything! Where have you been and what are you doing back now?' Hattie said sharply as she reached for the oil lamp next to the fireplace and lit it up in the kitchen to reveal her father sitting in his usual chair.

'Now, that's no way to greet your father. I thought you'd be glad to see me. After all, I've heard that you've been asking where I was at, according to half the street, as I walked past the nosy old devils cleaning their steps this morning,' Burt said and lifted himself in the chair. 'Are you not going to get on and light the fire and make a brew? I've been sitting here since well past twelve, waiting for you.'

'I will in my own good time,' Hattie replied, kicking off her work clogs and sitting in a chair, then rubbing her feet. 'What are you doing here? I don't suppose you have brought the savings back that we had above the fireplace?'

'What savings? I knew nowt about any savings. You can't blame me for that.' Burt shook his head. 'I'm here to tell you that I'm going to be wed. I've decided to move in and wed Betty Booth, on Cromwell Street. We've been friends for a while now, and she needs a fella to keep her company, and I'm in need of being looked after, so it couldn't be better for us both.'

'You aren't! How can you? You haven't known her that long. I bet she's got brass, else you wouldn't be bothering with her, or she's all too willing to look after you. What's going to become of me? I'm going to be on my own?' Hattie slumped down in her chair. It was cold in the house, and she started to shiver with cold and worry.

'You'll be all right. You're working now and that husband of yours will not see you short. He'll send you nearly all his money, knowing him. Who would have been daft enough to leave a well-paid mill job to go and fight the Huns? You are a right pair,' Burt scoffed.

'He's fighting for his country, Father, and so far I haven't had a penny from him or our Oliver. You should be proud of both of them. I've nothing to pay the rent with and hardly a penny for food because of the savings being taken.' Hattie looked at her father, who stood up from his chair.

'Well, that's your problem now. I've nothing to do with this house now. You'll get paid at the mill tomorrow, if you last that long, so the rent will get paid. Right, I've told you my business and you needn't bother about me any more, not that you will have been any way. Never mind about the brew, I'll go home and get warm and fill my belly with Betty's cooking.' Burt stood over Hattie as she bowed her head and went quiet.

He stood for a second waiting for Hattie to reply, but she said nothing, holding her anger and worry back until she heard him walking out of the front door, leaving her in desperation and feeling bitter towards her uncaring father. He just didn't care about her.

The next morning's work was soon done. Friday was always going to be the highlight of the week, the one day when the morning did seem to go fast. It was pay day, in more ways than one, if there was money waiting for Hattie at the Post Office along with her pay for her work at the mill. Her pay would just cover the rent, but there would only be a few pennies left over for food, coal and oil for the lamps. She couldn't live without Bruce's Separation Allowance, so while she was lining up to be paid by the firm's accountant outside the main office door, she was praying at the same time that there would also be a payment for her waiting at the Post Office. She noticed Maggie further back in the queue and remembered that she had promised to meet her to play football in the small amount of time they had at their lunch break. She'd forgotten completely that she had to go to the Post Office two streets away to collect Bruce's pay.

'Hattie Braithwaite, Carding Room. Six shillings, nothing docked this week, keep it up,' the accountant said as she stepped near his desk and he passed her a brown envelope with payment details written on the outside.

Money! She had money! He had no idea how good that was, she thought, as she felt the coins within the envelope and put it safely into her apron's pocket.

Joshua Swainbank looked out of his office window and noticed his latest employee, and smiled at her as she walked past. He knew that she would need the pay, with her breadwinners fighting for their country. She was a bonny woman, and her husband Bruce must have felt heartbroken leaving her behind and joining up with his brother-in-law. He nodded his head at her when she caught his eye and then went back to placing his order for khaki-coloured dye.

'Hey up, you got paid?' Maggie caught Hattie's arm as she passed her and smiled. 'It'll be grand to have some brass in my pocket. I can go for a drink tonight. That is after I've trudged back home and paid my mother rent. Are you still all right for a kick-around? Len's looking forward to it; he used to play with your husband.'

'I don't know if I'll make it today, Maggie. I need to go to the Post Office. Hopefully, some of Bruce's pay will be waiting for me there. Otherwise, I haven't got much to live on or pay the rent with. My father's left me on my own. He says he's getting married to the blinking woman that he's only been friends with for a short while. He hardly contributed anything to the rent anyway, but he took what savings there were in the house, and now I'm going to struggle to pay it, living on my own.' Hattie didn't usually bring up her personal affairs, but she was stressed about the thought of having to ask if there was a payment for her at the Post Office.

'Oh, the old bugger. As if you haven't enough going on in your life,' Maggie said and scowled, and moved a bit further up the queue. 'Monday, we'll have a play on Monday. Don't worry, none of us is going anywhere.'

'Yes, Monday, that would be better. Thanks, I really need to know if there is a payment for me.' Hattie blushed.

'It's right, you do that and put your house in order. I understand, my mother's always wanting rent from off me, even though we own our own house.' Maggie looked with care at Hattie. 'See you Monday.'

'Yes, I'm looking forward to it,' Hattie replied and then made her way back down the stairway to her carding room, still feeling the precious pay in her pocket. It would go on the coal bill and rent, and hopefully, a penny or two left over for food. She held her breath and returned to her carding machine, glancing at the clock – nearly midday. Come twelve thirty, she would have to lift her skirts, run and pray there wasn't a queue at the Post Office, so her pay wouldn't be docked the following week.

Hattie looked at the efficient woman going through the many envelopes of soldiers' Separation Allowance and already knew what she was going to say.

'No, sorry, no payment here for you, Mrs Braithwaite. Perhaps next week. Sorry, but things are taking time now. There are so many new recruits.' The clerk behind the oak counter looked at her with sympathy.

'Never mind, I'm sure there will be some next week. I hope it will be backdated.' Hattie could feel the tears nearly welling up in her eyes. How was she going to manage in the coming days?

'Of course, Mrs Braithwaite. I'm sorry, it's just the numbers being processed, of that I'm sure. There are so many allowances to deal with, they can be delayed.'

The clerk tried not to look at the young woman on the other side of the counter, hoping that it was a case of the payment being late in being processed, and that nothing had happened to her husband, causing the payment to be stopped.

'Thank you, I'm sure it is. I'll see you next week.' Hattie held her head high and tried to look positive as she walked past other war wives, all of them hoping that there would be pay for them waiting from their loved ones.

5

Maggie Fleming looked back down at the smoke-covered city of Bradford, the skyline just visible in the smog and incoming darkness as she climbed away from the busy city out into the countryside and back to her family home at Esholt. It was a seven-mile walk each way, enough to tire the strongest person before even starting a day's work in the warehouse at Swainbank's. However, it paid for her keep, and it got her out of the village that she despised and away from her mother, who never gave her a minute's peace.

She heard her mother's voice nagging at her as she caught her breath and put her head down and tackled the miles ahead. 'What I've done to deserve a daughter like you? Why can't you be ladylike and settle down with a good man?' This was thrown at her every day, and she was getting weary of having to explain that she didn't know the answer to either and that her mother should be happy she was as she was. Tonight, however, her mother and father would be glad that she was coming home with some pay. When High Mill had closed, it had made half of the village unemployed, so she was glad when Joshua Swainbank had invited her to work for him. It had answered several of her prayers, despite the long walk to and from work. Her father worked at the newly built car factory for Nanson, Barker and Company, making an automobile called The Tiny. Tiny by name and tiny by nature was the pay, and everybody wondered how long the work would be there for. Cars, everyone said, were going to be the future, but this model was by no means selling fast. Her pay was needed, but Maggie dreamed of leaving home. She didn't fit in, she had never fitted in, not even when she was small. She always enjoyed playing with the boys rather than the girls, and her mother used to always chastise her for coming home with her ribbon missing from her hair, her knees scraped and her skirts ripped. Now, with work in Bradford, she felt even more compelled to leave home; Bradford had so much more to offer. No one looked at her twice if she partook in a pint of bitter and had a smoke, not like in Esholt. Everybody knew everybody, and if they didn't know it, they pretended to. She sighed as she stood on the hillside before dipping down into her home village. The lights were lit and smoke from the fires was in the air. It was not as polluted as the air above Bradford, and she knew she should be grateful that she lived in the countryside and out of the city, as she passed the church with a small bell tower, St Paul's, before turning onto Cunliffe Lane and home.

'It's about time you were home. I don't like you walking at this time of day. You go in the dark and you come back in the dark. It's not safe for a woman to be walking on her own all that way.' Maude Fleming stood with her hands on her hips and looked at her wayward daughter. 'I don't know why you couldn't get a job in service, there's always somebody wanted in the better-off homes around here.'

'Because I don't want to be some snobby family's lackey, that's why not, Mother,' Maggie said and took her shawl from around her shoulders. 'I like my new job and it gets me out of this village.'

Maude tutted and shook her head. 'You always were an awkward one, and you are not getting any better as you get older. There's some mutton hash keeping warm in the side oven. What's left is all yours, me and your father have had our fill.'

Maggie got hold of the tea-towel that her mother passed her and opened the side oven door. The smell of the mutton hash made her mouth water as she lifted the enamel dish out of the oven and started to spoon it out onto a plate. She lifted her head as the door opened and her father stepped in.

'Tha's back then! Has mother told you my news? I've just been to tell Ted. It's a good day for this family.' Maggie's father looked at her as she sat down and tucked into her much-awaited meal.

'No, she's not said anything. What's the news then?' Maggie asked with gravy running down her chin, looking up at Jack, her father.

'I've been promoted to foreman at Nanson's. The foreman has gone and signed up, and I was next in line, so I wasn't going to turn it down, not with the rate of pay they offered me. The extra two quid will make all the difference.' Jack puffed his chest out and took his pipe down from above the fireplace and lit it with a spill from the fire, sitting down next to the fire.

'You were bound to get it, my love. You've worked for them since the day they started making those machines. It was well overdue,' Maude said and stood behind her husband while Maggie soaked the excess gravy up with a slice of bread.

'There will hardly be anybody there, surely. Most of the young men have left. Are you all able to keep producing that piece of tin with wheels? It's only a bike pretending to be a car, from what I can see.' Maggie sat back and patted her stomach. She felt a whole lot better for having something to eat.

'That's just typical of you, our Maggie, you never can say anything positive. It shows how much interest you have in my work. Every car we make now has a shaft drive and a Dorman engine. They get up to fifty miles an hour under the right conditions, and they are good little cars. The industry is going from strength to strength, and you should be proud that this family is part of it,' Jack said sharply. 'It's always put food on the table when you were growing up.'

'Aye, you should be proud of your father.' Maude took the clean plate from under Maggie's nose and scowled at her. 'Have you been paid today, because I'll have your board and lodgings. Not that it'll be a lot, working in a mill's warehouse, being a woman and all.'

'I have. Perhaps you won't want as much now my father's been promoted. I could do with a bob or two more. I don't ask for a lot to keep. Now that I have to walk into Bradford every day, there are a few things

I'd like to buy from the shops there.' Maggie looked up at her mother, who put into force all the house rules.

But it was her father who replied. 'Nay, lass, you eat like a horse. I should be asking for more, not less, and you are not here to help as much as you used to be. I suppose you'll be going to watch the football match tomorrow, and I can't count on you to help me whitewash the pantry?' Jack growled.

'I don't eat that much and yes I'm going to the match. It's the last one that our Fred is playing in. He's going to war next week. I don't want to miss it, and I've promised to meet a lad from work. He's a City fan,' Maggie said and felt in her pocket for her wages.

'Oh, a lad, now that's news. Who is he? Does he have a good job? Do you like him?' Maude held her hand out for Maggie's wage and counted it, passing her two shillings and sixpence back to her.

'He works with me, Mother, we like football,' Maggie sighed. Her mother was always hoping for her to be married off. 'Is that all that you are letting me keep? Surely you could give me three shillings of my own money. I've worked long enough hours for it.'

'We've a house and home to run, which, the way you are going, you'll never know anything about. You are going to be an old maid, Maggie, if you are not careful.' Maude looked with disdain at her daughter.

'Better an old maid than married to somebody you don't love,' Maggie replied sharply and decided that she would make her way to her bedroom, out of the way of her mother's sharp tongue and her father's dark looks.

'Just you watch your manners towards your mother, girl. She's to be respected,' Jack growled as she walked past him to the safety of her own room to lie and listen to her parents talking about her in hushed voices. For five pennies, she would leave home, but she had nowhere to go.

Manningham Lane was thronged with Bradford City football fans, all sporting a flash of claret and gold and wrapped up in their coats, ready to watch their home team play at Valley Parade. Street hawkers were busy selling favours for fans to show their devotion to their team. Wooden rattles were heard above the voices of the many fans. Most of them had come to see the last game that Fred Howell would play before he left his beloved team. Everybody was talking about men's football being suspended due to the war. The newspaper sellers were shouting loud and clear about the decision to be taken by the board of the Football Association.

'Oh, bugger, I knew that it had to happen, but not yet. I suppose we have no lads left, and football is not important when there's a war raging,' Len said as Maggie picked up a copy of the newspaper, read the headlines and then passed it back to the seller.

'Oh, no, what am I going to do now. Saturday's football match is the only enjoyment I get. Life with no football is unthinkable.' Maggie sighed and then spotted Bradford's manager, Peter O'Rourke, standing at one of the gates and greeting some of the fans with a good, hearty slap on the back and words of thanks as they shook their heads in disbelief at the news. Bradford City had a loyal following, especially since they had won the FA Cup in 1911, giving the club and city some pride.

Maggie said nothing as she and Len, who had been waiting for her outside the Picture House on Manningham Lane, walked up to Peter O'Rourke and shook his hand.

'Now then, Mags, have you come to watch Fred? It is a sad day to think that it's his last one playing for us. You'll have seen that this could be the last day for all the team to be playing. Bloody Kaiser Bill has put a stop to everything, including football. I only hope all my lads will return home safe. I heard that Bob Torrance was missing in action last week. To think he was voted man of the match when we won the cup in 1911. It's a waste of good men.' Peter O'Rourke hung his head and then lifted it to look at Len. 'Who's this then? Can he play football? I'll be looking for some new players when this war is over,' he said, looking Len up and down.

'This is Len. I work with him at Swainbank's Mill. He loves his football, like me. I can't believe that they are stopping men's football.' Maggie shook her head and felt near tears. Then smiled at Len and Peter. 'We are going to have a kick about when we have time in the mill yard.'

'Are you any good, lad? Although I only take on the best, war or no war, I might not be that picky if half of them come back wounded. It's a pity Maggie here isn't a fella. She's got a good eye and touch, and even though she's in skirts, she can bloody run. I've seen her playing with Fred when she didn't know I was watching.'

'No, sir, I only like watching and playing a little. I'd

never think myself good enough to play for Bradford City,' Len replied and shook his head.

'Well, that's a pity, lad. We could have done with you once this war is over. Should you not be at the front, instead of some of my lads?'

Peter O'Rourke looked at Len, questioning why a fit-looking lad was standing in front of him when half of his team were probably lying dead or injured on some war-torn battlefield.

'I've got asthma, sir. I can't run that far without gasping for breath,' Len replied and glanced at Maggie, who looked surprised.

'I didn't know that, you've never said!' Maggie exclaimed.

'That's because you've only just started working with me and I've not had an attack this week, thank heavens. I sometimes think I'm going to die when I can't get my breath.' Len spoke sharply in his defence. He felt ashamed that everyone looked at him as a fit young man who wasn't doing his bit for his country.

'Fair dos, then, lad. Not everybody can do their bit on the front. You keep working at the mill and keep industry going. Now, do you have tickets for the match?' Peter asked and knew the answer as he nodded to the man on the turnstiles.

'No, I'm just going to buy two.' Maggie put her hand into her coat pocket, but knew and hoped that the manager would let them both in for nothing, as he usually did.

'Go on, get yourselves in and get a good spot on the halfway line. I'm not going to cry over missing two ticket sales to the likes of you, and this might be the last game Bradford and Sheffield United play. Bad times, bloody bad times.' Peter shook his head and shouted to the man on the turnstile. 'Let two in, Mike. This is Fred's cousin.'

'Aye, I know, she never misses a match,' he replied and patted Maggie on the back as he passed her two tickets and let her and Len into the ground. 'You could be witnessing a piece of history today, a sad piece of history, the last game played here. It's apt that it's a local derby. Let's hope that your cousin Fred shows those Sheffield Blades what Bradford is made of before he goes off to show them Germans some real steel.'

'Ta, I wish he wasn't going,' Maggie said as she took hold of her ticket and walked through the gate to the open wooden stands of the stadium. She felt a sadness in the pit of her stomach as she and Len made their way down the set of wooden stairs to the halfway line over the green turf that held Maggie's heart. What was she going to do without football and her cousin? she wondered, as they took their place standing near the touchline and was thankful that she wasn't standing behind the goals and looked around the football ground as it started to fill up with Bradford fans. The opposing fans, in the red and white colours of Sheffield United, were in good voice as they sang out across Valley Parade. There was no feeling like it when two opposing football teams played one another. There was no better feeling than being proud of her team, proud of her cousin and proud of her country. Trouble is, her country needed everything that she held dear to her, she thought, as she watched the two teams run out onto the pitch, to the cheers of the supporters. Bradford, sporting their usual colours of claret and amber stripes with white shorts and black stockings with a claret and amber cuff, looked fresh and eager to play.

'Here we go. Look, there's our Fred. He looks raring to go. Oh, I bet he wishes he wasn't leaving and that this wasn't his last game.' Maggie sighed and then shouted encouragement as the ref tossed the coin to determine which end teams played. 'Good, we have the home end. That will give Bradford the goals and more incentive,' Maggie said and held her breath as the first kick of the ball was made.

Roars of Huhh! No! and claims of bad tackles were heard throughout the crowd and ear-shattering yells of encouragement and praise when the ball was being played well, with everyone ready to share their view on the state of play as players passed, missed the ball and made dirty tackles.

'Hey up, here comes your Fred. Look at him run with that ball. Go on, pass it. No, it's not out of play, go for it, you idiot!' Len shouted and hung onto Maggie's arm in excitement. 'Yes, go on! Goal! He's bloody scored, Maggie!' Len leaped up from his seat and the whole of Valley Parade was filled with the noise of cheering, all up on their feet. Everyone was shouting Fred's name as he ran back to his position, knowing that he had done well for his club.

'I'm so proud of him being my cousin. I wish I could play like him.' Maggie turned to Len and grinned.

'But you are a woman, what would be the point of that?' Len looked at Maggie and couldn't understand why she should want to be a footballer.

'I'll show you when we have a play in the mill yard. I'll beat you hands down,' Maggie sniggered.

'I'm in no doubt you will,' Len replied, the crowd surging as Sheffield attempted to equalise. Maggie was different, not at all ladylike, but she was good company.

The end of the match came all too soon, and everyone stood and sang the National Anthem as the players retired to change and return to their everyday lives.

'Four–One to Bradford. Now that's a win! One that Fred can be proud of, seeing that he scored two of the goals. Do you want to meet him? He'll be coming out from over the other side of the ground when he's changed?' Maggie turned and asked Len as they walked up the stairs from their seats and made for the now-open turnstiles.

'Me, meet him? He'll not want to see me,' Len replied and felt his stomach churn at meeting a semi-professional football player.

'He might not have much time, but I want to see him and say goodbye. I'm not going to get to see him again before he goes to Catterick Garrison before being shipped to France, so come on, he won't mind.' Maggie walked off down the gradual incline of the street towards the back of the ground and sat down on a nearby wall. 'They won't be long; they never are, because half of them have to get back to their work. Not that I know most of them nowadays. Watch out for Jimmy Speirs. Poor devil, he's signed up and going with our Fred. It's a bit of a contrast from being the captain of the FA Cup-winning team in 1911.'

'It's going to rain. We are going to get soaked,' Len said and looked up at the dark clouds overhead, pulling his jacket collar up against the inclement September weather.

'Aye, and I've a long walk back to Esholt, but I'm still waiting for him. You go home if you are not bothered about meeting him,' Maggie said sharply.

'No, I want to meet him,' Len said quietly and then asked the question that had been on his mind all day. 'Do you fancy coming home for an hour or so with me? Or we could go for a drink?'

'No, I don't think so, Len. I'm going to get home, thank you. Hey up, they are out!' Maggie jumped off the wall and shouted at her handsome cousin.

'Freddie, over here. Don't go to the station yet.'

Len watched the captain of Bradford pat Fred on the shoulder and say his farewells as Maggie ran to the side of her cousin. Both men looked ordinary in their jackets and trousers and were no longer the stars they were on the pitch.

'Mags, I should have known you'd be waiting for me. I can only spare you a minute. My father will be waiting for me at the station, so I can't miss this train.' Fred Howell flashed a smile at his wayward cousin and then glanced at Len. 'Hey up, you've got a fella in tow. He must be a brave man,' Fred said with a wry grin.

'Just friends and we work together, Fred. This is Len. He works at Swainbank's, in the warehouse with me, and likes to watch Bradford.' Maggie pushed Len forward, who held out his hand to be shaken by the tall dark-haired man who always sported a small moustache that made him look slightly debonair.

'Nice to meet you, sir,' Len said and shook his hand.

'Forget about the sir, mate. I'm a weaver and a footballer, nowt fancy. But it's good to meet you. If you are a friend of our Maggie's you'll do for me.' Fred looked at his watch. 'I'm going to have to go, Maggie. Here, give me a hug and I promise I will write.'

Maggie stepped forward and wrapped her arms around her cousin. 'Keep your head down and come back to us. Don't be going too far with any heroics, because I know you'll be tempted. I just want you to come back in one piece,' she whispered in his ear.

'I promise I won't, but I might teach those Germans how to play football. You look after yourself, Maggie, and all the best to you, mate. Football has become a thing of the past,' Fred shouted sadly as he walked backwards and waved his last farewell to Maggie and Len.

'I hope he's wrong and I hope he survives the war,' Maggie said quietly and wiped away a tear.

6

Monday arrived all too soon for Hattie. She had managed to pay the rent when the owner of the terraced house knocked on her door, but had little left to live on. Her life had been turned upside down with her father leaving her nearly penniless. Now, all she thought about was where her next penny should be spent wisely. As well as praying every minute of the day that her husband Bruce and brother Oliver were safe. She had cancelled the knocker-upper and had sparingly used the milk that was delivered on Saturday morning. Now, as she hurried out of the house in near darkness to work, she hoped she would manage the day's tasks on the crust of bread and beef paste in her pocket. The work at the mill was hard; she was always on her feet, checking the carding machine and shouting to one of the carriers when the baskets were full enough to be taken above for spinning. Although she had seen everyone working in the mill before, she hadn't realised until now just how much effort it required. She could understand why her husband and brother were so exhausted every evening and now regretted chastising them for not doing jobs that needed doing around the house. To make matters worse, it would soon be the end of September, and lights and warmth would soon be needed even more. She only hoped that her payment from the front line would arrive by Friday, and that it would be backdated. If only she had received a letter from Bruce, it would have made her feel better. It was the not knowing where he was and if he was safe that troubled her most. She pulled her shawl around her. She was right, the seasons were changing, and soon cold winds would be blowing through the northern streets of Bradford.

She turned the corner and saw the lights were already lit at Swainbank's Mill and that the line of workers were slowly making their way into their daily toil. Walking briskly down the street, she could just make out the form of Maggie, not quite running but at the same time rushing to work, thinking that she was going to be late.

'Bloody hell, I thought I wasn't going to make it in time. I can't afford to have any of my pay docked.

I hardly have anything for myself as it is,' Maggie said and caught her breath as she lined up behind Hattie.

'I know. It's not the best paid of jobs, but at least it's work. I need the money too. I didn't get any separation payment from my husband this week, and so I'm trying to balance the books and run my home on just what I earn,' Hattie said quietly and moved forward, holding onto her clocking-in card as she reached the open doors of the mill.

'You need to tell my mother that; she takes nearly every penny from me,' Maggie replied and sighed. 'Times are hard, especially if you've been used to having a husband paying your way. Are you still all right for this dinner time? I'm really looking forward to it.' Both women shuffled nearer the factory doors and knew a hard day's work was awaiting them.

'Yes, it will take my mind off my worries,' Hattie replied and placed her card into the clocking-in machine, and noticed that the clock said five fifty-five a.m., just in time to get to the carding machine and get down to work. 'I'll see you in the yard at twelve thirty, twenty minutes having a play around, and ten minutes for dinner, that should do us both good.'

'Aye, it will. Now we had better get to it,' Maggie said and made her way into the warehouse.

The production of khaki serge was starting within the mill, giving all the staff a new purpose. It was good to know they were helping with the war effort as all departments prepared the wool, dyed it and spun it before sending it on its way to Higher Mill in Thornton.

'I don't think we have been as busy for a long time,' Sara Turner said as she summoned a worker to collect the combed wool to be taken up above to be spun. 'I'll be going home absolutely jiggered tonight. I hope my lass will have some supper ready and waiting for me.' She walked over to the neighbouring carding machine and adjusted one of the combs that seemed to be causing problems for Anne Birtwistle, the woman who worked the carder next to Hattie. Her voice was hardly heard above the busy machinery.

Hattie could only think about how much she would like to go back to a ready-cooked meal and a warm, welcoming home. Instead, that evening she would be going home to a cold house. She had not lit the fire that morning, and as for supper, it would be one of the make-do variety. She would probably boil the one egg that she had in the small larder.

Sara came back to her side after fixing the comb

that was causing the problem. 'At least your father is still with you. He'll be waiting for you when you get home. Else it would be a lonely life with both your husband and brother at war.' Sara smiled. Her new apprentice was learning quickly and didn't need much of her attention, unlike Anne next to her, who complained about everything, even though she had worked there for at least a year.

'No, he's gone and left me. I think he's got a new love in his life, so I am on my own. It does feel strange. I've never been on my own before.' Hattie spoke so quietly that Sara had to ask her to speak up over the sound of the machines.

'Oh, Lord, you'll be quiet, if you are on your own. Will you be all right ? Have you heard from your fella yet ? It always takes a while. They train for a week or two and can hardly find time to breathe, let alone write, and then they're out on the front line. I was worried sick when I didn't hear from my lad for a week or two, and I bet that any payment you've been waiting for from him is taking its time. The army is quick to fight but not to pay,' Sara said with some concern in her voice.

'No, I've had neither. I was starting to worry. It's the not knowing or hearing anything, and then my father deciding to leave was just an added blow. Not that I miss him that much. He's never been much of a father to me,' Hattie replied and felt like crying.

'Aye, I know that your brother used to curse him many a day when he worked in here. He never had a good word for him, despite him being his father. I bet your mother had a hard life living with him when she was alive.' Sara shrugged her shoulders. 'Families, you couldn't make it up. Never mind, it's nearly dinner time, and I'm more than ready for mine. It's been a blinking long morning now we are in full production. It's good to see. I thought we might close at one time. This order from the War Office could be the making of this mill.'

Hattie just smiled. She was ready for her dinner. It was not a lot to look forward to, but at least she had found out that it was usual practice for army pay to be late and for letters not to be sent.

'Is that all you are eating? Do you want a bit of my apple pie? At least my mother feeds me decently, even if she does take every penny from me.' Maggie sat next to Hattie and Len on the loading bay wall in the backyard of the mill and offered Hattie the piece of apple pie that she had decided to leave in favour of a smoke on her pipe before their planned game of football.

Hattie looked at the piece of pie and heard her stomach growl in anticipation of being fed more.

'Go on, take it. I'll be fed apple pie for ever. We have two Bramley apple trees in our garden. It's all we get fed at this time of the year.' Maggie passed Hattie the pie wrapped in greased paper and then put her filled pipe in her mouth and lit the tobacco with a match from a vesta case. Both Len and Hattie watched in disbelief as she drew on her pipe and sat back content, while Hattie filled her stomach.

'How long have you been smoking a pipe?' Hattie asked as she savoured every crumb of the pie.

'For a few years now. My grandad, just before he died, introduced me to it, much to my mother's disapproval. It's grand after a meal, I can see why he smoked it. I'll just have a minute while our dinner settles and then a play before we have to get back to work.' Maggie leaned back and looked at the disgust on Len's face. 'What's wrong with you?'

'Nothing, it's just I've never seen a woman smoke a pipe before. It isn't really . . . ladylike,' Len replied and hoped that he had not offended.

'Well, who laid down the rules on how to be

ladylike? It must be a fella because I can't see any woman knowingly wanting to be trussed like a chicken in corsets, not able to have a gill or smoke how they like. All that's not for me,' Maggie replied and watched as Hattie finished her donated pudding.

'Fair enough. I've just not seen it before.' Len shrugged his shoulders.

Hattie looked at Maggie; she was different, and she quite admired her outspoken ways. 'I like the smell of baccie, but I'd never smoke. That's something I miss with no man in the house.'

'I bet it's quiet at your house at the moment?' Maggie enquired and watched as Hattie went across the yard's cobbles and retrieved the tired-looking football.

'It is until my father comes back. But I'm rather hoping he doesn't, even though I could do with his help with bills.' Hattie kicked the ball to Len. 'Come on then, show us what you are made of.'

'He went to watch Bradford and the Sheffield Blades with me on Saturday. It was their last match for a while. He should have picked up some tips.' Maggie grinned as Len jumped down from the wall, his clogs sparking as he hit the dry cobbles, and she dampened down her pipe with her finger and then put it on the wall top.

'Come on, Hattie, let's run rings around him.' Maggie kicked the ball from off Hattie's feet and goaded Len to come and tackle her. Which he did, but in vain.

'You'll have to be faster than that, mate,' Maggie chuckled as she passed the ball back and forward to Hattie and then ran over to the other side of the yard for her to pass it to her. Len ran between both women, trying to retrieve the ball with no success, until he stood and swore at them both.

'You are making me look like a fool. Tomorrow, we will bring some chalk with us and draw goalposts on that far wall. I'll be the goalie, that's more my position. I can't tackle you two, you are far too vicious for my liking.' Len caught his breath and looked up at the factory clock tower. 'That's made short work of our dinner time,' he said as the clock struck one.

'Same again tomorrow?' Maggie said, noting the colour that had come into Hattie's cheeks.

'Yes, I'll look forward to it. Makes me forget my worries.' Hattie grinned and then patted Len on his back. 'Definitely the goalkeeper or our manager, because you can't kick a ball if all hell had you.'

'All right, don't rub it in, I feel daft enough.' Len sighed as they all went back to work. 'You both played dirty anyway. You really kicked my shins.'

'Soft lad,' Maggie replied and put her arm around him as they both walked back into the warehouse.

Hattie ran up the stairs to her level and hoped that Sara wouldn't reprimand her for being a minute late back at her machine. As it was, she was nowhere to be seen, but Anne Birtwistle was standing between the two carding machines.

'I've kept an eye on your machine. Sara had to go up to the top office. I thought that with you being late, I'd cover for you. I've cleaned the wool for you, it just needs feeding through the combs.' Anne looked at her new workmate with a questioning look.

'Thanks, Anne. I was only a minute or two late. We've just been kicking a ball about in the yard for something to take our minds off everything.' Hattie started feeding the raw wool into the machine and suddenly stopped as she realised that Anne had not cleaned all the dirt and muck from the fleeces at all.

Anne stood and smiled, with a wicked look. 'I only cleaned the first fleece, you needn't think I'll help you out if you are going to be friends with her down in the warehouse, when you hardly say anything to me. She's a right oddity, more man than woman,' Anne said with a spiteful look.

'It's only because we are too busy when we are here that I don't have a lot to say to you. Anyway, Maggie is all right, she can play football. Come and join us tomorrow, you might enjoy it. We had a good laugh showing Len from the warehouse up. He can't kick a ball for toffee.' Hattie pulled burrs and a piece of briar out of the next fleece and then fed it into the carding machine. 'Come, you'll enjoy yourself.'

'I might, I'll see. Hey up, Sara is back. I bet she comes straight to you; she favours you. I've watched her. She was never like that with me.' Anne, whose words did not at all match her pretty face, quickly went back to her own place, leaving Hattie feeling awkward as Sara came to her and asked if everything was all right.

'Yes, I'm fine, thank you.' Hattie glanced at Anne. She didn't know why, but she seemed to have made an enemy of her, through what she didn't know.

That evening in the darkness and cold of her home, Hattie realised just how alone she was. She had no money, the house was cold and empty and even at work, it would seem that Anne, who worked next to her, disliked her, through no fault of her own. She lit a candle to see her to bed and decided that was the best place to be. Her stomach was growling after the meagre helping of supper, and it would soon be morning and back to work. The only good thing to look forward to was the laugh at lunchtime with Maggie and Len. As she blew out the candle and pulled her quilt over her for warmth, she hoped that Anne would not take her up on her offer of coming to join them in the yard. She would spoil the few minutes of peace, of that she was sure.

The following day came with typical Yorkshire weather. Clouds hung low and dark, while the rain that had started as soon as the mill's doors had opened was still pouring.

'Well, that's buggered that,' Maggie said and leaned against the warehouse door and watched the rain pour down. 'I've got to walk home in this as well. I'm going to be soaked.'

The cold rain that had fallen over Bradford had stopped play at the factory and the workers were forced to stay at their work.

'You'll be soaked before you've walked a hundred yards, you'll get your death of cold,' Hattie replied and felt downhearted.

'I know. God knows why I decided to get work here, but I was desperate, and to make things worse,

I fell out with my mother again last night.' Maggie kicked the side of the door and growled.

Hattie thought for a minute. 'You don't have to walk home tonight. Why don't you stay at mine? It would make more sense. I've a spare bed, it'll save you getting wet through. Although I've hardly anything to eat in my kitchen.' Hattie looked at Maggie and wondered if she was being a bit hasty. After all, she hardly knew her, but the walk to Esholt in this weather was not to be savoured even by her worst enemy.

'Could I? Do you mean that? Bloody hell, it would save me from facing my mother again and keep me dry.' Maggie's eyes twinkled with delight at the thought of not going home and facing her parents, as well as not getting soaked to the skin.

'Yes, I've a spare bedroom, and tonight, whether I can afford it or not, I'll light the fire. Autumn is here. I'll be glad of the company.'

'Oh, Hattie, that will be grand. I tell you what, I'll buy us fish and chips for our suppers. My way of saying thank you. I've just enough left from last week's wage.' Maggie beamed from ear to ear. 'Fish and chips and a night away from my moaning mother, couldn't be better. Apart from the weather, if only it would fair up for a game of football.

'That will be just lovely. Oh, fish and chips, a real treat. Couldn't ask for anything better.' Hattie could feel her mouth dribbling at just the thought. 'I'll wait for you at the mill entrance.'

'Right you are, I'll look forward to it. It might do my parents good to worry about me for one night. It'll serve my mother right for her hard words.'

'They will be worried about you, though.' Hattie looked at Maggie as she grinned like the cat that had got the cream.

'It will do them good. I'm just used by them, let them worry. Thank you so much for putting me up for the night. I really appreciate it. See you at six, and I can't wait for our supper either. It will be a treat for me.'

Hattie and Maggie walked quickly through the rain-sodden streets later that evening with their prize of fish and chips wrapped up in layers of newspaper, tightly clutched to their bodies, waiting to be eaten once they arrived home.

'So this is the way you live? At least you have a good view over Bradford from living up this hill-side; that is, when the smoke from the chimneys isn't hanging in the air.' Maggie watched as Hattie unlocked her door and, once open, bent down to pick up a letter that had come through the letterbox.

'Yes, it's all right up here.' Hattie's reply was half-hearted as she tried to read the handwriting on the letter and realised in the half-light that it was from her Bruce, the letter she had been waiting so long for. 'It's from my husband. He must be safe. Thank God for that.' She sighed in relief as she lit the hall lamp and felt relief at the thought that Bruce had written to her.

'There, you see, you've got supper, company and a letter from your old man. Just shows you how things can change in a second. You looked so glum this afternoon.' Maggie looked around her. It was a modest terraced house like most mill houses in Bradford, but it was clean and well-kept.

'I'll just put a match to the fire and get it going. We should soon warm up. Do you want to get two plates down from off the dresser and knives and forks from out of the drawers, and the salt and vinegar are above the fireplace?' Hattie reached for the box of matches from the fireplace and struck a match to the already set fire and watched as the flames took hold, making the small room look more homely and warm, as she pulled the already filled kettle onto the stove.

'Don't be daft, we want nowt with all that washing up. We'll eat them straight out of the newspaper with our fingers.' Maggie reached for the salt and vinegar and sat down at the kitchen table. 'It's the only way to eat fish and chips. Come on, before they go cold.' She pulled on Hattie's sleeve. 'I'm absolutely famished.' Maggie unwrapped both portions and smiled as Hattie sat down and started to eat.

'Oh, these are so good straight out of the paper. I always have to get plates out when everybody is at home.' Hattie licked her fingers and enjoyed every mouthful as the room warmed both with friendship and the heat of the fire.

'I can never treat myself to these, we have no fish and chip shop in Esholt. Believe me, it was a treat for me too. I hate living at home. I think I'll look for somewhere to rent in Bradford. Especially now my father has got a better job with his work. You can outgrow your family home, and that's what I've done.' Maggie spoke quietly and sat back in her chair, feeling full and content as Hattie poured them both a cup of tea.

'I hope you don't take sugar, because I haven't any. In fact, I don't have a lot of anything in the whole house. I've been left on my own, paying the rent, and I don't have much else to live on at the moment.' Hattie looked up to the mantelpiece, where the letter from Bruce was waiting for her, but she was waiting till she could read it on her own. She hoped that it contained good news and that he would tell her that both of the men she loved were safe and well.

'It must be hard for you.' Maggie hesitated. 'I don't suppose you'd be willing to take me in as a lodger? I'd pay my way. I wouldn't cause you any bother, and we seem to get on, having the same interests.'

'I don't know, I haven't thought about a lodger. I suppose it would help with the bills.' Hattie watched as Maggie got her pipe out of her skirt pocket and lit it, sitting back in the chair, getting warm and listening to the grandfather clock steadily ticking. 'Can I let you know in the morning? I need time to think about it,' she replied, looking at the letter and wanting to know what was going on in her husband and brother's lives before replying.

'Of course you can. It was just a thought,' Maggie replied and hoped as she had never hoped before that she would say yes to her staying at number 2 Gladstone Street. It would make sense to both of them after all, and she had taken a shine to Hattie Braithwaite.

7

Hattie watched as Maggie lit a candle and made her way up the stairs to bed. She had been good company over the evening, and the fish and chips supper had been more than welcome. She just questioned if she could have Maggie as a permanent lodger; she was a little forthright with her views and ways. Now, in the silence of the terraced house and with the clock striking eleven, she was going to read what her darling husband had written. Her heart skipped a beat as she reached for the letter on the mantelpiece above the dying embers of the fire she could ill afford to have lit. It had an English stamp on it, telling her that Bruce was not yet in France, she noted with some relief as she ran her finger under the seal and, with shaking hands, read the contents.

Dover Port
England

My dear Hattie,

This will be the last letter that you receive from me before we go to the Western Front. We are encamped on the outskirts of Dover, awaiting our orders and a ship to take us across to Calais.

It has been a hard few weeks down here. You wouldn't believe what we have had to endure, up before it is even light, only to be drilled and shouted at until we have lost the will to answer back and just to obey like a whipped dog. The officers tell us that it is nothing compared to what we are to face, but it is hard to comprehend anything worse, although a walk down by the port has prepared me for what I can expect.

The harbourside at Dover is heaving with troops, departing and returning, looking jaded and tired; they seem to have lost their souls as they return to their barracks and hopefully home for a brief period of normality before returning to the front. Ships full of the injured are also at the docks. It is a terrible thing to see, men injured, limbs missing or blinded by the mustard gas that Gerry is using against us. Along with men, there are horses by the dozen, awaiting to be shipped; the poor creatures like us know not what they are about to face. Supplies for the front are also piled high, everything from tins of bully beef to uniforms, arms and medicines. It is truly a different world from that of the mills of Bradford and I am starting to realise that both Oliver and I would be better at home than doing the patriotic thing and fighting for our country. But somebody has to stand up to these Germans and keep our land free of oppression, so enough about me.

How are you coping at the mill? You will find it different from running a house and home for us three? Is your father still moaning and being demanding as usual? I'm sorry I had to leave you, my darling. There is not a minute of the day that I don't think of you. Hopefully, when this war is over and I'm back home, we can perhaps visit the seaside one weekend. I know how much you like the sea.

Oliver sends his love. He's taking to being a soldier like a duck out of water; he's even joined the camp's football team. He will be organising a game against the Germans before we know it.

I hope that your weekly allowance has come through to the Post Office. Some are saying that it does not come through straight away, so hopefully there was enough left in the savings box to see you through until payment arrives.

Once over there and on the front line, I'll send details for where to write to or send an occasional treat from home, which will be most welcome. I'm missing you so much, my love. Your photograph is in my breast pocket, so you are close to my heart at all times. I will always love you.

Your dearest

Bruce.

Hattie looked down at the letter, and a tear dropped on the writing, causing the ink to splodge and blur the last two lines as she held it close. How she missed Bruce – she loved every inch of him. Little had she known when they used to play together on the streets of Bradford when they were young, he would end up as her husband. He sounded as if he didn't want to go to war now; that seeing the goings-on at Dover docks had opened his eyes to the true nature of war and had watered down his bravado. How she wished he could come back home and things could be how they used to be. No sooner had they married than he had gone, and now she was on her own. At least Oliver was still full of patriotic fervour, and it was no surprise to her that he had already found fellow footballers. She missed their cheek and their laughter, and just to have her husband lie beside her and caress her, even those nights had been all too brief.

'Please protect and look after them both,' Hattie whispered and sobbed. Without them, there was no point to living, she thought, as she picked up the candle for bed and put the guard around the dwindling fire. Life was empty, the house was empty, and she longed for her husband and brother to return.

'Bloody hell, I never sleep past five. I usually have to be halfway to work by now. Can't give you full marks for your breakfast, though, Hattie. It doesn't beat my mam's. What were you thinking of for dinner, more of the same?' Maggie bit into the piece of bread that Hattie put in front of her for breakfast and sipped her cup of tea, wiping her chin as a sup ran down it. 'Have you been living like this since your husband left? You can't live off nothing, you know?' Maggie was fond of her food and couldn't believe how little Hattie had in the house.

'It's only until the army payment comes, as it takes time for it to be processed. Bread and tea always does me in the morning, and there's enough bread and cheese for our dinners.' Hattie looked at Maggie and felt a little ashamed at not offering her guest more to eat. 'Besides, we aren't late up, it takes ten minutes to walk to the mill from here. If you need something for your dinner, there's a baker's at the end of this terrace. They are open at this time of day to catch the mill workers going to work.' Hattie felt her cheeks flush. 'I'm sorry, I haven't a penny to my name. My father took every penny when he left, and I had to pay the rent on Friday.'

'Did you think any more about my suggestion? I'd be no bother, you could charge me rent and make sure your house is warm and even save a little if the payment from the army comes.' Maggie pulled on the dry bread as she chewed it and looked at Hattie. It would benefit both of them if she would only say yes.

'I thought about it all last night. Bruce says his payment should be made, hopefully soon, but even he says it is taking its time, and I can't continue like I am. I can cope on bread and cheese for a week or so, but not for ever. It's just if Bruce, Oliver or even my father wants or has to come home, what would I do then?' Hattie sighed.

'Simple, you tell me to leave and I go home to my parents. I might have to return shame-faced, but that will only make them say "I told you so". Hattie, there would be no problem if I had to be thrown out, but it would help us both so much if you let me stay for now.'

Hattie knew what Maggie said made sense. It would help her out of her present predicament, she thought, as she sipped the last dregs of her tea and considered it.

'You'd go home if I needed the bedroom back? And I'd have to charge at least ninepence a day if you were to eat with me as well.'

'Yes, that sounds fair to me, and I'll buy us fish and chips on a Friday. A treat for both of us.' Maggie's face lit up at the thought of no longer having to live at home and endure the long walk to work. 'I'll even buy you your dinner today. I've twopence left in my pocket. Hopefully that'll get us both a meat pie from the baker's, because this bread is as dry as my bum.' Maggie grinned.

'Just pay me the rent on time, that is all I will expect, and we will take turns in making meals for us both.' Hattie smiled as Maggie grabbed her hand from across the table and squeezed it.

'Oh, thank you, thank you. No more trailing back and forward to Esholt and having to listen to my mother's jibes. Rent will be paid on time. I don't know if you will appreciate my cooking, but I'll have a go and I'll help keep the house tidy. I'll be no bother, I promise.' Maggie sat back in her chair and felt like her world had just changed. She was to live in Bradford and be her own woman, instead of having her mother lecture her every five minutes. 'I'll go home tonight, pick up a few belongings and bring them to work with me tomorrow. I can't wait to see the surprise on my mother and father's faces. Can I pay you the first rent on Friday? Although I'll try and borrow some money from my mother, if she'll let me, to pay for some food until our wages.' Maggie spoke her thoughts out loud and grinned with excitement. 'And somebody to play football with! A kindred spirit!'

'Let's keep it as friends, I don't know about kindred spirits.' Hattie blushed and smiled. 'Are we having a kick about this lunchtime?'

'Too right, we are, but we need to get some more workers interested in playing. Len is useless; he's only good in goal. And even there he's got butter fingers and he can't judge which way we are going to make the kick.'

'I tried to get Anne Birtwistle to play with us at lunchtime, but she didn't show much interest. She seemed to know you, though.' Hattie looked up at the clock. 'We'll have to get going, especially if you are going to call for a pie for your dinner.'

'Oh, I know her; she'll not say a good word about me. We had a difference in opinions, should I say, when I met her in The Cock and Bottle on Barkerend Road. It was not over football, that's all you need to know,' Maggie replied and reached for her shawl. 'I used to get a good pie from a bakery in the part of Bradford they call Little Germany. There are plenty of bakers there, all catering for the mill workers. Trouble is, they are, as the name suggests, mainly

German or Polish that have businesses there. Life is a little bit awkward for them at the moment. Some have even had their windows broken. Folks don't realise that they have fled their own homeland for a better life and have nothing to do with the Kaiser and his war.' Maggie walked towards the door and hesitated as she opened it to the cold September morning. 'Thanks for agreeing to let me stay here. I couldn't have walked every day this winter from Esholt to work. Besides, it's time I left home, else I'll end up an old maid.' Maggie patted Hattie gently on her arm and smiled. 'Now a pie for you and me, and then I'm as skint as you. Although I'll ask my mother to give me some money to tide us both over until Friday, and then hopefully you'll have both your pay and your separation payment from that husband of yours.'

'The pay will be most welcome, but I just want him to keep safe. He said they are due to sail to Calais and then to march out to the front. God willing, both he and Oliver will keep safe.'

'They will. I'm sure they have one another to look for each other. That's what we will be like. It will work out well for us two sharing everything.' Maggie stepped out down the street, and Hattie pulled her shawl around her tightly and hoped that Maggie would be proved right as they made their way to work.

'What do you mean you are leaving home! You just can't walk in, sit down, eat your supper and tell us that this is your last night with us.' Maude looked at her daughter in disbelief.

'I can and I am. Hattie, whom I work with, has offered to put me up while I'm working in Bradford, so for that I'm thankful. No more traipsing over fell and dale to get back home every evening. It makes sense, winter will soon be here, and besides, it's time I moved out.' Maggie looked at her father, who had not said a lot about her declaration of independence.

'You are sure, Maggie, it is not a fella? I'll not have a daughter of mine living over the brush.' Maude shook her head and glanced at her husband for support.

'Now, you are talking rubbish, Mother. You know as well as I that the likelihood of her doing that would truly be a miracle.' Jack sat back and smoked his pipe, slow and long. 'Let her be off, we can manage without her rent now that I've got a promotion. She'll be better out of Esholt; folk only talk.'

'What do you mean by that, Father? They have nothing to talk about when it comes to me. Although what they don't know, they make up. That's why I'll be glad to see the back of the place.'

'I've said enough, but if you want to go, then go. Bradford is happen the right place for you.' Jack wasn't going to be drawn, but he often heard the men at work talk about his daughter and comment on her lack of feminine ways.

'But I'll miss you, your help about the house, and I'll miss your rent money, not to mention your company.' Maude sighed.

'You'll miss the rent money, I'll give you that, but we don't have much in common, Mother. We never have long conversations, and you like to keep this house just the way you want it. I should leave, like my father says. I may come back at weekends to make sure you are both all right. I'm not thousands of miles away.' Maggie got up from her seat. 'I'll put some things together to take with me. I'll be leaving a bit earlier in the morning, so don't get up and see me off.'

'We can bring you some of your things on the horse and cart. I'd like to see where you are living,' Maude replied, suddenly realising that her one and only daughter was leaving them behind and that she had just fed her her last meal under their roof.

'I don't need anything except my clothes and bits and bobs, I'll bundle them up in a sheet and drop them off at Hattie's before I start work. I'll send you my address in a letter once I'm settled. You'll be welcome to visit.' Maggie watched as her mother looked down at the table, already feeling the loss of her own child. 'I don't suppose I could ask for a shilling from out of the savings, just to see me fed and pay part-board until pay day?'

'You suppose right, lass, tha can't. You've made your bed, now you must lie in it,' Jack said sternly and didn't look up from the fire as Maggie went to her room and started to gather her belongings.

'Father, that was hard. We could give her a bit of something; she'll need to eat,' Maude whispered.

'It'll not do her any harm for once, to go without. If she's boarding, she'll get her meals in with her rent. Let her be a mother, she's old enough to know what she's doing.' Jack picked up his daily paper and hoped that Maude would say no more about Maggie leaving them. She was often the talk of the factory with her different ways; she might be his lass, but sometimes he doubted it.

It was pitch black as Maggie made her way down the stairs with her bundle. She quickly lit a candle and had one last look around her family home. She was going to miss it, but she'd be back once she had got settled in with Hattie. Sundays would always be hers to do as she pleased. On the table, she spotted a note and a food parcel, just as she wondered whether to help herself to breakfast.

I couldn't let you go unfed, and there's that shilling you asked for. Don't tell your father.

Take care, Love Mum.

She read the note with a lump in her throat as she picked up the shilling and put it into her pocket. She loved her mother too, but it was hard to show her emotions towards her. Perhaps it wasn't her mother who was the hard one; it was her father who dictated how the house was run. She picked up the food bundle, and a tear ran down her cheek. She was going to miss her home in truth, but it was time to move on. No more walking in all weather to work, and she'd be able to do what she wanted without anybody judging her. No, she would be better living in Bradford, and Hattie's home was ideal, and it would help her out until her menfolk returned. Life would be better for one and all, she thought, as she took one last look around the kitchen and blew the candle out. It was time to change her life for the better.

8

Maggie had landed on Hattie's doorstep good and early and had left her belongings to be put away on her return later that evening. Now, they both sat on the warehouse steps of the mill, sharing the meal that Maggie's mother had sent with her.

'You are going to miss home if this is how your mother fed you every day.' Hattie happily bit into a piece of Victoria sandwich cake and smiled at her new lodger.

'No, I won't. I think my father has been wanting rid of me for a while, by what he said last night. I always thought we were quite close, but I must have thought wrong,' Maggie said quietly and looked up as Len joined them both, sitting down next to her.

'Why, what did he say?' Hattie enquired.

'Oh, nothing much, but I think he's probably glad to see the back of me. My mam was worried about managing without the rent money, but she was good enough to put this food up and give me enough money to live on for the week. So she must have had second thoughts about being hard on me.' Maggie sighed and wrapped what was left of her dinner up in paper. 'I'll have a walk home in a week or two and convince them that I can live and look after myself.'

'They are welcome to come and visit whenever they want. I hope you told them that,' Hattie said and then looked at Len as he nudged Maggie's arm and prompted her to look at the newspaper that he had started to read.

'Yes, I did,' Maggie replied and looked over Len's shoulder. 'What are you getting all excited about?'

'Just look at it in the paper. It says that with all the football players going to war, the FA are going to close the grounds until the end of the war. Then it goes on to say that some factories, especially up here in the north, are putting women's teams together to play and raise money for worthy causes. That a game was played up at Ulverston in Cumbria between a local munitions factory and local women and raised substantial funds for charity. It says there is another to be played on Christmas Day, with all takings going towards the war effort.' Len sat back. 'So you are not the only ones who can play football.'

'Is there a picture? What did they wear? Is the FA supporting them?' Maggie snatched the paper from Len.

'That's all it says, although it does mention a munition factory in Preston, called Dick Kerr's, that is also showing interest in having a football team. Imagine if the women took over playing football from the men, while they are away fighting.' Len shook his head.

'The FA would never let them. I think I remember reading about a woman trying to get women's teams to play all over the country, and she was just laughed at and put up with and humoured. It will never happen.' Hattie shrugged.

'It won't if we don't fight for it and train like proper footballers do. We could have a team, there's plenty of women working here. I bet we could easily get a team together.' Maggie's eyes twinkled with the thought of playing actual football on a pitch. '"The Yorkshire Ladies' Football Club" – that could be us.'

'We'd never get a team together. Where would we play? This yard isn't big enough, and none of us really know the rules.' Hattie sighed.

'You can't call it the Bradford Ladies' team because we don't all come from Bradford, and we can't call it after the mill, because I can't see Joshua Swainbank backing us. I suppose the Yorkshire Ladies would be good enough,' Len mumbled. 'But I couldn't play then. You couldn't have a fella in your team!'

'We'd get you a wig and some lipstick.' Maggie hit Len on his shoulder and laughed. 'You can't run because of your asthma, anyway. You'd have to be the linesman.'

'You are not getting me wearing a wig and lipstick. The linesman will do. But it's all pie in the sky as of yet. There are only two of you, no ground, and you've no boots or anything to play in, let alone anyone to tell you where you are going wrong. It's just a dream.' Len pinched his paper back and looked at the main headline.

BATTLE LINES BEING DRAWN ON THE SOMME, BRITISH LIVES EXPECTED TO BE LOST.

'I hope to hell everyone we know is safe,' Len whispered and looked at Maggie and Hattie.

'My Bruce and Oliver hopefully will not be in the middle of that yet, they were just about to be shipped out when he wrote me the letter I received on Monday. I pray they stay safe.' The excitement of the football report was soon lost as Len read that the front line between the Germans and the French and English was twenty-five miles of trenches and barbed wire. The reality was that men were dying for their country, and football was not top priority.

'Sorry, just thinking about football. If we do get a team, we play to help our lads. It's the least we can do,' Maggie declared. 'Even if we can save one life, it's better than just doing nothing. Hattie, we will put our heads together and come up with a plan. What do you say?'

'All right, if other women can do it, we can. I don't know how, but we will. But right now we will have to get back to work, unless we want to lose pay.' Hattie stood up and wondered what she had just let herself in for. 'We haven't even looked at the football this dinner time, we will have to do better than that in the next weeks.'

'It'll take a while, and ten minutes in this yard is no good for anything. We need somewhere proper to play and more than ten minutes at dinner time,' Maggie said as she looked back at the yard and walked into the mill to her work with her head full of ideas that she would discuss with Hattie later that evening.

Hattie looked across at Anne Birtwistle and gave her a brief smile. The noise of the machines made conversation hardly possible as they both returned to their work and got on with the job in hand. In between feeding the carding machine cleaned wool, Anne quickly came across and placed a note in Hattie's hand, looking worried as she did so and without saying anything before returning to her work.

Hattie looked at the note and opened it up to read it after feeding the next fleece through the carder. She stared at the words.

> *Be careful with Maggie Fleming; she is not to be trusted. If you need to know more, stay back for a while after work, and I'll tell you all.*

Hattie glanced across at Anne and wondered if she was just trying to make bother or if she was telling the truth. There was only one way to find out, and that was to hang back after work and speak to Anne. She definitely knew something about her new lodger, and it was best that she listened to her. Hattie nodded her head at a worried-looking Anne as she put her thumbs up and then got on with the job at hand.

The mill whistle blew, and silence gradually came to the mill as the weaving and carding came to a stop. Hattie noticed Anne waiting for her to turn off her machine for the day and gave a glance her way as she said evening to everyone before walking to the stairwell where Anne waited for her.

'What's this all about, then, Anne? What do you think is wrong with Maggie?' Hattie asked outright as the weavers from the top floor pushed past them to get out of work and home as fast as they could.

'I thought you had a right to know; that is, if you don't know already? Seeing that you have taken her in as your lodger,' Anne said with her eyes downcast and wondering if she should have said anything at all. But she felt spurned by Maggie, her one-time close friend. 'I presume you don't know what she is like, as you are a married woman, but that won't stop her if she takes a liking to you,' Anne whispered and looked at Hattie, hoping that she wouldn't have to go into detail and that she had said enough.

'What do you mean, Anne? Stop her from doing what?' Hattie asked.

'She prefers women to men, and if you have taken her eye, she will soon talk herself into your bed,' Anne whispered and blushed.

'That will be just gossip, because she doesn't act like a conventional woman. She does say it as it is. I can assure you, even if she does have those tendencies, I am a happily married woman and I have taken her in just to help with paying the rent.' Hattie felt herself slightly worried and embarrassed; nobody ever talked about suchlike.

Anne whispered again, a little louder. 'Think of your reputation and the gossip; everyone knows what she's like. The whole of Esholt will be glad to see the back of her.' Anne turned and looked out of the long window at everybody streaming home, unaware that Maggie was making her way up the stairs and had heard the last comment.

'So that's what you think, is it, Anne? I don't suppose you have told Hattie that we are close friends, and the reason why you are telling her this is that you think you have reason to be jealous of her. I was hoping to catch you on your way out of work, and when you didn't show, I decided to come and talk to you. To tell you that I've moved to Bradford to be closer to my work and you.' Maggie looked perplexed.

Hattie just stood and looked at Anne and Maggie. She had had no idea that they were friends, and certainly not that they were that close.

'You are just saying that. I thought that Hattie was your new muse.' Anne blushed; she was never open about her relationship with Maggie. It was dangerous.

'Don't be so stupid. Hattie is providing a roof over my head, and besides, my father has been listening to the rumours as well, and I know he's glad to see the back of me. Bloody gossips!' Maggie put her arm around Anne's small frame. 'Besides, as well as hunting you out to tell you I was moving in with Hattie, I was also wanting to tell you we are putting a football team together and we need someone who can run and dribble the ball like a whippet, and I know you can.' She smiled at the nimble Anne and would have liked to have kissed her, but not in front of Hattie. She didn't know her well enough and didn't want to lose her home through her passions.

Hattie felt uncomfortable, watching them both. She hadn't realised that Maggie had known Anne all along when she had complained about her when talking about work.

'This one here, we need in our team, if she stops talking rubbish. She used to work at my old mill and ran the lads ragged with her ball-passing skills. How about we ask her home, Hattie? We can run to an extra mouth at the table tonight, now I've brought some money with me.' Maggie grinned at Hattie and then looked at Anne as she shook her head.

'No, please don't bother yourself asking me home. My mother will be waiting for me. Perhaps another night,' Anne replied and saw Hattie almost breathe a sigh of relief, before sharing her thoughts about Maggie's idea. 'A football team, for this mill? You'll have to get permission from him upstairs, and I don't know if many women will be interested.' Anne sighed as Maggie squeezed her hand.

'You will have to come around to our home another evening. Just let Maggie and me get used to our ways, and then you will be more than welcome. As for football, if you can play, then we definitely need you. Why didn't you tell me when you knew what I was doing during my dinner break?' Hattie asked.

'Because I thought Maggie had fallen out with me, and you were my replacement. Sorry for being a bitch the other day. I hope my act of jealousy didn't cause you any problems.' Anne hung her head.

'No, not at all, and you have no worries when it comes to me.' Hattie felt stupid. She had known Maggie seemed uninterested in men, but had not realised that she preferred a female lover. Nobody had said anything, just sniggered and wished her well with her new house guest. Just as long as she didn't think she was the same way inclined, it would not worry her; she needed her money too much. Plus, perhaps Anne would be better to work with from now on.

'Ah, well, that's sorted then, and all is out in the open, but we don't make it common knowledge, do we, Anne?' Maggie smiled. 'It's best Hattie knows. If you want to throw me back out onto the streets, I'll understand.'

'No, just keep to yourselves, that's all I ask. I'm happily married, and that's the way I want it to stay. Now, I'm going home and will make some supper. We had better get a move on. Everyone has left except the accountant and Joshua Swainbank.' Hattie listened to the empty mill. It was silent, and the air was filled with woollen fibres gradually settling onto the quiet wooden floors.

'Aye, let's get home, now that it's settled. And now that you, Anne Birtwistle, have been put straight.' Maggie took her pipe out of her pocket and started to light it as the three of them made their way down the stairs and out of the open mill doors to clock off.

'I need some bread from the baker's,' Hattie said, realising that Anne and Maggie needed to talk on their own. 'I'll get a move on and leave you two.' The bread had already been bought that morning, but it was an easy excuse to leave the two lovers to make up, and she needed some time on her own to realise just what she had taken on with Maggie Fleming coming to stay with her. Her life had completely changed since Bruce had gone to war, and it was getting more and more complicated by the minute. Women like Maggie were labelled 'Tommie' and, as a player on a women's football team, her father would definitely not want to know her now, she thought. As she turned the corner she glanced back at Maggie and Anne, sitting on a seat just outside the mill, their heads bowed together in private conversation.

9

Hattie watched as Maggie sat across from her and ate the dish of potato hash that had been cooking in the side oven all day while they were both at work. It had no meat in it, but at least it was filling with the help of a loaf of bread brought home by herself.

'I will give you your due, you didn't bat an eye when Anne was telling you about our relationship. I expected to be out on the street when she said something about me.' Maggie didn't raise her head as she ate. She didn't want to make eye contact with Hattie, feeling that she had perhaps not been quite honest with her.

'It's nothing to do with me, as long as we keep it that way. I need your rent, and besides, we seemed to hit it off and have a lot in common, apart from when it comes to that! Your personal life is up to you, I'm not interested,' Hattie replied and looked across at Maggie as she lifted her head and stared at her.

'Then we have an understanding. I'll pay the rent, help out and promise not to flaunt Anne in front of you. But in the meantime, let's concentrate on this game of football. We've got to get a team together. It will be the best team in Yorkshire. We can both see to that.' Maggie smiled at Hattie. 'It was like music to my ears when Len read that out of the newspaper. We've got to do it! We already have three good players, we only need eight more and somewhere to play.'

'Only! We need boots and clothes, and a field to play in is not going to be easy to find. This will all take money. We could really do with a backer. If only Joshua Swainbank would back us, that would solve all our problems. I don't know anybody hardly in the mill, especially upstairs, where they weave. There might not be anybody else in the mill that even likes football, let alone thinks they can play.' Once Hattie had walked away from the mill, she had started to think the idea of a women's football team was a step too far. Women were still battling to get the vote, let alone play football like men.

'I think I can perhaps solve where we play, but I can't promise. I'll find out this coming Saturday. What we need is some posters put up around the mill. But we will have to ask Joshua Swainbank for permission, so he will have to know.' Maggie sat back in her chair. 'Do you fancy going to see him tomorrow at dinner time, and we will ask him for permission and see how he feels about his mill having a women's football team?'

'What, me and you? We have only just started work there. He'll think we are going to cause bother with talk of taking over the men's game.' Hattie felt her stomach churn. The less she had to do with management, the better, her brother and husband had always told her. Even though Joshua Swainbank was known to be fair to his staff.

'He'll not be struggling for ever. The first supply of serge went to Higher Mill this week, and the Government will be paying him well for his supply. Besides, I know he likes his football. It's how I met him and got this job.'

'How do you know that?' Hattie asked and was intrigued to learn how Maggie knew so much about the mill owner, who kept himself to himself, especially after his partner left under a cloud and his wife and child died.

'I was having a drink in The Diplomat, and he was talking to some of the locals about Bradford City and its players. I don't know why, because I was a bit worse for wear, but he seemed to take a shine to me and offered me my job.' Maggie grinned. 'Although I think he was desperate for workers.'

'Perhaps we should both go and see him, ask about putting posters up advertising a team and just see how he feels about it? I don't mind talking to him, my brother and husband never had a problem with him. They always said he was a fair man, but that he was still management and the owner.'

'A boss is never fair, he likes to line his own pocket first and then give the crumbs to his workers.' Maggie scowled. 'But saying that, he needn't have taken me on, so perhaps he is. What about it then, shall we go and see him tomorrow? Start the ball rolling, as it were?'

'Nothing ventured, nothing gained, I suppose. I'll pick up my courage and go with you. We will make a formidable team.' Hattie smiled.

'That we will when we get a full team. That Ulverston Football Team will wonder what's hit them if we ever get to play them.' Maggie couldn't wait to see Joshua and hopefully put posters up. Anne had told her there was an ideal goalkeeper who worked in the weaving room. She would speak to her on the way to the top offices. An ex-goalkeeper of a hurling team from County Kerry in Ireland, as tough as old boots, but just what they needed. They would have a team, a class-one team if she had her way.

Sara Turner watched as Maggie waited for Hattie at the stairs and urged her to join her as the dinner time break began. They were an odd pair, she thought, as she watched Hattie nearly run to join her. It would be dinner together and a kick of the old leather ball. They acted more like lads than grown women, Sara thought, as she walked past Anne and noticed her watching them both disappear.

'Bloody crackers, liking to play football in their half-hour. You'd think they would just need a sit and a bite to eat like everybody else.' Sara nodded her head to the two who had disappeared out of sight.

'They like their football, so do I. Tomorrow, I might join them. It will make a change to get a bit of fresh air instead of sitting here eating my sandwiches,' Anne replied and grinned.

'Fresh air, in Bradford, now that will be a first. The buildings aren't black with soot for nothing. And as for football, it's a man's game. Women are not built for all that running and tackling. Don't even think about it, Anne. There's nothing to you anyway.' Sara shook her head. The times were mad, with suffragettes walking through the city wanting equal rights, and now women playing football.

'Aye, but we are taking men's jobs now they are at war. Tell those lasses that work in munitions that they are not good enough to do a man's job and you'd soon be given a mouthful.' Anne, for once, answered back and looked at the disdain on Sara's face as she moved off down the row to go and have her dinner. Anne sat on a wool bale and ate her sandwich and hoped that the meeting taking place was going well; that is, if Joshua Swainbank had given Hattie and Maggie the time of day with their fanciful idea of a football team. Trust Maggie to start in a new job and cause chaos as soon as she arrived. She never made life easy for herself, but Anne loved her dearly.

Hattie felt her heart beating quickly as she and Maggie reached the top of the stairs and looked at one another before knocking gently first on the office door and then, when not heard, a lot louder.

'Perhaps we shouldn't be even thinking about a football team,' Hattie whispered as they saw shadows from behind the frosted glass door and started to lose their nerve.

'It'll be right, I tell you, it'll be good for the mill.' Maggie nearly reached for Hattie's hand to squeeze, but quickly decided against it as a figure came behind the door and the handle turned.

'Yes, what do you two want? Do you not know it is your dinner break?' Mary Mason opened the door, still eating a fish-paste sandwich, and looked at both the new girls. 'You are not giving your notice in already, are you? I hope not. Jobs are hard to find, you know, you should be grateful for what you've got.'

'No, no, we just hope to speak to Mr Swainbank. We have an idea, but we need his permission to put it into practice,' Maggie said, able to see Joshua Swainbank sitting in his office, and hoping that he would give them his time.

'Well, you can tell me first, and then we will see if it's worth wasting his time. He's a busy man, you know.' Mary was Joshua's guard dog, and everyone knew she hardly let anyone bother him if she didn't have to.

Hattie looked at Maggie and decided she would say what they wished to speak to their employer about.

'We were wondering if Mr Swainbank would give us permission to put a poster up asking if any women who work here would like to join a football team?' Hattie felt her cheeks flush. Talking to the elderly prim woman made their request seem of little importance, with what else was happening at the mill and with war raging.

'A football team! A women's football team! Now I've heard it all!' Mary Mason shrieked and laughed, making Joshua Swainbank look over towards the open office door and wonder what the noise was about.

'Have you got time to even think about playing football when you are working? If you have, then we are not working you hard enough.' Mary peered over her glasses. 'You young women are a new breed to me. We used to know our place, looking after our parents and family, respecting our husbands, and now things are turned on their head. I only work because I'm a spinster and need to support myself.'

'No surprise there,' Maggie whispered to Hattie and grinned.

Hattie gave Maggie a warning glance. 'If we can find somewhere to play, it would be good for morale. Please, all we want is permission to put up a poster,' Hattie pleaded and noticed Joshua Swainbank coming to see what the conversation was about.

'I don't think so, you might be telling me that it's football when it could well be one of those suffragette meetings. We have a hard view of those within this mill; they have been known to disrupt work and give women silly ideas.' Mary shook her head and then turned when she realised Joshua was standing behind her.

'Thank you, Mrs Mason. Perhaps I can take it from here? Did I hear the word football? Is this what it's all about? I've noticed that the football was being used by you two at dinner times. I've seen you out of my office window. As long as you play in the half-hour dinner break, I have no problem.' Joshua looked at the two women and smiled. They were like chalk and cheese: Hattie Braithwaite, blonde-haired, pretty of complexion and petite, while Maggie Fleming was dark-haired with stunning bone structure, high-cheek-boned and distinctive looks. She also had an air about her that made her stand out.

'Sir, we apologise for the bother.' Hattie bowed her head and kept her eyes downcast; she knew he was the boss and held authority over all his workforce. She held her breath. 'Maggie and I were wondering if you would mind if we put up a poster asking other women, aside from ourselves, if they would be interested in forming a football team. A lot of the mills are organising football teams, but we wouldn't ask for anything more than your permission to do so at this stage.' Hattie held her breath. 'We'd only meet at dinner time and in our own time out of work, and we wouldn't cause any bother with current politics.'

Maggie looked at Joshua Swainbank. 'And perhaps I should apologise again for being worse for wear when we first met. However, you know from that meeting that I know my football. I'm sure we could have the best team in Yorkshire, a winning Yorkshire Ladies' Football Club.' Maggie didn't drop her eyes and instead looked into Joshua's and hoped that they could both convince him.

'Well, ladies, this is a first. I don't quite know what to say.' Joshua looked at Mary Mason as she shook her head and went back to her desk. 'The yard won't be big enough for an eleven-a-side team, so I don't know how I can help further. But by all means, put a poster up, and see if you get anybody else interested. I'll be surprised if you do, most of my employees have families or dependants at home that probably wouldn't be suited if they even think of playing football.'

'If we can just put a poster up, that would be wonderful, and we promise it won't get in the way of work. There are three of us who can already play quite well, so we only need another eight to show interest, and we have our eye on a likely goalkeeper,' Hattie said quietly and looked up at Joshua Swainbank. He was an attractive man in his sharp-cut suit and a brocade waistcoat. His hair was thick and dark, and his eyes were the bluest of blue as he looked at her.

'I didn't think that you would be one for football, Miss Braithwaite. You aren't built to take knocks, you must be careful. It's a man's sport.'

Maggie sighed, typical of a man to think that. 'She's better than any fella, quick to see good passes, and she can run with the ball.'

'I used to play with my brother and husband when we were younger. I've always enjoyed playing with a football.' Hattie smiled and tried not to blush as Joshua stared at her.

'Very well, then, go ahead and put your poster up, but I'll be watching for any disruption to your work. The first sign of it interfering with the running of my business, and I will stop it.' Joshua stood and watched as both women thanked him and then walked out of his office.

'Now, why have you encouraged them, Mr Swainbank? It will go to their heads. They are both new to the firm as well, and we don't know much about them yet. They both could be dreaded suffragettes for all we know.' Mary Mason sighed and then went back to her fish paste sandwiches.

'I don't think Bruce Braithwaite's wife will be, she's not the kind, but perhaps you may be right about Maggie Fleming. She's a different mixture. Whatever, it will give some of the women something to combat the worry while their men are away.' Joshua sighed. 'I'll keep my eye on it. The yard is just under my office window. While they play in there, I can keep my eye on them, don't you worry.'

'You'll regret it, mark my words. They'll be late back for their work, and take advantage of you, just when you need every hand to the looms,' Mary Mason growled.

'We'll see, Mary. It will keep me amused watching them, if nothing else.' Joshua grinned; he had already seen Hattie and Maggie tackling one another in their work clogs. Neither were shy of going for the other's ankles. They weren't as fragile as they looked, especially Hattie.

'Have we got time to go and see this weaver that Anne told you about? It's nearly one, and I bet them upstairs will be watching our every move now.' Hattie stopped and put her head around the stairwell, and looked across the main weaving room. The looms were quiet, but the weavers were making their way back to their positions, with lunchtime being over.

'No, we'll not risk it, we will both catch her after work. I think that's her with the bright red hair. Anne said she was a redhead and had the loom next to the far window.' Both looked at the woman who was standing by her loom and about to turn back to work.

'She's not that young. Are you sure it's her?' Hattie exclaimed, watching the woman with sturdy arms start weaving, as the noise of the looms started filling the air again.

'Yes, that's her. We will catch her later, as we walk out of work.' Maggie pulled on Hattie's sleeve. 'Come on, else we will be docked pay, whether we have been talking to the boss or not.'

'All right, I'm coming. I'll meet you outside at six. We'll put a poster together tonight as well,' Hattie shouted as Maggie ran down the wooden stairs, her clogs clattering as she went.

'Yes, tell Anne we have the boss's blessing, will you?'

'Yes, of course I will,' Hattie said as she reached her level in the mill and walked into the carding room, trying to look unflustered and hoping to escape the gaze of Sara Turner. She glanced at Anne, who mouthed the words 'All right?' Hattie nodded her head and smiled, putting her thumb up as she started about her work. A poster would be put together that night, and then it was a case of seeing if a team was viable. Maggie had come along at just the right time. She had solved her financial problems and given her an interest other than work and home. Now, she just prayed that the two men in her life were safe and not about to take part in the largest battle of the war to take place at the Somme.

Hattie, Maggie and Anne were three of the first out of work. They stood together and watched as the workers from the mill streamed out of its doors.

'There she is, that's Lorna O'Donnell.' Anne pointed and pulled on Maggie's sleeve. 'She's a real bruiser, nobody would dare tackle her.'

Maggie and Hattie glanced at each other and hoped that the tall, stocky woman with a mop of wild red hair wouldn't literally be a bruiser as they approached her, walking on either side of her.

'What's your two's game then? What you want with me?' Lorna O'Donnell stood still and looked at the two women who had singled her out as she made her way home.

'We hear that you used to be pretty good at hurling back in Ireland.' Maggie studied the pale-faced woman who had the greenest eyes she had ever seen.

'Aye, but what's that got to do with you? I left that behind when I left Kerry. Besides, there's no hurling played over here, in this godforsaken country.' Lorna studied the two women and wondered what they were about.

'There might not be hurling, but we are about to put a women's football team together. We also heard that you were in goal, and we are short of a goalkeeper. Do you fancy joining us?' Hattie smiled at the woman with the broad Irish lilt and hoped that the answer would be yes.

'By Jesus, you hear a lot about me, to say I don't know either of you. There are no secrets in this place. It's just a good job I'm not part of the Fenians, else you'd be accusing me of all sorts.' Lorna shook her head. 'A football team, do you say? Now that's a novelty.'

'Yes, a football team. Hattie and I have been playing in the mill yard during our dinner times and are about to put up a poster, seeing if anybody wants to join us. It was Anne over there who had heard you used to be a goalie for a hurling team. So we could do with you in our team.' Maggie looked across to Anne, who started to walk forward to join them.

'You'll need a much bigger pitch than the mill yard, and who says I'm any good? A women's football team, you'll be the laughing stock of Bradford. I've never heard owt like it.' Lorna grinned and looked at the three who had obviously lost their senses.

'I don't think we will, women's football teams are springing up all over the country. There's already been a game played at Ulverston only the other week, and other teams are springing up to replace the men's teams. As for a field to play in, I've got my contacts. I hope to sort that out this weekend.'

Hattie looked at Maggie. She was trying really hard to get Lorna interested, even mentioning her elusive contacts.

'Ah, let me be, and I'll have a tink about it. In the mill yard at dinner time, you say? If you see me there, then you'll know my answer.' Lorna smiled at all three and then pulled her shawl around her. 'Now, I'll be away, my old man will think his throat's been cut, let alone my two young'ens. The idle idiot can't peel a tattie even when I've been at work all day.' Lorna grinned.

'I hope you will join us,' Maggie said and touched her arm gently.

'Aye, well, we'll see,' Lorna replied and then walked off with the rest of the workers down the cobbled street.

'She'll not be joining us,' Hattie whispered as she watched her walk away. 'She's got a husband that's still at home and children. He's dodged going to fight, but I don't know how.'

'Don't be so defeatist. She'll be joining us; she'll not take any notice of her husband by the sounds of it,' Maggie said quietly. 'She's our goalie, I'll tell you now.'

10

It was Friday dinner time, and Maggie and Hattie stepped back to look at the poster, wondering if they were a bit mad for even thinking that some of the women who worked at Swainbank's Mill might be interested in playing football.

'I think it says all it needs to,' Hattie said and pulled her shawl on. She hadn't time to talk to Maggie as she was on her way to the Post Office to see if her Separation Allowance had come through from the front line.

'To the point, if nothing else,' Maggie replied and grinned as she read the words again.

DO YOU LIKE FOOTBALL?

DO YOU THINK YOU CAN PLAY?

GIRLS AND WOMEN ARE NEEDED TO MAKE A TEAM FROM THIS MILL.

JOIN US IN THE MILL YARD EVERY LUNCHTIME BREAK TO FIND OUT MORE AND TO BECOME ONE OF THE YORKSHIRE LADIES' FOOTBALL CLUB.

'Yes, it reads just grand. Now we will have to wait and see if anybody turns up. It will take a while for everybody to spot it, even though it is next to the clocking-in machine.' Maggie glanced at the clock.

'I'm going to have to go. I need to know if Bruce has sent me some money, although I'm not as desperate as I was last week, now you are helping with the rent and everyday things.'

'Get gone, then, I'll go and sit with Len and Anne and see if anybody comes to see what we get up to. I hope Lorna shows her face; she's just who we need in goal, I'm sure of it.' Maggie watched as Hattie flew out of the mill and made her way to the Post Office. She'd made her welcome in her house, and Maggie was thankful. There wasn't that uneasy feeling there had been at home, and both women enjoyed one another's company of an evening, filling it with talk of their dreams for a better future and, of course, dreams of the greatest women's football team ever to play in

Yorkshire. Now, whether the latter would ever happen was anyone's guess, she thought, as she walked through the warehouse to the mill yard doors and saw just Len and Anne sitting on the landing bay eating their snap.

'Lorna not here then? I really thought she would be. Perhaps her husband has told her not to join us.' Maggie sat down next to Len and Anne and unwrapped the boiled eggs she had prepared for her lunch, then started eating them.

'Lord, they smell, Maggie. Anything but boiled eggs at dinner time,' Len said. 'It won't be Lorna's husband that is stopping her from playing. He looks like a little feeble man. In fact, the coppers came here once for Lorna. She'd hit her husband over the head with the frying pan when he had answered back, and he ended up in the hospital, and she nearly got charged with assault until he decided to drop the charges, rather than make publicity about himself. You don't really know what you are taking on there. Be thankful she hasn't shown her face.' Len looked at Maggie and couldn't help but wonder what he had let himself in for, let alone Maggie.

'That's the kind of reputation we want our goalie to have. Nobody would dare touch her. I hope she decides to join us. Once folk have read our poster, they will start showing up. I'm sure they will, and then we will just have to pick the cream from them and train, train, train until we are perfect. Nothing less will do, especially if I'm going to be captain,' Maggie added quietly and hoped that nobody would dispute giving herself the position of captain.

Hattie stood in line and watched the clock's hands moving closer and closer to one o'clock as she moved up the queue of women waiting to be paid their husbands' army payment. She held her breath as she got to the counter and smiled at the cashier.

'Payment for Hattie Braithwaite from Private Braithwaite 43567 16th West Yorks Regiment,' Hattie said and watched as the cashier behind the counter flicked her way through the many pay envelopes and to her immense relief eventually stopped at her name in the alphabet.

'Yes, here you are. Oh, and there are actually two payments for you, one from a private Oliver Gilbert?' The cashier looked at her and smiled.

'My brother, bless him, did not need to send money home. I'll put it away for him into savings, and then he will have something for himself once he returns home.' Hattie smiled and put both payments into her skirt pocket. As the Post Office clock struck one, it looked as if she was going to have to run back down the street if she was not to be noticed as absent from her position at her carding machine. Hopefully, Anne would cover for her if Sara realised she was not back in her place.

'Where have you been? I told Sara Turner that you were indisposed on the toilet, so say the same when she walks back this way,' Anne shouted in her ear above the sound of the clanking machinery, having crossed from her machine to Hattie's.

'Ta, there was a queue at the Post Office,' Hattie replied and then got on with her job with a lot lighter heart. The rent was easily going to be paid that evening, and the payments meant both of her menfolk must be fit and well. Two fewer worries for her, she thought, as she went about her work and thought of the few hours she and Bruce had lain in one another's arms and when he promised to return to her.

Meanwhile, in the trenches of no man's land, Bruce watched the rats scurrying along the trench and reloaded his rifle, looking at Oliver as he did so. They had been given the basic training and then shipped out to hold the line against the Germans, ill prepared and fearful of losing their lives.

'They never told us that it was going to be like this. What they should have said was join together, serve together and bloody well die together.' Bruce was wide-eyed with fear. His regiment, commonly known as the Bradford Pals, was in the thick of it as shells rained down and the wisps of mustard gas hung in the air.

'I'd rather be back working in Swainbank's Mill, Ollie. I reckon nowt to having my head shot off my shoulders,' Bruce said and wondered whether he dared put his head above the protection of the trench.

'It's hell! Why on earth did we sign up? We are just cannon fodder for the bloody Germans. That village of Serre has been obliterated; it's just ruins, and for what, a few extra yards taken, only to be taken back by tomorrow by Jerry. All that keeps me going is thinking of home and Hattie,' said Oliver.

'Aye, she should have got her pay from us both now, and I've written to her. It will be grand to hear from her.' Bruce looked to his left and right and heard the sergeant shout his orders and slap his swagger stick next to his thigh. He, too, looked more than worried as he walked along the trench, giving orders and making sure that his men were ready for the next assault.

'I've not told her that we are over here yet. I don't want her worrying. We'll stick together, Ollie. When they shout "over", we make for the next shell hole and stay there and keep our bloody heads down.'

'Aye, we'll look after one another. I'll be with you. We've lost too many pals already in this war, but they'll not get us two.' Ollie felt his stomach churn, and he wanted to be sick as the sergeant shouted to get ready for the next assault. Bruce and he had witnessed soldier after soldier lose their lives on the battlefield of the Somme in the few days since they had arrived. Bodies of those they knew lay on the muddy, rat-infested fields, with horses and soldiers caught in barbed wire, both crying with pain and fear until a sniper put them out of their misery. It was a living hell, and thank God, Hattie would never know the truth of real war.

'Attack, attack!' the order ran out, and both men looked at one another and clambered over the trench top and prayed to God that they would survive the following few hours as they stumbled and ran across no man's land. What both of them wouldn't give to be back in Bradford, sitting in the kitchen of number 2 Gladstone Street with the woman they both loved.

'Oh, pie and peas, what a treat, Hattie.' Maggie looked at the steaming plate of mushy peas and meat and potato pie that Hattie had bought from the market stall seller on her way home.

'A Friday treat, seeing as both Oliver and Bruce have sent me some money. I have their address to write to now as well, it was in with their pay. I heard the woman at the Post Office counter saying that the GPO send all the mail to their home depot in Regent's Park and then it's taken by ship from Folkestone or Southampton to those that are fighting in the trenches. Amazingly, my letter will be read by Bruce as he sits in a trench in France.' Hattie looked at her treat of a supper and hoped that both Oliver and Bruce were eating well, as she poked her fork into her pie.

'I don't think it will be meat and tattie pie, probably a tin of bully-beef from what I've heard.' Maggie looked at Hattie, who was putting on a brave face. The whole of the country was reading the news from the Somme, getting more grave by the day.

'As long as they and all our menfolk are safe.' Hattie tried to smile. 'You know, if we do get our football club started, let's see if we could make some money for charities linked to our brave men. A small charge on every gate, although I don't expect to see masses coming to watch us.'

'Whoa! Masses, we don't even have a goalkeeper yet or a full team, let alone anywhere to play. Although tomorrow, I am to solve that.' Maggie was enjoying every mouthful of her supper and was so thankful that she did not have to walk home to Esholt to her parents' home.

'And how are you going to do that, may I ask?' Hattie sat back and quizzed her determined lodger.

'I have friends with grounds not being used at the moment. Leave it with me. Although I will probably get a ribbing when I ask for a favour.' Maggie reached for her pipe from above the fireplace and lit it, sitting down in the chair next to the open fire. 'If it wasn't raining out there, I'd say we have to go for a gill, but I'm quite content here. Perhaps tomorrow night, a quick one at The Diplomat, and Anne can come with us. Hopefully, it will be a celebratory pint if I can get my way tomorrow.'

'Oh, I don't know about that. I've never been in a public house in my life, it's not really ladylike,' Hattie said and blushed.

'Ladylike, and you want to play football in front of crowds of people. You'll not be playing in your skirts, you know, we'll need knickerbockers, more freedom for movement.' Maggie drew on her pipe. 'I spotted some twill that looks like it's been forgotten about at the back of the warehouse the other day. If we do get a team together, it would make good knickerbockers. Are you any good at sewing?'

'Knickerbockers! Over my dead body! Everybody will laugh at us, and what men that will come and watch us will come for the wrong reason,' Hattie exclaimed.

'They'll come more to watch us making fools of ourselves running about in skirts. Of course we need knickerbockers and a shirt, even a hat if it's colder weather,' Maggie laughed.

'Oh, my Lord, what would my Bruce think of all this? I'll have to write and tell him and Ollie. It will give them both something to laugh about.'

'Aye, you do that, it will keep their spirits up. They will need all the good news they can get.' Maggie sat back and closed her eyes. Tomorrow, when she did her business with Peter O'Rourke, she would be asking a great deal of his friendship, and she hoped that he would take her words seriously.

11

'Are you not going to tell me where you are going and who to see?' Hattie looked up at Maggie as she swept the kitchen floor clean.

'No, if you don't know nowt, then you'll not be disappointed if I don't get my way.' Maggie pulled on her brown hat with a felt rose attached and swore as she pulled on her coat. 'Bloody weather, I could have done with it not raining today. Things are glum enough without the clouds hanging over us.'

'What do you expect? We live on the backbone of the Pennines, it's right Yorkshire weather.' Hattie leaned on her brush. 'Could be a good omen for the Yorkshire lasses.'

'I don't know about that, it will be hard work playing on a rain-soaked pitch with a heavy leather football. We'll need to pray for fair days when we play, else we will come off the pitch absolutely jiggered.' Maggie pulled her hat even further down over her ears and stood looking out of the doorway at the rain bouncing off the cobbled street.

'Well, get yourself gone and put wood in the hole,' Hattie said, meaning close the door. 'You are letting the cold in, and the house is nice and warm since the coal man arrived first thing with the regular order. I was so glad I had money to pay him.'

'All right, wish me luck! If I can get us somewhere to play, we will go out and celebrate. Have a quick gill and take Anne with us, I'll call and tell her on my way back if it's good news.' Hattie pulled her collar up and faced the weather with a determined look on her face.

'Good luck, whatever you are up to. I'm going to make a brew and sit and write to Bruce while you are out. I miss him so much, and it seems like a lifetime ago since I said goodbye to him at Bradford station.' Hattie sighed and put the kettle onto the fire. While the house was quiet, she would say what her heart was feeling and tell Bruce and Oliver her news. She took pen and paper from the kitchen drawer and, with a cup of tea next to her, started writing.

2 Gladstone Street
Bradford
7 October 1916

My darling Bruce,

It seems an age since we said goodbye to one another, and I count the days until you return to me.

Thank you for your letter, which I received safely, and I am now in receipt of your pay and that of Ollie's through the Post Office. Can you tell Ollie that, unless I am desperate, I will put his money into a savings bank until he returns. It will be a nice nest egg for him to return to.

I'm still working at Swainbank's Mill, I've found some good friends there, and the work, at least, is not as dirty or dangerous as working in munitions. You can tell the poor girls and women who work making munitions, their skin has a yellow glow and their hair changes to a dirty-looking ginger. It hardly seems fair when they are putting their lives on the line, just like you, my dear, for their country. Although they don't face those dreadful Germans like you do, my darling. I read the headlines in the papers and pray every day that you and Oliver are safe and keeping your lovely heads down while looking after one another.

Father left home not long after you went. I believe he is living with Betty Booth, down on Cromwell Street. It was a bit of a shock when he left, but at least I am not beholden to his demands and moans. When you come home, my love, the house will be ours, as Dick Middleton, the owner, changed the rent to my name the first week you were away.

Now, for my news that will make you smile, I have become friends with a rather independent young woman called Maggie Fleming. In fact, she is renting my father's bedroom and keeping me company in the evening. Her money helps with the rent and buys one or two luxuries, like fish and chips on a Friday night. However, this will make you smile. She is absolutely mad about football! So much so, that we play every dinner time in the mill yard and at the moment we are asking if any other women would like to join us and make a proper football team. Joshua Swainbank let us display a poster asking if anybody wants to join us. So far, we only have the women that we know play, but hopefully, more will join us. Maggie is really determined to make us a winning team, 'The Yorkshire Lasses', or something like that, and that we should play professionally, just like men.

Oh, my love, I miss you so much. A week of being married to one another before you left hardly seemed fair. I pray that you come home safe to me and that we will soon be in one another's arms. I pray that God will keep you and Ollie safe. Don't put yourselves at risk and volunteer for any daring feat. You are always in my heart, and I long for your gentle touch.

I love you,

Hattie

Hattie felt the lump in her throat rise in her mouth and saw tears drop onto the table and wiped one off the paper she was writing on, not wanting the ink to smudge and give a tell-tale sign to Bruce that she had been crying. He had enough to worry about just keeping alive without knowing she was heart-broken. She walked over to the bookshelf and opened a book that was filled with tissue paper and the pressed flowers from her wedding, and took a dried spray of forget-me-nots from between the pages. They had been so vibrant in her wedding bouquet; now they were sending a message to her husband on the war-torn front, a message that she would never forget him or stop loving him as she placed them in the pages of her letter, folded them into an envelope and kissed the seal before placing it on the mantel-piece, ready to post. They might be hundreds of miles apart, but in her heart, they were together.

Maggie walked along Manningham Lane, making her way to the home of Bradford City at Valley Parade. There were no crowds gathered for a match, no hawkers selling their football favours, and no shouts of the paper seller as she walked towards one of the two stands that backed onto North Parade. A few weeks ago, the roadway would have been full of fans and recruiting officers looking for men who had escaped the draft. She walked towards the gateway into the stand, thinking it would probably be locked, but was surprised to find the gate open. She looked around her and felt a slight feeling of doing something wrong as she pushed open the gate and walked into the hallowed grounds of her beloved football club, without permission or payment. There were two wooden stands at the ground, and the rest was a standing area, where hundreds of people wrapped up against the cold had stood and watched their team, a sea of flat caps and mufflers, with shouts for their favourite player and boos! and ha's! as goals were saved or lost. Today, there was an eerie silence, and in the middle of the pitch, a puddle of rainwater was forming with no groundsmen available to clear the precious turf. Maggie stood for a moment and remembered better days when she had urged on Bradford and her cousin as they ran back and forth up and down the pitch. Would half of those players ever return? she wondered, as she stood in the rain.

'Hey, what are you doing in here? Do you not know the pitch is closed?' The voice of Peter O'Rourke shouted at her from behind her.

Maggie turned and looked at the manager of the club, who was carrying a net of footballs and making his way down the stands.

'Sorry, the gate was open, and I was hoping that you'd be here. I need to speak to you.'

'Oh, sorry, Maggie. I didn't realise it was you. I was just having a tidy up and a sort out. There's nothing much else I can do this Saturday. I'm going to be blinking lost without the lads to manage, it's what has made my life worthwhile of late. Not that I should be complaining. At least I'm not gambling with my life on the front line. Thank God for breaking my leg when I used to play and it not healing properly.' Peter put down his net of balls, sighed and looked around the ground. 'Look at it, rain-soaked and miserable, just how I feel.'

'Yes, there's a strange feeling in the air, I must admit. This part of the town will never be the same without a football or rugby match on a Saturday.' Maggie walked towards him. 'But perhaps that needn't be, if I can ask you a favour and you tell me what you think of my idea.' Maggie looked at Peter and hoped he would not think that she had gone completely mad. It was him, after all, that had said she could have played for Bradford, if only she had been a man.

'Oh, it's a favour that you are asking. Well, let's talk about it over a cuppa, out of this rain and cold. I've got the kettle keeping warm on the side of the stove in the clubhouse. Come on down with me, and you can tell me what you want while we both have a warm-up and a brew.'

'You'll not laugh when I tell you, because I've never been more serious in my life,' Maggie said as she followed Peter down the steps and onto the sodden pitch, heading for the white-painted clubhouse with advertising banners displayed on it for Wills Cigarettes and Aniseed Balls, as well as the empty fixture board.

'Aye, I don't know. What a bloody day for you to come out on, Maggie. What are you doing here that is so important?' Peter pulled the brown enamelled kettle onto the top of the wood-burning stove and blew the dust out of two enamel cups, and eyed Maggie. What did she want with him? He'd no jobs going if that was what she was thinking.

Maggie stood and looked around the clubhouse walls. There were pegs on one wall of the wooden shed, where the players hung their clothes, and benches where they sat and discussed tactics. On the other side of the room, there were badges and shields won in previous games. It was a Bradford fan's idea of heaven as she spotted the shirt worn by Jimmy Speirs, who had scored the winning goal in the 1911 FA Cup.

'If you are looking for the cup, it's not here. A copy is at my house for safekeeping. But aye, that's the shirt my best ever player wore, claret with an amber yoke. It was a different kit that day, it brought us luck, I'm sure of it. The poor bugger will be up to his knees in French mud with bullets flying over his head now.' Peter sighed and passed Maggie a cup of steaming hot tea. 'I've no milk so I hope you'll be able to drink it black.'

'This will be grand, it will warm me up. Thank you.' Maggie sipped hesitantly and smiled.

'Well, what's this about then? What are you doing here and what has it got to do with me?' Peter looked at the strong-willed young woman and waited as she sat and shuffled in her seat, building up to ask him her question.

'We are going to be starting a women's football team at the mill, and I need your help.' Maggie held her breath and hardly dared to look at Peter.

Peter looked at her open-mouthed. 'A women's football team! And do you think that will be popular? I know you like your football, lass, but I think you are in a minority.'

'No, I'm not. There are a few women who like knocking a ball about during our dinner time, and in the newspaper the other day, it was saying that there are two teams that play one another regularly up in

Ulverston. It seems to be a thing that is only going to grow over time. I bet all the women in the munition factories will be putting teams together. I just want our team to be one of the first.' Maggie looked hard at Peter and saw his face had a smile on it.

'Oh, aye, and what has all this to do with me? I've never managed a team of women apart from my old lass and daughter at home, and even those test me to my limit.' Peter grinned.

'I was hoping that you would let us use these grounds to practise and play our games on. The mill yard is all right with just the three of us kicking a ball to one another, but not when we have got a full team together . . .' Maggie said, and then realised that she felt as if she was asking the earth, and it just sounded like children playing in a school yard.

'Three or you, eh! You need a few more to form a team, and you'll need boots, balls, and what will you all wear? You'll never replace men playing.' Peter shook his head and then looked at the anger on Maggie's face.

'Oh, yes, we will, we are just as good as any fellas' team, you'll see. Hattie Braithwaite is one hell of a player, and we have our eye on a lass from Ireland, who used to play hurling; she's going to be our goalie. No one will dare tackle her.' Maggie's voice softened. 'I think you'll regret missing out if you don't jump onto the wagon now. It's not every day you get a chance to sign up the best women's team in Yorkshire.' Maggie looked hard at Peter O'Rourke. 'We wouldn't expect to be paid! It would bring crowds in just out of curiosity.'

'You are mad, Maggie. I should have known that you'd miss the football. But honestly, lass, I don't know how I can help you. The ground belongs to the FA Board. I'd have to ask them for permission. The last time women played, I think they regretted even considering the suggestion. I don't want my name being laughed at by those boards of theirs.' Peter shook his head.

'The ground looks so sad without anyone playing on it. Could we at least, if I can gather a team, have one match here, just to see if we can complete a full ninety minutes? Just the once, Pete, please, nobody needs ever know if you don't say anything,' Maggie pleaded.

'Aye, I don't know, I'd lose my job if the FA ever found out.' Peter looked at Maggie; he liked the lass, she had a passion for the game like him.

However, she was just the wrong sex.

'Please, just one game. Just to see if I have a team,' Maggie pleaded.

Peter shook his head. 'One game and that's all. And you keep it quiet.'

'Oh, thank you, Peter. You won't regret it. Just so that I can give my girls some feel of what it would be like to play a real game.' Maggie sat back in her chair and took a long sip of tea. She knew that Peter would not let her down. One game with him watching should prove that she meant business and that his ground would be full of supporters and players again.

Peter smiled. 'One match and make it on a Sunday, just for you to see if they are worth anything.' Hopefully, Maggie would not get too interested, and the idea would fizzle out, Peter thought as she stood up and looked as if she had been given a king's ransom.

'A Sunday it is, and I swear you'll not regret it.' Maggie beamed as she left the clubhouse. She had got the ground. Now she needed her players and the rest she would figure out as they progressed. And progress they would.

Maggie stood on the doorstep of Anne's home and waited for the door to be opened with a smile on her face and her heart beating wildly. Anne opened the door and quickly drew it towards her, so that her mother couldn't hear who she was talking to as she yelled, 'Who is it, Anne?'

'It's only a salesperson, Mother. I'll get rid of them,' Anne shouted into the kitchen and gave Maggie a glaring look.

'A salesperson! Anne Birtwistle, I could kiss you, I love you so much, and I'm so happy,' Maggie said and didn't care who heard.

'Shh. My mother and the neighbours, keep your voice down. What are you doing here? I've told you not to call, else my mother will only suspect something, because you don't hide who you are.'

'I don't care, and neither should you. Anyway, I had to come and tell you my news.' Maggie held her breath and then exploded. 'We can play on Bradford City's pitch. I've just asked Peter O'Rourke and he's let us have a go with a full team on it, just once, but it's a start. He'll see how good we play and will want us back.'

'Oh, Lord, you haven't even a team, Maggie, or anything else. Don't you think you are running before you can walk?' Anne kept glancing back, hoping her mother wouldn't hear the conversation.

'Once I can say we are playing at Valley Parade, everyone will want to play.' Maggie grinned.

'Tell them to bugger off, Anne, we don't want anything,' Anne's mother yelled, and Anne heard her reach for her walking stick in order to back her up with the unwanted visitor.

'I'll have to go! Well done, I suppose.' Anne turned and smiled at Maggie.

'Meet me tonight at The Diplomat. Sneak away when you can and have a drink with me to celebrate.' Maggie touched Anne's hand as she turned to close the door.

'I'll try. I can't promise,' she whispered and then closed the door on Maggie, leaving her standing and smiling like the cat that had just drunk the cream.

'I never go to the pub. I've never been in one in my life,' Hattie protested later that evening, as Maggie almost shoved her through the doors of The Diplomat and waltzed her up to the bar, before pointing to three chairs and a table in a quiet corner of the snug.

'Once will not hurt you. You never know, you might get to liking it. Do you have any idea what you want to drink?' Maggie asked as she watched Hattie walk over to the corner they had spotted.

'Whisky. I've always heard about folk drinking whisky or gin. It can't be mother's ruin if I drink it, seeing I'm not a mother yet.' Hattie grinned.

'I think a sherry will be enough for you. I'm not propping you up on your way home.' Maggie pointed to the jug of the locally brewed ale and nodded, and then asked for a small sherry for Hattie, paying the barmaid with a smile.

'Anne should be joining us shortly, now that it's gone dark. She'll be waiting until she gets her mother to bed, and she goes to sleep. She doesn't know about me. Anne says she'll not like me as soon as she sees me.' Maggie took a drink of her dark brown porter and wiped the creamy head from around her lips.

'I can't see why she shouldn't like you. You are easy to get along with,' Hattie replied and looked at her small glass of sherry and tried to summon up the courage to have a drink.

'I think it's Anne, she doesn't want her mother to even suspect how close we are.' Maggie took another mouthful and looked around her. 'You know what some folk are like, they gossip and imagine all sorts.'

Hattie blushed. 'Well, it's their problem and as long as you are happy; but as I say, not under my roof, please.' She picked up her sherry and took a quick sip, nearly coughing as the warmth of the liquor hit the back of her throat.

'That'll warm you up. Good job you didn't have a whisky, that would have caught in your throat.' Maggie grinned and looked around her. She half expected to see Joshua Swainbank sitting in the wide armchair next to the window, but he wasn't to be seen. Instead, there were a few familiar faces at the bar and in the opposite corner to them, a body of six or seven rough-looking men with Irish accents, all whispering and deep in conversation. She couldn't help but wonder why they weren't fighting for their country, like every other man. Conscription dodgers, she whispered to herself, the lowest of the low. Her face lit up as she noticed Anne walking towards them, looking flustered as she came closer.

'Lord, I thought my mother was never going to go to sleep. Anyway, I'm here now. At least it has stopped raining and I can relax for an hour or two.' Anne sat down in the spare chair and looked at Maggie and Hattie. 'Good news then! We have got somewhere to play, and not just somewhere, but the main pitch in Bradford.' She gently touched Maggie's hand and smiled.

'Aye, Peter was only too willing for us to give it a

go,' Maggie lied through her teeth. 'He'll be glad to see the crowds come back when we really get good at our game.' She went to the bar, ordered Anne her usual drink of sherry and stood and watched as Anne and Hattie talked together. She'd give Hattie a month or so and then she was sure that she could convince her to let Anne stay with her until the early hours. She returned to the table and placed the drink in front of Anne and watched as Hattie took another sip of her sherry, not screwing her nose up this time as she did so.

'I quite like this now, I've got used to it.' Hattie sat back and felt the colour rising to her cheeks.

'You need a lemonade next time. Can't be getting you tipsy. You are not used to it, unlike me,' Anne replied and then saw the group of men in the corner. 'I don't like the look of them lot, they all sound Irish. Fenians, I bet, and I think that's Lorna O'Donnell's husband with them. I've only seen him once, but I'm sure it's him.'

'Don't worry, Anne, we will walk you home when we've had our celebratory drink. Aye, you could be right. They seem to be plotting something. They've been huddled together and whispering all night. You can't trust the bloody Irish, but I still want Lorna

O'Donnell as our goalie. That mop of ginger hair and her attitude would frighten anyone with any sense.'

'She's not said yes, yet,' Hattie replied and looked at the group of men.

'No, but she will. She loves a good game, just like me.' Maggie glanced at the men and thought the same as Anne. Trouble was brewing in Ireland, and the Irish had plenty to say about it.

12

Lorna O'Donnell looked around her two-bedroom home, to find her husband asleep in the corner of the kitchen. He'd been gone all night, but she didn't know where. His breath stank of drink, and his language had left a lot to be desired as he had entered the family home in the early hours of the morning. It was a usual experience for Mick O'Donnell. Through the day he was a quiet man without a word to say for himself, but with a drop of drink in him, he thought he could take on the King's Army and would have done if he was given a chance. He had two lifestyles, and it was the darker one and his associates during those times that frightened Lorna. The man might have left Ireland, but Ireland had not left the man, and that was where her troubles lay.

'Look at the waste of a man, he's not fit to be your father,' Lorna spat at her daughters of thirteen and eight. 'Never get married to the first man that catches your eye. Get one with brass, not looks, that's where I went wrong. Ta, he's a useless man.'

Both girls looked at their father and then their mother, not wanting to cross either, as Lorna kicked her husband's outstretched feet and swore before filling three checked handkerchiefs full of cheese and soda bread together for their dinners.

'My mother told me he was a useless slob, but did I listen? No, I did not, and now I'm paying the price. I should have stayed back in Kerry and married Frank Farrell. He was a better man by far.' Lorna glanced at her two daughters, who could not get out of the house fast enough; the youngest, Ella, to school, and the oldest, Freda, to her newly started job helping a local seamstress. They didn't like their mother when she was in a temper, knowing all too well to keep out of her way, else pots and pans would fly through the air and she would not be concerned who they hit.

'You make sure the fire is still lit, Ella, when you get in from school and then go for a ha'penny of tea and a loaf of bread, because your useless father won't be stirring so far. No wonder he can't hold a job down.' Lorna gave her husband another kick and then placed two pennies on the table for her daughter to spend on the groceries. 'Put them in your pocket, our Ella, else he'll nobbut spend it on another gill.' Lorna sighed. 'Now you get to work, Freda, and you go to Sara O'Keefe's until it's time for school. I'll not be leaving you with this useless lump.' Lorna reached for her shawl and made sure that both girls were fit for the day that lay in front of them as she ushered them out of the terraced door and watched them go their separate ways until it was time for her to step out and get to work at Swainbank's Mill.

Lorna , full of anger over her husband's drunken night, pulled her shawl around her and stepped out. The bloody man was just playing into the neighbours' way of thinking of the Irish: lazy, drunken, potato-eating paddies, and she wasn't happy. She'd worked hard all her life and left a life that she had loved behind her in Ireland for the sake of uprooting and going to live with Mick O'Donnell in his new home in Bradford. It was only when she had arrived straight off the boat at Heysham that she realised that all he had promised her was not what it seemed. The house had been a squalid, near-dilapidated terraced house in the worst part of Bradford, and the work he said he had turned out to be wherever he could get it. Nobody wanted a paddy, thinking they were lazy and drunk, which they were not far wrong about when it came to her Mick. But her eyes were still full of love for him, and as the months turned to years, she found herself, like every good Catholic, pregnant and a mother to two grand girls. Those she would not change for the world, but when it came to her husband Mick, she had been tempted a time or two to hit him so hard that he would end six feet under or floating in the underground passages of Bradford Beck on its way to the river Aire at Shipley. Her temper had been well known at home and in her position as goalie in her local hurling team, and many a person had commented that it would end her in trouble if she let it. Her mind turned to the conversation she had held with the dark-haired lass who had approached her about playing football. Sure, she'd been curt with her; football was nothing like hurling, and she would never have seen a hurling game in her life. It would probably be a waste of her time, and age was against her now, whether it was hurling or football. It would rile Mick, though, if she were not at home being a wife and mother to his children. The girls were both old enough to look after themselves now, so perhaps she should give it some thought. It would serve the bugger right if he had to fend for himself for a weekend. She quickened her pace as the lights of Swainbank's came into view. She'd see how she felt at dinner time and perhaps just go along and see what the eejits were up to, she thought, as she clocked in and made her way up to the weaving gantry. Just for once, she might just do something that she enjoyed.

'It's only just gone half past, give them time,' Maggie soothed, though she gave Anne a worried look.

'You might have to have me in your side, but I'm still not wearing a wig.' Len sighed and watched as Hattie kicked the ball hard out of frustration and swore as it went to the bottom of the mill yard.

'It'll not come to that, believe me,' Maggie replied and looked at the clipboard that she had brought with her in the hope of putting names down to make a team.

'We need to say what positions we are happy to play in. I've no idea where I'd be best playing,' Anne said and sighed. 'I've got a rough idea, but not sure.'

'The way we are going, we will not be playing at all! That manager at Valley Parade will think of us as stupid women who know nothing if we can't get eleven of us interested.' Maggie retrieved the ball and then looked up at the open warehouse doors.

'Well, what's wrong with you eejits?' Lorna said loudly as she walked through the doors with two fellow workers next to her. 'I came because I heard there was some football to be played, but all I see are glum faces.'

Maggie looked up and smiled. 'Lorna, I'm so glad that you have made it, and with friends.'

'Aye, this is Molly Brennan, strong with her left foot, she tells me, and this is Bridget Baines, never kicked a ball in her life, but she can run like a whippet, so she'd make a good winger.' Lorna patted both of her friends on the back. 'But this is of little consequence. If this yard is all we've got to play in, we're cooked, because it's no good to man nor beast,' she muttered and looked around her. 'And your football is fecked.'

Maggie and Hattie stood together and looked at the three new players, and breathed in.

'No, we have got no other than Bradford City's pitch to play on. The manager, Peter O'Rourke, agreed with me that we could play there when I went to see him on Saturday. We just need a good team to play now.'

'Well, you are looking at it, or at least half of it, and there will be others wanting to join when they realise that it isn't just a kick about with a bag of wind in the mill yard. What are we playing for? You never put on your poster; not just for the hell of it, I hope. I'm not showing my bloomers for nothing. There has to be a purpose.' Lorna sat down on the side of the loading bay along with Molly and Bridget.

'We thought if we got a team going, we'd play to boost troops' funding or help the Sally Army or the Red Cross, anything that is a deserving cause for our lads and menfolk fighting,' Hattie said and watched the three women look at one another and nod in agreement.

'And who's this? He can't pass as a woman with that chin stubble!' Lorna looked at Len and grinned.

'I'm Len. I work with Maggie downstairs in the warehouse. You will have seen me most mornings when you go into work. Maggie has made it clear that I'm not to play, but she says I can be a linesman.' Len looked at the wild-looking, strong woman. He had seen her and heard her working most mornings, but she obviously hadn't given him a second look.

'Ah, good man, we'll need a linesman and we'll need a decent referee that doesn't take sides. But the big question is who, if we do get a team, are we going to play against? Unless we get enough interested women to make two teams?' Lorna looked at Maggie for answers.

'Ulverston has a ladies' team. They are playing on Boxing Day against a local team, and I bet they would have a match against us in the new year,' Maggie said off the top of her head. And all her followers looked at her with open mouths.

'Ulverston? Where in God's name is that?' Lorna asked in disbelief.

'It's in Westmorland, near the lakes,' Maggie said quietly and wished she could retract her words, as she knew nobody would want to travel that far and getting there would be nearly impossible.

'Ah, now you are full of blarney,' Lorna said and shook her head.

Molly put her head to one side and looked at Bridget. 'Didn't you say that your mate who works in the bottling factory was talking about women's football? Arthur Hey that owns it has a lot to do with Bradford City, I've heard my father say.'

Bridget, who was quietly spoken, suddenly came to life.

'Yes, she works at Hey's Brewery next to Manningham Mills. Her boss has shares, I think, in one of the football grounds, but I don't know if it's

City or Bradford Park Avenue. I'll ask her. I think she said they were thinking of putting a football team together and their boss was going to be backing them.'

'Well, I hope he doesn't have anything to do with Bradford City, else Peter O'Rourke will have second thoughts about us playing there.' Maggie looked crestfallen.

'I might have got it completely wrong, and I was only half listening. I wasn't that bothered when she was talking about it at least a month ago,' Bridget said quietly.

'A month ago! And I thought we were quick thinking about it.' Maggie sighed. 'This coming Saturday, I'll go and tell Peter O'Rourke that we hopefully will have a team and that we want to play on Sunday. Please let us have eleven in number by then! Are you all with me?'

Everybody nodded their heads.

'We need that ground, and hopefully we will have enough women playing for us by then. I need you all to get other women to play for us, and then we can prove we are serious. But we can't just take anybody, we have to be as good if not better than the men, and that's going to take practice and dedication.' Maggie looked at her team, and they were her team; she had taken charge of being captain automatically, and she was going to make them the best team in Yorkshire if she had her way. Better than Hey's Brewery Ladies anyway.

'I'm sorry, Maggie, the Board and the FA won't let me have you play here at Valley Parade. I know I promised you, but I just can't let you.' Peter O'Rourke couldn't look straight at Maggie. He hated going back on his word. But things had changed following a conversation with his main director and the board of managers.

'I don't understand, you said it would be all right and now you are telling me that we can't even play for one time on the pitch, just to see if we are worth anything?' Maggie was frustrated and angry. She knew Peter wasn't telling her everything.

'I know, but I just can't, lass, my hands are tied. I've been told no, and that's all I can say.' Peter put his head down. The truth was, Arthur Hey, owner of Hey's Brewery, had spoken to him after hearing rumours and insisted that if any women's team was going to play at Valley Parade, it was going to be his team, not a rabble from a woollen mill. It would seem that Maggie was not the only one who had seen the interest in women's football and had seen the publicity that it would bring. He'd reminded him sharply just how much he invested in the football club and hinted that his job might not be needed in the times they were in.

'It's the boss of Hey's Brewery and the bottle firm, isn't it? He's got his own team and the brewery is backing them. You can't say no to them. I bet he owns half the club! And yet you nearly laughed at me when I mentioned it last weekend.' Maggie was annoyed.

'Aye, lass, I can't lie, it is. He's got me over a barrel. I hate going back on my word, especially when you have a team. But if you get a good team, you could play them here, I'm sure. Phoenix and Dynamo Manufacturers are getting a team together too, so you are not the first with the idea in Bradford.' Peter shook his head. 'I'm sorry, but have you thought about asking at Park Avenue? I'm friends with Tom Maley, the manager, and he loves his football. I'd go and see him and tell him I've sent you after feeling bad letting you down.'

'That ground isn't as good, it's been used for cricket and rugby in the past, and it's the other side of town.' Maggie sounded deflated.

'The ground isn't that bad, and he had a damn good team. They were ninth in the league this year and above us. It's the only thing I can think of. Perhaps you could give it a try. You don't know that you've even got a playing team yet. I'll warn you with this as well, the FA are going to be charging a pound for a practice night per team and three pounds for you to play a match, so I hope you lasses are prepared to put your hands in your pockets if you are serious about it. Not that Tom agrees with them, he falls out many a time with those who he thinks talk nonsense when it comes to the game. He's a Scotsman, says what he thinks, but has a heart of gold.'

'I wanted us to play here at The Valley and I didn't think we would have to pay to use the ground. We would have to have a whip around before each match, and the lasses can barely afford to live, let alone pay out of their own pockets to play a game of football. Without a backer, we don't stand a chance.' Maggie could only see the demise of the team as she looked around the ground she loved.

'Nay, don't give up. I know you can play football, go and see Tom. He's your man, he's even thinking of organising matches for the lads that have come back injured with wounds. He's a good man.' Peter sighed.

He had hated admitting the truth, but he was just a pawn in a different game.

Maggie lifted her head. 'Right, I'll go and see him. I'll not be defeated.'

'That's the spirit. Just mention Celtic to him or take somebody with you who's Scots, his sympathies lie with his homeland,' Peter said and watched as Maggie made her way across the dew-covered field. He wished her well, he really did, and he knew that it would not be the last time he saw the wild Miss Fleming and that next time it would probably be with a football at her feet.

13

Lorna, Hattie and Maggie stood on the tram. It was Saturday afternoon, and all the women had abandoned everything that needed doing, despite housework and family needing their attention.

'Your man's not a Scot. With a name like Maley, he's as Irish as me,' Lorna said and held onto the hand strap of the tram as it jolted over the points to the far side of Bradford.

'Peter said he's a Scotsman, and I remember that he used to play for Celtic. He had a lot to do with forming them as well,' Maggie said and peered through the tram windows, making sure they hadn't gone past their stop.

'Ah, well, there you go. Celtic is nearly a hundred per cent Irish. The whole club is made of Irish Catholic players. We will have something in common, the love of the Emerald Isle.' Lorna grinned. 'I'll talk him around, now don't you worry.'

'You don't really need me. I could have stopped at home. It might be a wild goose chase anyway,' Hattie moaned. 'He might not even be at the ground.'

'It's Saturday afternoon. If he's as mad on football as Peter O'Rourke says he is, he'll be there. It's like a vicar going to church on a Sunday,' Maggie said and then urged the two of them to the back of the tram as she summoned the conductor to let him know they wanted to alight.

'We are nearly on the outskirts of Bradford. It's going to be a trip every time we play,' Hattie groaned. 'Perhaps we should have a rethink.'

'Stop complaining. Come on, we are here now, and to be honest, it looks bigger and better than I remembered it. I've only been here when they played a derby match. At least they have a stand at one end, and there's plenty of room around the wooden fence to watch. That's the cricket pitch and pavilion. They won't even have a team to play that now.' Maggie strode out in the direction of the club, passing rows of terraced houses that were clinging to the edge of the mill town.

From within the ground came the sound of men's voices, and all three women looked at one another.

'They can't be playing a game? They've been

stopped,' Hattie said as they walked over to the open fenced end of the ground and stood beneath the trees that edged the green space, pulling their shawls about them as the late autumn wind blew the falling leaves around.

'Well, look at that. They are soldiers playing and they are injured, some are even on crutches,' Maggie gasped as she watched wounded soldiers kicking balls to one another and shouting and laughing even when they missed catching the ball.

'Doesn't that touch your heart? Look at them, bless them, I never knew there was anything like this going on down here.' Hattie caught her breath and thought about her husband and brother and just hoped that they were safe.

'A good afternoon, ladies, it's a braw wind that blows you my way. Have you come to watch the football or maybe admire our brave men? Although I must tell you most are married.' Tom Maley walked up behind the three women and smiled. He was tall with dark greying hair and his blue eyes shone as he reached for his pocket watch from out of his waistcoat pocket to check the time. 'Nearly time for the lads to call it a day. Their transport will be coming for them to take them back to the convalescent home at Shipley.'

'I think what you are doing is wonderful. I know my husband and brother, if they got injured and returned home, would welcome the idea.' Hattie looked at the caring man as he stood with them and watched his raggle-taggle team of wounded soldiers.

'Aye, they need hope, and something to take their minds off the horrific things they have witnessed. But try and tell the FA that. They think I shouldn't be allowing these lads to play, but I have different plans.' Tom Maley held his hand out to Hattie. 'Tom Maley, manager of this ground and a rogue one at that.' Hattie took his hand and shook it. 'You have men serving? I hope they are safe.'

'I do, my brother and husband, somewhere in France. I don't exactly know where, but I pray they are safe.' Hattie turned to Maggie and Lorna. 'These are my friends Maggie Fleming and Lorna O'Donnell. We all play football together, which is why we are here.'

'Ladies who play football! Now it is an honour to meet you, ladies. The FA did you wrong back in the day, as well as my lads. However, I hear that there is a resurgence.' He shook Maggie and Lorna's hands and looked at Lorna as she smiled and greeted him.

'To be sure, they don't know what they are

missing. We play football just as good as any man,' Lorna replied and grinned.

'Ah, a lady from the old country, a fellow spirit. My team play in green and white stripes to remind me of my Celtic roots, and indeed, when I managed a team up in Scotland, it was Celtic. I'm proud to say both player and manager.' Tom then turned to Maggie. 'And you, my dear, have you got this love of football that takes over our lives?'

'I do, and that is why we are here. We are putting a ladies' team together with workers from our woollen mill. It will be a winning team because, so far, all our players are determined to show that we can play just as good as any man.' Maggie stopped and looked at Hattie and Lorna for support.

Lorna sighed and put her hands on her hips. 'Ah, just tell Tom how it is. That your so-called friend Peter O'Rourke has let you down and that you are looking for somewhere for us to play?' Lorna shook her head. 'I need to get home to my brood as soon as I can. That useless lump of a man didn't come home last night.'

Tom looked at Maggie. 'So you know my old friend Peter. Now there's a man. Unlike me, his hands are tied good and firmly with his directors and the

FA. He will have to do as he's told. They have given me so many warnings in the past I think they have given up with me. Plus I own my ground, so I do as I like.' Tom smirked and put his hands in his pockets. 'Come and meet some of my players. They all look to have had enough and are waiting for the transport back to Shipley. They will be glad to have new faces to talk to.' Tom looked at the group of close friends. 'Just for a second, I'll not hold you up.' He smiled at Lorna. 'That man of yours will return if he's got any sense. He wouldn't want to lose a woman like you.'

Hattie nudged Maggie as they walked across the field. Tom Maley must need glasses, or he was just using his winning charm to get his way.

'Oh, he's just a man, never thinks,' Lorna said and walked next to the man she had taken a liking to.

The ten soldiers sat on the steps of the stands and looked up at Tom and his guests as he approached them. Some looked weary with bandages and wounds upon their heads, and some had crutches by their sides. They had all experienced the atrocities of war, and playing football, no matter how badly, was like a miracle to them. Smoke from shared cigarettes rose around their heads as Tom approached them.

'Now then, my lads, do you know what we've got

here?' Tom stood in front of the group as they eyed Maggie, Hattie and Lorna over.

'No, but you are greedy, Tom. Three women at once,' a cheeky Tommy shouted and lay back smoking his cigarette with a bandage around his head.

'Now then, lads, a bit of respect! These ladies are thinking of having their own football team. I don't know much about it as of yet, but I suspect that they have come to ask if they can play on the ground.' Tom nodded at the three women who beamed at him. 'But what do you lads think? Would you lads like to come and watch them play? It would boost your spirits!'

'Aye, of course we would,' said the head-injured Tommy. 'It would give us a meaning to our life and make for good morale throughout us all.' He stubbed out his cigarette and looked at his fellow patients. 'Do you not think, lads?'

A few of the soldiers smiled and grinned and lifted their heads, gazing at the three women who stood embarrassed as they all glanced at them.

'Aye, just what we all need. Do it, lasses. We'll all come and watch; that is, until we are fit enough to play a proper match again ourselves,' one of them replied, and the others shouted their approval.

'Well, that tells you what these lads think. And

I'm sure that they are not on their own.' Tom looked up and saw that two ambulances were pulling up to take their war-weary patients back to the comfort of their rehabilitation. 'Look lively, lads, your transport awaits.' Tom went over to another group of soldiers and patted the ones who lagged on their backs. 'Same time next week.' And then went to the ambulance drivers to thank them for their help.

'Do you think he's going to let us play here?' Hattie whispered and watched as the injured men climbed into the ambulances.

'He wouldn't have asked them that if he wasn't toying with the idea,' Maggie whispered back, smiling as Tom walked back and the ambulances pipped their thanks.

'Ah, well, that's my boys back home safe and sound. It does them good and gives them exercise for the time they are here. Builds their confidence and their morale. Some are in a precarious mental state because of the war and what they have seen. It's the least I can do for them. But enough of them, ladies. Now what's this you are saying about playing women's football? I hear that it is surfacing again. The FA must be desperate to keep their grounds open and bring money in. Hypocrites, that's what they are.

They should have had more faith in the fairer sex the last time women wanted to play. Way back just before the turn of the century.'

'And do you have faith in a women's team? Because, as you have no doubt gathered, we are here to ask if you could let us play on Park Avenue? Peter O'Rourke has already said yes to a team from Hey's Brewery playing there, despite my asking him first. One of his directors has not left him any room to move with owning the brewery.'

'Aye, I can understand that. Now, as you might gather, I'm not a fan of the FA, but I will have to ask for their permission and our board members' permission, but they won't give you any bother. Do you need someone to manage you and train you? I'd be willing. It would keep my hand in the game. It'll cost you nowt, just a bit of gratitude and for you all to do as I say and give me no lip or sulking.' Tom looked at the three women who had smiles so wide he thought they were going to crack.

'Are you sure? Is there anything you need to know about us? Do you need any money or our boss to get in touch with you? Not that he's that interested in our game,' Maggie replied and couldn't believe Tom had been that easy to ask.

'No, just come next Saturday, with a full team and with something more appropriate to play football in. We've got the footballs, maybe not the boots, unless you fit a size seven or above. We are not used to women's smaller feet.' Tom looked at the women's feet and wondered what he had just done, but he believed everybody, no matter what their sex, should have a fair chance in life, and he had nothing better to do on a Saturday afternoon, and football was his life.

'Thank you, thank you, you'll see we will be the best football team in Bradford, in Yorkshire even.' Hattie shook Tom's hand and could have hugged him.

'Aye, and the first chance we get, we will give Hey's Brewery a run for their money. Just to show Peter O'Rourke what he's turned down,' Lorna said sharply, but wanted to be on her way home.

'He's all right is Peter, a good friend, just doesn't stand up for himself. I've had to since changing this club from a rugby club to a football club. It was a matter of survival. Now, get yourselves home, and I'll see you all next week.' Tom bent down and picked a stray football up from next to the fence, and watched as the three women linked arms together and all shouted a rowdy thank-you to him.

He'd hopefully made a few people's days better, and that was what life was all about.

Lorna O'Donnell walked back into her home. She could hear the sobbing of her youngest daughter, Ella.

'What's to do, my darling?' Lorna put her arm around her youngest and sighed. 'I told you I wouldn't be so long.'

'It's Da, he came home, went upstairs, packed his suitcase and said he was leaving. But Ma, I saw a gun in his case. What does he want with a gun in his case?' Ella sobbed. 'He shouted at me and told me to mind my own business when he saw me looking at it.' She caught her breath and cried as she curled up under her mother's arm, burying her head in the comfort of her mother's bosom. 'Ma, he's gone, he's left us.'

Lorna kissed her daughter's brow and then lifted her head. 'He's best gone, my love, he's never here anyway, and when he is, he never works and tells everybody that he's got the wife from hell. We will survive, your sister's working now, and Lord knows what he's got himself involved in. He's a selfish, weak man, and it's hoped that he doesn't come back to us.'

Lorna closed her eyes and sighed. So he'd made his choice, Ireland and the Fenians over his family, and the fact that if he stayed in Bradford, he would need to go to war. In Ireland, he would be able to hide with his own and evade the draft. He put saving his own skin before the love of his family. How she wished that she didn't love that man of hers so much.

14

It was Sunday morning, and Hattie lay in her bed listening to the church bells chiming. She was tired and couldn't be bothered to climb out of her snug bed. The rain was battering at the window, and she could hear that Maggie was already up and in the kitchen. She heard her raking the ashes in the fireplace and was thankful that she was seeing to the fire as she closed her eyes and turned onto her side. She hadn't slept well, and when she had slept, she had dreamed of soldiers lying wounded in the trenches, with them shouting for help and her not able to do anything for them as she ran to help them, only to find her legs didn't work. It had been terrifying as the soldier's face, which had been that of the cheeky one at the football pitch, had transformed to Bruce's and had begged her for help. It had felt so real, she thought, as she pulled her covers over her and wriggled back down into the warmth and security of her bed. She closed her eyes and dozed for a while. It was warm, and it was Sunday; no need to do anything, she thought, as a quiet knock on her bedroom door made her open her eyes and sit up in bed.

'Good morning, I thought I would treat you. So when you weren't stirring, I moved my shanks and decided to get the fire going and to make us breakfast for a change.' Maggie walked in with a loaded breakfast tray and was still in her nightdress with her long black hair flowing over her shoulders and a smile on her face.

'Oh, I've never had breakfast in bed before.' Hattie pulled her nightdress straight and felt slightly embarrassed as Maggie put the tray on the side of her bed and sat next to it.

'Don't get excited, it's only a slice of toast each and a cup of tea, but it's better than nothing. It's a filthy day out there; a right firesider, as my father would say.' Maggie looked at Hattie. 'Go on, get tucked in.' She pushed the plate of toast towards Hattie and then picked up her cup of tea. 'Now, this is nice, isn't it? Two women having a civilised Sunday breakfast together.'

'It is, but I should have got up and made breakfast.' Hattie took a bite of toast and pulled the covers up more around her, giving Maggie a telling look.

'All right, stop it. I'm not going to pounce on you. We are having breakfast as friends, nothing more. Besides, I am true to Anne. In fact, I thought I would go and see her today. Her mother usually goes for a Sunday natter to her friend's, so it's an opportunity for us to have a little time to ourselves.' Maggie smiled.

Hattie felt the colour rising to her cheeks. 'I didn't think that for one minute. I'm just not used to having breakfast in bed.' She reached for her tea and took a sip. 'It would be a good idea for you to go and see Anne. You could tell her about our meeting yesterday. I still can't believe that we have somewhere to play. We need something to wear, and boots, and quickly. Nobody has money to be spent on either, so I don't know what we will do.'

'We need a full team first. We haven't even got half of one yet.' Maggie looked at Hattie. 'I was thinking that perhaps you could ask Joshua Swainbank to buy us boots. You could convince him by saying that he could advertise Swainbank and Gregson at the club and look as if he's doing good things for the community and the war effort by sponsoring us. By the amount of cloth going out of the warehouse, he's making brass at the moment.'

'Why me? You are the one who has all these ideas. I wouldn't dare,' Hattie replied and took a second slice of toast. Now she felt more comfortable with Maggie's presence in her room.

'Have you not noticed he looks at you in a certain way? Anne commented about it the other day. She said he had come down and talked to Sara Turner about something, but she noticed he kept looking at you.' Maggie spoke quietly and watched Hattie's face.

'He was probably asking how I was doing and telling Sara to keep an eye on me with this football thing going on. I never noticed; I was too busy working, unlike Anne. Besides, he knows I'm married, and that my Bruce is at war along with Oliver. He's not like Patrick Gregson, his old partner. Now, he did have a roving eye,' Hattie protested.

'Just thought you could ask on your own and turn on the charm, eleven pairs of sturdy boots will be nothing to him. As for something to play in, I'll bring that roll of blue serge back with me one evening and give it to Anne. She's got a sewing machine. We will have to play in skirts until she gets us shirts and knickerbockers or shorts made.' Maggie sighed and lay back. 'It's warm in this bedroom with being over the kitchen, it's warmer than mine, and you can see down into the street.'

'It's mine and Bruce's bedroom. I'm not swapping, and I am not going to be seen wearing blue serge knickerbockers. Shorts, maybe, but we need two colours and socks to match. Do I really have to ask Joshua Swainbank for boots?' Hattie put her tea cup down.

'I'll promise no knickerbockers, if you ask Swainbank. How's that for a deal?' Maggie grinned.

'All right, then, but I bet he says no.'

'We won't know if we don't ask, will we?' Maggie got up off the bed and picked up the now nearly empty tray. 'I'll have a wander to Anne's now. The dragon should have left the lair by the time I get dressed and have walked there. Or at least I hope so. I'll see what she says about making a football strip for us all. It doesn't have to be fancy.' Maggie turned in the doorway. 'You take your time getting up. I heard you crying in the early hours of this morning. You must be worrying about your man and brother. They'll be back, I'm sure, unharmed and full of stories.'

'It was seeing those soldiers. They were so injured and they looked as if they had been to hell. All I could think about was Bruce and Ollie and what they would be going through. I'm sorry if I kept you awake.'

'You didn't, but I did worry about you. Try and keep your spirits up. Surely the war can't go on for ever.' Maggie closed the bedroom door behind her and sighed. Poor Hattie, she didn't deserve all the worry that she had. Perhaps a game of football would take her mind off it and make her feel that she was doing something by raising funds to help keep her men on the front line out of harm's way.

'I like our time together. You do know if I could let you live here, I would? It's just my mama, she is so against you.' Anne curled up in the protection of Maggie's arms and looked at her with love in her eyes.

'She thinks I'm a bad influence, that I'm a wicked woman,' Maggie chuckled. 'I should tell her that her daughter is not as innocent as she seems.' She bent down and kissed Anne's brow. 'How and when are you going to tell her about us playing football? Surely she will have something to say about that when she finds out?' Maggie stroked Anne's hair and smelled her perfume.

'I'm not going to tell her. I've said that I'm joining a ladies' sewing class that repairs soldiers' uniforms. I saw the advertisement on the billboard across from work, and it fits in perfectly with the times that I think we will be playing. Now, I'm not so sure if I have to go to Bradford Park Avenue, it's a bit of a walk.' Anne sighed. 'She would have a fit if she knew what I was really doing.'

'That answers the next question I was going to ask you and gives me another worry,' Maggie muttered as she looked into the open fire. She felt content with Anne lying beside her on the sofa, but at the same time, her mind still dwelt on their upcoming new venture.

'Why, what were you going to ask me?' Anne rested her face on her hand and looked up at Maggie.

'I was going to say, could you sew the team eleven shirts and eleven pairs of shorts; not knickerbockers, because Hattie won't wear knickerbockers and I've made a deal with her.' Maggie grinned slightly.

'You know, I'd do anything for you, and our team if we get one put together, but my mother . . . she would soon guess what I was about if a pile of football clothing started to appear and the sound of the treadle sewing machine never stopped.' Anne paused and thought for a moment. 'No, I daren't, I just daren't . . . she would kill me or, at the best, make me homeless. I'm risking things as it is with lying about my whereabouts.' Anne looked perplexed. 'What's the deal that you've done with Hattie? What's the poor woman got to do for you and your mad idea?'

'I've asked her to go and see Joshua Swainbank, just to see if he would put his hand in his pocket and buy us some boots. We can't play in our clogs or good boots. I'm afraid I led her on slightly, saying that Joshua Swainbank had been seen taking an interest in her. So she was the best one to ask.'

'Maggie Fleming, you are such a devil. No wonder my mother doesn't have a good word for you. Joshua Swainbank will never look at another woman, I fear. His heart is for ever broken over the death of his wife and child. And Hattie's married to her man out there fighting for us all.'

'I know, but we need to get things done. I'm not having Hey's Brewery team being better than ours. Not when it was my idea first. We will get a team by fair means or foul, and we will be the best,' Maggie replied with determination.

'Football is taking over your life, Maggie. It's only a game,' Anne laughed.

'Oh, no, it isn't for me, my dear. It is my life and always has been.'

*

It was Monday morning, and Maggie and Hattie stood with a pen in their hands adding more information to the poster that was placed with good faith on the factory wall at work.

'There, that should get a few more interested.' Maggie stood back and looked at her handiwork as she stuck a drawing pin into the wooden frame and made sure that her spelling was correct.

> PLAY FOR YOUR PRIDE AND SHOW THE WOMEN OF HEY'S BREWERY HOW WE WOMEN IN WEAVING CAN REALLY PLAY FOOTBALL.
>
> FOOTBALL PITCH SECURED AT BRADFORD PARK AVENUE FC WITH COACHING AND MANAGEMENT BY THE FAMOUS TOM MALEY. NO KIT OR BOOTS REQUIRED, BOTH WILL BE SUPPLIED.

'Oh, Maggie, you are lying through your teeth. We have no kit, nor boots, and just how famous is Tom Maley? I'd never heard of him before,' Hattie whispered as a group of women looked at the poster on their way to their work.

'Twelve thirty in the mill yard, join us there,' Maggie shouted to them as they walked away and she took Hattie's arm. 'I know, but we will get both eventually. You'll talk Joshua Swainbank around today, and I'll wangle a kit for us from somewhere. As for Tom Maley, of course he's famous. He was manager of Celtic. That might be over the border in Scotland, but we will keep that to ourselves for those who don't know.'

Hattie shook her head. 'You are always chasing your luck. I really don't want to go and confront Mr Swainbank this dinner time. Why don't we send Anne or Lorna? Especially if he has been looking at me strangely. You don't know what's going through his head.'

'Just go up there and ask him, just for boots, we can't play without them. He will be in his office. His keeper, the old bag of a secretary, will watch his every move, but try and talk to him alone, especially out of the earshot of the accountant,' Maggie hissed. 'Let me know how you get on after you've seen him. We've got to get to our work now, else we will be in bother.'

Hattie watched Maggie leave to go to the warehouse and sighed. Maggie was good at making the bullets, but never fired them herself, she thought, as Sara Turner walked past her and pointed to the works clock.

'Two minutes to get to work, Hattie. You had better be quick, else I'll be docking your wages.' Sara glanced at the notice's new signage and shook her head. 'Don't jeopardise your job for a game.'

'No, indeed not, Mrs Turner, I don't intend to,' replied Hattie and almost ran to her job in the carding room.

It was the 12.30 dinner break, and as the machinery came to a short halt, Anne touched Hattie's arm and whispered, 'Good luck.' She watched Hattie step away from her machine and take a deep breath. 'We know you can do it,' Anne shouted after her as she watched Hattie make for the stairwell and climb the stairs to the management office.

Hattie tapped on the office door, and Mary Mason glowered at her through the glass panel before coming to answer her tap.

'Yes, what do you want this time? You do know that Mr Swainbank's time is precious, that he hasn't got time to be wasting on insignificant things?'

'I'm sorry, I just need to ask him something, something personal.' Hattie peered past her and could see that Joshua Swainbank had his office window open and was leaning out of it and yelling at somebody down below.

'Could I not deal with it? I should be your contact before Mr Swainbank.' Mary Mason nearly jumped a mile as she heard her boss let out a yell and watched as he patted the accountant next to him hard on his back in the adjoining office.

'Yes! Bloody good goal! That lass can play.' Joshua Swainbank looked joyous as he partly hung out of his window and watched Maggie run rings around Len from out of the warehouse and deftly left-footed a goal past him, hitting the mill wall with a resounding thump. He waved down to Maggie as she looked up at him and tucked the ragged football under her arm, before walking back to a crowd of women sitting on the warehouse steps, who were watching her in awe.

'It seems we have all lost our senses. I'll tell Mr Swainbank you are here,' Mary Mason said and looked with disdain at Hattie, who was trying to calm her nerves.

'Hattie Braithwaite is here to see you, Mr Swainbank. I expect it is something to do with this wretched football team. It will certainly not be to do with her work!'

Joshua and the accountant came away from the window and sat down at their desks. Both looked flushed and embarrassed that they had been caught watching her friends playing football.

Joshua pulled his waistcoat down and looked seriously at Hattie, but with a slight smile on his face.

'Miss Braithwaite, you have decided to join us again, without your friend this time? I can see she is busy playing football in her lunch hour, and with quite a crowd.'

'There are more women than just us usual four!' Hattie gasped and hoped that she or Maggie was not in trouble.

'Indeed, there looked to be at least fifteen or more, enough to make a football team anyway. Now, to what do I owe for the pleasure of this visit?' Joshua smiled. 'Perhaps you would be more comfortable if you took a chair? You look slightly perplexed.' He pointed to a mahogany straight-back chair in the corner of the room, and the accountant got up from his desk and placed the chair right in front of Joshua's desk, lightly coughed and gave his apologies to Joshua as he left his office and joined Mary Mason to have his dinner.

'Now, tell me what brings you here in your own time when I'm sure you would rather be out there in the yard with your friends or eating your dinner?' Joshua sat back in his chair and looked at the striking young woman. She was indeed good-looking with pretty blonde hair and blue eyes, and he understood why his best warehouse man had married her.

'Have you had news of your husband and brother? I trust they are safe. The sooner this war is over, the better.' Joshua tried to put Hattie at ease as she played with her wedding ring on her finger and plucked up the courage to ask him her question.

'Yes, I have. Both are well, thank you. I wrote to my husband at the weekend. No reply yet.' Hattie lifted her head and looked across at the handsome mill owner. 'I'm sorry, I'm not liking being in this position, but I'm afraid I've been elected to ask it.'

'Elected, eh! Must be important!' Joshua grinned. 'Go on, I don't bite, tell me what it is you want. I presume it is once again to do with this football team that I am harbouring within my walls? I must say, Miss Fleming can shoot a goal if nothing else. I was impressed.' Joshua noticed how uneasy she was.

'Well, we're wondering . . . now that we have got a ground to play at and it would seem enough women are interested, if you would perhaps consider funding our team some football boots. It would promote the mill, and I'm sure Tom Maley would let you put up a banner with the mill's name at Bradford Park Avenue.' Hattie hardly dared look at Joshua as she tried to justify her request. 'Hey's Brewery have got a ladies' team and have beaten us to Valley Parade, otherwise we were going to go there. Their owner is going to back them, and there are other factories thinking along the same lines. It would be a shame for you not to have your name on the match day programme,' Hattie quickly added and watched as Joshua sat back and thought about it.

'So, you've convinced Tom to let you play there, have you? He's a good man, always has the good of the community at heart. Unlike the owner of Hey's Brewery. He's got fingers in all sorts of pies.' Joshua leaned forward and looked at Hattie. 'You know, when you first came up with this idea, I thought I'd just play along with it, because nothing would come of it. However, now I can see how determined you all are, and I'd do anything for a team of my women to beat those of Arthur Hey. He is always strutting about like an important bantam-cock.' Joshua smiled and knew that his accountant wouldn't like what he was going to say, but it was his firm, and at the moment, they were making good money through the war.

'Aye, I'll buy your boots. Tell Tom Maley to order them and send me the bill. He can put my name in the football programme if he thinks of printing some, and I'll come and watch the matches. I've nothing else to do with my Saturday afternoons since my wife died.' Joshua admitted to himself he was feeling just a tad excited about going to see a women's football match, especially if it was his workers and if they all played like Maggie Fleming.

'You will? That is absolutely brilliant news. It was the one thing that was going to hold us back, as nobody can afford to buy boots from out of their wages . . .' Hattie said and then blushed.

'Boots you will definitely need, and if you were proper footballers, the club would buy them for you.' Joshua laughed and then said, 'I pay what wages I can afford, and you women will play the best football you can. Go and give the team the good news, and I hope my accountant won't curse me.' He smiled and looked across at his accountant as he sat back down at his desk and said nothing. Joshua then rose from his seat and went to open the office door for his guest as she blushed yet again and showed a faint smile on her lips.

'Thank you, sir,' Hattie said quietly as her heart thumped with excitement over the good news.

'My pleasure doing business with you, Mrs Braithwaite. I expect I will be seeing you again over this matter.' Joshua smiled. He wished all his business partners were as beautiful and respectful. The team deserved his support, he thought, as he looked at his accountant and knew he was going to have to justify himself on the madcap scheme. However, he couldn't overlook the passion that the women had for their football, which was not unlike what his old self had felt, before tragedy had struck his life.

15

'What's wrong with you, Lorna? You don't look at all happy. Blinking heck, woman, we have got a field to play on and with the news that Hattie's just told us, we even have the boots, and a team of eleven if not more.' Maggie stood in front of Lorna, who had her head in her hands, her ginger hair cascading through her fingers as she raised her head.

'Ah, it's a long story, but to cut it short, it's my eejit of a man. He's bloody well upped sticks and left me. While we were down at Park Avenue, he came home, packed a suitcase and left. The man's a fool, I should never have married him.' Lorna stood up, and even though she was a hard woman, she looked near to tears.

'Oh, Lorna, will you be able to manage without him? Perhaps he'll regret leaving and come back.' Maggie put her arm around Lorna and saw Anne shoot her a glance as she left to go back to work, making her shrug her shoulders to say there was nothing in it.

'I don't want him back, we are better off without him. He doesn't work or only when he wants to, and he's mixing with a bad lot. He's best away from my house and our children. I'm ashamed that he hides from enlistment. He might be an Irishman, but his children are brought up in this country. I hope the bloody boat that takes him back to his precious Ireland sinks with him on board right in the middle of the Irish Sea and that he's never found.' Lorna stood up and looked at Maggie. 'He's a bad lot, Maggie. He's a bloody Fenian that won't fight for his country, like other good men!'

Maggie stood back, everybody else had quickly gone back to work, and now there was just Lorna and her on the warehouse steps.

'It must be bad if you are wishing him dead. There are too many of our young men dead. Hattie would do anything to have her fella back, and as for me, well, I've never been bothered by men.' Maggie smiled slightly and put her hand on Lorna's shoulder.

'Perhaps you are the wise one out of us.' Lorna stepped up the loading bay steps and shook her head. 'Jesus, I could do with a drink, a touch of the good stuff. I've done nothing but worry since he's been gone.'

'Do you want me to come around to your house tonight? I could bring a bottle of something with me, and you can talk and tell me your worries. I'll come on my own. Hattie will probably want some time to herself anyway.' Maggie felt sorry for her new Irish friend. Everyone had told her that Lorna O'Donnell was as hard as nails, but it seemed she had her worries just like anybody else.

'Oh, no, I don't want to bother you with my troubles. Sure, they will work themselves out. I do have a good bottle of potcheen from back home if you want to join me, but I'm not responsible for your legs having a mind of their own when you drink a drop or two of it. Lethal it is, I've been keeping it hidden from my Mick. It would have been wasted on the likes of him.'

'That sounds like a good drink to me. I'll come around about eight and just stay an hour with you. We'd better not have too much to drink, with it being work in the morning. And don't worry, you can tell me anything. I'll not say anything to anybody. We all have our secrets.' Maggie followed Lorna up the steps and back into the mill. This team was about more than just a game; it was about comradeship and support for one another. Without that, a football team would be nothing. Her cousin had taught her that.

'Where are you going at this time of night?' Hattie looked up from darning her socks that evening and watched as Maggie pulled her shawl on.

'I'm going to see Lorna. Her old man's walked out on her,' Maggie replied. 'She sounded as if she needed someone to talk to, and it's the least I can do.'

'You hardly know her. Do you think you will be able to help her? She could perhaps do with someone who knows her really well,' Hattie said and put down her darning.

'There's more to it than that. He's involved in these renegade Irishmen. And she said she just needed a drink and to talk to someone who would listen. So how could I refuse? I can, believe it or not, make a good shoulder to cry on, and she must feel comfortable with me.' Maggie stood in the doorway. 'I won't be long. It's work in the morning and we can't let Joshua Swainbank down, now he's taking an interest and backing our football team.'

'I'll wait up for you. I might even write another letter to Bruce, and tell him where we are playing and that we have now got hopefully a full team, if some of those women that came along today can play. Any news, I'm sure, will be welcomed by him.' Hattie concentrated back on her needlework and hoped that Maggie would not be too late back home.

Maggie walked in the light of the gas lamps down the cobbled streets to one of the most deprived areas of Bradford, called Longlands. The back-to-back houses were marked for demolition, but a few were still being lived in, like the one that Lorna and her family were living in. The sanitation of the street left something to be desired, Maggie thought, as she picked her way up the street to number 4 and climbed the step up to the front door. Knocking hard, she heard a girl's voice shouting, 'I'll get it, Ma.' And the door opened, letting a stream of light out into the dreary, depressing street. A young girl in a white smock and with a head of wild ginger hair just like her mother's stood in the doorway.

'Ma, there's a woman here. I don't know who she is.' Ella yelled over her shoulder and waited until her mother joined her at the door.

'Of course you do, turnip head, it's Maggie from the mill. I told you she was coming. Your ma and her are going to have a good craic and put the world straight over a drink. Now you find something to do with yourself and don't pester your sister. She's reading in the front room.' Lorna smiled. 'Come in, Maggie. That's my youngest, Ella, although I sometimes think she wasn't born with many brains.' Lorna scuffed her youngest's head as she skipped past her. 'You found us then in this godforsaken hole? They don't mind where they put us Irish. These houses were supposed to be pulled down years ago, but folk are still living in the odd one or two.' Lorna held her hand out for Maggie's shawl and hung it up behind the front door on a wooden peg.

'At least you are in the centre of the town here, not on a hillside like Hattie, and you have Westgate around the corner. You might be able to get a house there if you have to leave.' Maggie couldn't help but notice that, although the houses were due to be demolished, Lorna kept hers tidy and homely. The fire was lit, and the clothes rack hanging from the ceiling was hung with drying and airing clothes, while there was a bunch of late flowers, chrysanthemums, in a jug on the kitchen table.

'Ah, with all that's going on in my life, I don't know if I want to stay here in Bradford. If he doesn't come home and they make me move out, I'll go and live somewhere else in the country, or I might even take the girls back to Armagh, get some good, clear Irish air in their lungs, cause there's none to be had in Bradford. Mucky place, it is.' Lorna opened her pot cupboard door and took out two small glasses, and placed them on the scrubbed kitchen table before reaching behind a curtain below the sink and taking out a bottle filled with a clear liquid. She smiled.

'The only place to hide it. He never went under the sink, which was full of things for work, and he'd never be seen doing that. The useless, lazy fecking man.'

Maggie watched as Lorna poured two good portions of the clear liquid. 'Sláinte,' she said and picked up a glass and knocked it back in one. 'Lord, I needed that,' she said and smiled as Maggie took a sip and pulled a face, and felt her throat nearly alight as the potent homebrew went down.

Maggie coughed slightly and then croaked. 'Heavens, Lorna. That's some drink. I think my throat is on fire.'

'Aye, it's a drop of the good stuff. You can't get this in any of your pubs over here.' Lorna poured herself another and offered a top-up to Maggie.

Maggie signalled to pour her only a small one, but Lorna filled her glass up.

'Ah, you need a big'un if you are anything like me. Get it drunk,' Lorna said and sat back in her chair. 'I appreciate you coming around tonight. I needed some company after that man of mine had left me. It's not the first time, and it will probably not be the last. He's hiding from being enlisted, the bloody coward, as well as being mixed in with the wrong lot. I don't know if he will return to me or not. I don't even know if I want him back this time.' Lorna took a slower sip and watched as Maggie got used to the heat and taste of the deadly brew.

'He's in too deep with the Fenians; and he has always listened to them. This time, he's gone too far, if he had a gun on him, like my Ella said she saw. He must be in deep, and I'm not getting involved in the like. He's best gone from my door.'

'He had a gun! Bloody hell, Lorna! Would he think of killing somebody with it?' Maggie gasped. 'They should all be bothered about fighting the Germans, not plotting about Ireland's independence.' Maggie stared at Lorna. 'I wouldn't want him back either, but can you manage without him?'

'It'll make no difference if he's here or not. I hardly ever saw a penny from him anyway. My girls are growing up now, and we will survive. This football team will help take my mind off my worries, and it looks like it is shaping up now.'

'Aye, Hattie managed to wangle boots for us all from Joshua Swainbank this afternoon. He's going to be backing us now. He knows we are not the only mill trying to get a team together.' Maggie smiled. 'You never know, we might all become famous, and then your fella will come wandering back, with his tail between his legs.'

'He can please himself what he does. I hope he stops wherever he is and keeps his family out of his political ways. I'll not have anybody's blood on my family's hands, except that of a German. You'll be having another drop before you go home?' Lorna grinned and watched as Maggie got a liking for her homebrew.

Hattie sat in her chair as the clock struck midnight. Her eyes were getting heavy and the fire was dying down. It was no good, she was going to have to go to bed and hope that Maggie was all right. It would soon be morning and work. As long as she was safe, she thought, as she climbed the stairs and left the front door unlocked for her missing lodger.

The next morning, there was no sight of Maggie as

Hattie quietly opened the bedroom door and peered into Maggie's bedroom. The bed had not been slept in, and downstairs, there was no sign of Maggie ever coming home.

Work was calling as she looked at the clock and hoped that wherever Maggie was she was safe, and she decided to lock the door and make her way quickly to the mill. She scanned the row of workers that were lining up, but there was no sign of Maggie or Lorna as she slowly made her way into the mill and quickly gazed around the warehouse before climbing the stairs to the carding room.

'Morning, Hattie,' Anne waved and shouted as she switched on her machine and then came to stand by her side for a quick minute before starting work.

'Did you manage to get the boots from him upstairs? I bet you didn't. I couldn't catch you to ask you yesterday,' Anne said above the noise of the mill, as the carding machines started work and wool was brought up from the warehouse and placed at the workers' stations.

'I did, he says that Tom Maley has to order them for us, and he will pay for them,' Hattie replied. 'I caught him watching Maggie scoring a goal. He was hanging out of his window and getting excited about it. He's a football fan. Maggie was right.' Hattie hesitated. 'Have you seen Maggie this morning? I'm a bit worried. She didn't come home last night.' Despite Maggie going to see Lorna, she could only imagine that she had stayed the night at Anne's.

'No. What do you mean she hasn't come home? Where is she? She knows better than to come to my house when my mother's about.' Anne looked worried. 'Do you think we should call the police? She could be lying dead on a street corner.' Anne gave a questioning look and stood wondering where and what had become of her lover.

'Damn, I thought she might have stayed with you after visiting Lorna. I hope they are both all right. I saw neither of them in the line-up for work this morning. She said she was going there to listen to Lorna's worries, but she said she would not be late.' Hattie glanced at Sara Turner, who was making her way to them, and nodded to Anne.

'Better get a move on. We will look for both at dinner time,' Anne shouted as she picked up the first fleece of the day.

'Morning, ladies. No time for football chat. It's work now, especially if you want to earn those new boots. Mr Swainbank is too generous for his own good, if you ask me,' Sara commented and scowled as she watched Anne scurry back to her machine. Mary Mason had wasted no time in telling her that Hattie Braithwaite had persuaded the mill owner into backing her madcap scheme of a football team. With that in mind, she was not going to give any of the so-called players an inch of leeway. Women, playing football, how ridiculous, she thought, as she watched both buckle down to their work.

'Yes, Mrs Turner,' both said in unison and decided not to chance talking until dinner time.

Dinner time couldn't come quickly enough for Anne and Hattie, both concerned about their friends. They headed to the warehouse, before going to the yard to see who had gathered for a game of football and tell those gathered that free football boots were to be theirs if they hadn't already heard. There was still no sign of Lorna or Maggie as they both made their way to the warehouse.

'You don't think Lorna bats for both sides, do you? She is a rough diamond,' Anne whispered and looked worried as she glanced at Hattie, fearful that her lover had found a new home.

'Don't be silly.' Hattie blushed. 'Lorna has family; she wouldn't look twice at Maggie. Besides, Maggie thinks the world of you.' Hattie strode out across the warehouse floor and through the many piles of fleeces and rolls of cloth, hoping to track down Maggie before going to play football.

'I know, but my mother spoils things for us. If she's not here, we will have to go to the police and check if Lorna has definitely not made it to work,' Anne whispered as they saw Len walking towards them.

'Are you two looking for Maggie? She's sitting over there on a wool bale, nursing the headache from hell, and it serves her right. She says she's not even been home last night, she and Lorna rolled into work half an hour late.' Len grinned.

'Oh, thank heavens. We thought something had happened to them.' Hattie sighed.

'No, she's just been felled by Irish potcheen and blarney all night. And now she's mad with herself for being docked wages and letting the side down in more ways than one.' Len smiled. 'I'll go and see who is with us for football today and tell them that there's no practice this dinner time, but for them to be down at Bradford Park Avenue for one o'clock on Saturday to play some proper football. It's no good this dinner time. The goalkeeper, Lorna, was last seen rushing to the toilet to be sick, and up to an hour ago, the warehouse was whizzing around in Maggie's head. Tom and I have covered for her all morning.' Len walked through the wooden-floored warehouse past the strong metal pillars that supported the whole building and made his way to the backyard and loading bay.

'I'm here, you two. Don't believe a single word he says, I'm not that bad,' Maggie shouted and looked up from the greasy woollen bale to focus on her friends' faces.

'You idiot. You had us both worried, we thought the worst,' Hattie said sharply.

'I'm sorry, I meant to come home, but I didn't bet on Lorna's potent homebrew. It just floored me, and when she offered me to stay the night on her sofa, it seemed a good idea.' Maggie looked up at the two who were glaring at her with their hands on their hips. 'I'm sorry.'

'You look terrible, grey and shattered. You'll not be doing that again in a hurry. I hope Lorna isn't as bad, else there will be mistakes in the serge that she's been weaving all morning.' Hattie sighed.

'You did sleep on the sofa, didn't you?' Anne asked and then went to sit next to Maggie and put her arm around her.

'Of course I did! Stop worrying. I'm more mad at myself because we were both late to work. That's no way to thank Joshua Swainbank when he's about to put his hand in his pocket for our boots.'

'You have only yourself to blame. I hope he doesn't go back on his promise once he realises that you two are in such a state. Were you celebrating buying the boots? Or was Lorna drowning her sorrows? You have both drunk yourselves stupid,' Hattie said with annoyance in her voice.

'Oh, she's got problems. That's why I stayed so long. But I don't think she will be taking the main one back, or shouldn't if she has any sense. Her husband's a right wrong'en, him and the lot we saw him talking to in The Diplomat. No wonder Lorna acts so hard, she's had to.'

'Fenians, blinking Irish, they are all the talk in the newspapers; what with the war raging, and the Irish wanting independence. I hope that our football team gives people a bit of relief from their worries and raises money for good causes,' Hattie said and looked at Anne.

'Yes, and that this one and Lorna don't hit the bottle again, else we'll have no team to play with,' Anne replied.

'One player, or in this case two players, does not make a team,' Maggie whispered. 'We all have to play as a team and back one another up. That's what makes a football team great.'

All three nodded and agreed – they had to be strong, determined and to trust one another, if they were going to be a winning team.

16

Hattie and Maggie viewed one another with smiles on their faces. Dared they go through Bradford dressed like that? Both had decided to put on a pair of Bruce and Oliver's trousers rather than play in their long skirts that day. But now they were wondering if they dared walk out in them.

'No wonder men wear trousers, they are ten times more comfortable.' Maggie viewed herself in the wardrobe mirror. Admiring the brown and black chequered pair of trousers and her black blouse, she looked at her figure that she had never made public before.

'I don't know, men can see our legs, we are going to be talked about when we are on the tram. I'll be glad that we will be coming back when it's nearly dark. Perhaps I should put my skirt back on.' Hattie looked at her long black skirt that she had just taken off for the sake of ease of playing football, and was tempted to dress as usual.

'Once we are there, it won't matter, you'll get tangled up in those skirts of yours. As it is we are having to wear our best boots and they aren't exactly made for running around a football field in, but then again neither are our clogs. If anybody comes in corsets today, they might as well turn around and go home. You can't breathe in them at the best of times. You'll not get me ever wearing them.' Maggie smoothed her hands over her hips and smiled. 'You know, I quite like this look.'

'Trust you. I'm going to put my long coat over the top, and then hopefully nobody will see.' Hattie left Maggie admiring herself in the bedroom mirror and went downstairs to find her purse and put her coat on.

'You know, if you are not happy wearing trousers, what are you going to feel like wearing shorts or bloomers when we actually play in front of a crowd?' Maggie ran down the stairs after her.

'That'll be different, we will all look the same, and we will be playing football. It's just that we will stick out like two sore thumbs today on the tram and folk will talk,' Hattie said quietly as she pulled her coat on and put her purse in her pocket.

'They talk about me all the time. It's like water off

a duck's back. I often hear the word dyke whispered, but I ignore it. It's their problem, not mine. It still hurts, though. I can't help being like I am.' Maggie, for once, blushed and let her feelings be known.

'Oh, Maggie, I never judge you. We are all different in our own way, and as long as you are right with me, then I've no problem with your private life.' Hattie looked with sympathy at her friend. She hadn't realised that she was sometimes hurt by people's reactions towards her.

'Come on then, enough of this doubting ourselves. Let's go out with our heads held high and show Tom Maley just how well we can play and make sure that he trains the other lasses well. I hope Anne has managed to persuade her mother that she's going to a sewing class. She would have a fit if she knew the truth.' Maggie sighed and grabbed her jacket and pulled it on.

'It's hard when you have to do as your parents dictate, even at our ages. I'm just thankful that my father hasn't shown his face back here yet. Life is so much easier without him living here. I'm sure he killed my mother with his austerity and miserable ways.' Hattie smiled and put her arm through Maggie's as they left the house. They were two friends stepping out to change the world's view on football, and today they were going to play until their hearts burst.

'Fecking hell, it's not a fashion show, it's football.' Lorna looked at some of the workers from Swainbank's Mill and sighed. Some of the women had come dressed in their Sunday best as if they were going to church or afternoon tea, not about to play football. She stood with Hattie, Maggie and Anne and shook her head as Tom Maley walked up and down the row and looked at them all and asked their names and wrote them down on his clipboard. She herself was dressed in a wool jumper, a long skirt and a woollen hat. She automatically knew she was going to be in goal, so she had come dressed warmly.

'I had to come dressed like this, else my mother would have wondered where I was going,' Anne replied and put her head down, knowing that her calico blouse and blue skirt were not the thing to wear for football as Tom turned and lined up the mish-mash of women.

'Right, ladies!' Tom hesitated and shook his head. 'I don't know how you think half of you are going to play dressed like you are. Football is a dirty game; your posh frocks and skirts are going to get filthy and tattered if you play properly. Maggie and Hattie have assured me that Joshua Swainbank has offered to pay for your boots, so next week, hopefully, we will have decent footwear. I need all your foot sizes before you go home. When it comes to what you wear on the field to play in, I had an idea after Maggie and Hattie left last week, and I hope that you will agree to it.' Tom glanced over at Maggie and Hattie, nodded his head in the direction of the clubhouse and changing rooms and said, 'Follow me.'

'What's he up to?' Hattie said as the troupe followed him across the field to the clubhouse and chatted with enthusiasm and giggled with excitement.

'Right, ladies, there is no way you can play football dressed like you are, although I do recognise that some of you have made an effort on that front. Therefore, I have been looking in our old linen baskets. You can't wear the latest strip of Bradford Park Avenue, but there is no reason why you can't use the old one that I very nearly gave to the rag and bone man.'

Tom stood in front of the sixteen women and opened the two linen baskets' lids as they all waited in the wooden changing rooms and looked around them, gasping as he picked up shirts that had been worn by men who were now mostly at war.

'Now, these are our old colours. We play in green and white hoops nowadays.' Tom held up a heavy twill shirt in colours of black, amber and claret. 'These aren't far off Bradford City colours, but we have a black band unlike them, and our shorts are white, socks match the shirt.' He watched as all the women nudged and whispered to one another.

'There's at least thirty sets of strips in here. I will give you them to play in, in the hope that you will all find a size that will fit you, or that you can alter them to fit. I trust some of you ladies can sew? Keep them baggy, though, you need to be able to move freely in them.' Tom lowered his eyes; he wasn't used to discussing sizing issues with women.

'Oh, that's wonderful. That is one big problem solved. I didn't know how we were going to play in our skirts, and I don't want to dress in my husband's trousers again. The looks I got as we came here today, and I've got to go back in them yet.' Hattie stepped forward and held a pair of shorts up, and looked at the length. She thought she looked an idiot in trousers and had worried at people looking at her on the way there, but shorts! 'Men are going to come to see how much of our legs they can see, if we wear these. Are we daring enough, ladies?'

Hattie shouted and grinned as she held them up next to her.

'Yes, of course we are! We are The Yorkshire Ladies' Football Club!' a voice from the back of the row shouted as they all agreed and pushed forward to rummage in the basket to secure sets of the football kit.

'I'll go and wait outside, if you ladies want to change into what is your closest fit. There's a drawstring in the shorts' waistband, pull it tight until it fits, we don't want any mishaps when you are running down the pitch.' Tom spoke quietly and then left the women as they gathered around the baskets. He'd never heard so much noise coming out of his changing rooms and was starting to wonder what he had let himself in for.

'Oh, we will all be showing our legs, how disgraceful,' Anne chuckled and then nudged Maggie. 'My mother had better not find out, else she will have a fit.'

'You know, it's good of Tom to give us these strips, but they are very similar to Bradford City's and what if Hey's Brewery play in City colours, because I can see them doing that?' Maggie put on a shirt, shorts and socks under her arm, and looked at them.

'Nobody would know who was playing who apart from spotting the black band.'

'That's true.' Hattie held a shirt up that was not far from her size and watched as the rest of the team found something to fit them and then bashfully started to disrobe and pull the shorts and shirts on. Looking at one another and grinning, they felt a little vulnerable at only wearing so few clothes.

'We need it to be known that we are from Bradford, but we need to make the shirt our own,' she said as she unbuttoned her blouse and stepped out of her husband's trousers.

Anne, hiding behind one of the changing-room doors while she took off her clothing, shouted, 'I can sew something on everybody's shirt to make them different. A sheep to represent that we work with wool? Or how about a Yorkshire rose? It could be on the backs of all the shirts, and then the crowd could pick us out.'

'A Yorkshire rose, now that is a good idea. Our nickname could be The Yorkshire Roses. Every good football team has a nickname,' Lorna answered as she stepped forward in her shorts and socks, with her original boots from her hurling days on her feet and still with her jumper and woolly hat on.

Everybody looked at her.

'You've not got your shirt on,' Maggie said as she pulled her trousers down in front of everybody and stood with her shorts in her hands.

'That's because I'm the fecking goalie. Has anybody got a problem with that?' Lorna looked around at everybody. 'The goalie always wears a jumper and a hat, it will keep me warm while you lot are running around like idiots.'

'We haven't a problem, but perhaps Tom has other ideas about you being a goalie.' Maggie pulled her shorts on and watched as Lorna shook her head.

'Then he'll be an idiot, because nothing ever gets past me. I'm the goalie, all right. I'm not running up and down that pitch, I'm too old.' Lorna stood her ground and made for the open door, followed by most of the team.

'She's the goalie indeed, and if Tom has any sense, he'll not argue with her.' Maggie smiled at Anne. 'A Yorkshire rose on the back of our shirts would be just right. Will you be able to do that? I'm just thinking what your mother might say. Will she not get suspicious if a load of football shirts arrive at your house to mend?'

'I'll say it's part of my sewing group, that I'm doing

a favour for a local football team. She'll not know any different, none of her little group will associate with any sport, so I'll get away with it.' Anne took a deep breath as she made for the door and stepped out into the cold autumn day, with the least clothing that she had ever worn in public, and hoped that nobody who knew her would be watching as she made an utter fool of herself trying to play football.

Tom Maley gazed at the group of sixteen women and looked at them huddled together, trying to keep warm in the sharp autumn winds.

'Right, ladies, it's no good you all standing together, spread yourselves out and let's see what you are made of. This will warm you all up. Line up on the pitch edge and let's see you do four laps of the ground, for me to see how fit you are. Then I need to see ten squats, get those leg muscles strengthened.' Tom listened to the moans and watched as his team looked at one another in disbelief. 'It isn't just about kicking a ball, you've got to have stamina.'

'If you think I'm going to run around the pitch, you can think again. Goalies don't need to be that fit,' Lorna replied and stood with her hands on her hips.

'And who said you were going to be the goalie?

I'll decide that when I've seen what you can do. Now, line up and get on with it. No moaning, ladies, ten minutes and you should all be back and doing squats. Now, go!' Tom put his foot down and watched as Lorna cursed under her breath, but walked over to the pitch edge with the rest of her team and started to run.

'Go on, I'm timing you all. For fit mill girls, this should be nothing to ask of you. Every bit of stamina will be needed if you are going to play for ninety minutes on a full-length pitch.' Tom took his pocket watch out and watched as the women ran around the pitch, some with ease and some struggling more and more with every lap.

'I never thought he'd be making us do this. I thought we would be kicking a ball about. So far I haven't even seen a bloody football,' Maggie said, catching her breath as Hattie and Anne tried to keep up the same pace while Lorna lagged behind everybody else and was getting redder and redder in the face as the final lap was completed.

All the women grouped, catching their breath and looking at one another. They hadn't been prepared for all this.

'I'm shattered. I don't think I can do any squats.

Are they like I imagine? Squatting down on your legs and then jumping up?' Anne moaned and felt quite weak at the thought of all the exercise.

'Yes, I've seen my cousin doing them. They strengthen your leg muscles, but I bet we ache in the morning.' Maggie caught her breath and looked across the pitch, and stood in front of Tom.

'Right, what are you waiting for? Ten squats, then you can have a rest.' Tom looked hard at them and watched, knowing some of the team had hardly had the strength to complete the laps. This was sorting the weak from the strong, and he knew that some would not be returning the following week, once they realised the regime that being a footballer involved.

The three best friends looked at one another with a determined gleam. They weren't going to give in on their first day. Neither was Lorna, gasping for breath and red in the face, as she joined in with gusto.

'He's a fecking bastard, but I'm not going to let him win. I'm the goalie, and well he knows it,' she said as she stared at Tom and bit her lip, and did ten squats with her legs trembling underneath her and determination on her face.

Tom kept a straight face as he watched his ladies'

team going through agony, and shouted, 'No pain, no gain. You need to be as fit and as lean as the butcher's dog. This is basic training, and then we will see what your individual skills are. Expect this every time you come to practice. There's more to it than just being able to kick a football or keep it out of the nets. So, if it's not going to be for you, let me know before you go home, and then neither of us wastes our time. A football pitch is one hundred and fifteen feet long and seventy-four feet wide, and there won't be an inch of it that you won't cover. You need to be fit, ladies, fit and hard. If I'm to be your trainer, you are going to be the best and fittest ladies' team in Yorkshire. Otherwise, there is no point in any of us being here.'

Tom walked between the two rows of women doing their squats with his hands behind his back. They were going to hate him by the end of the day, but it was all going to be for their benefit and his too if they proved to be a winning team. Nothing would give him greater satisfaction than to coach the best women's team in Bradford and to play Hey's Brewery Ladies at either Bradford City's ground or at Park Avenue. That would show the FA and his rival, Peter O'Rourke.

The changing room was a little subdued as the training came to an end. Some of the women were moaning that they had been asked to do too much, especially as they worked five days, if not six, in quite a manual job anyway.

Maggie, Anne, Hattie and Lorna listened as they removed their shirts and shorts and wondered if their idea of a football team was going to be dead in the water as aches and complaints were exchanged. There might be too many women for a football team attending this week, but they wondered if there would be enough to make a complement of eleven for a team the next time they gathered because of the vigorous exercise asked of them.

'Tom was hard on us today. I doubt some will return next week,' Hattie whispered as she laced and tied her boots.

'He had to be to see how fit we all are. When I was playing in Ireland, we had to do a similar thing. It's just that I had forgotten, and I'm a lot older now and have given birth to two children. Not to mention what living with that bastard of a man has done to me.' Lorna groaned and put her hands on her back as she stood up and looked around the room.

'It'll not be as hard next week, so I hope that you'll

all return,' she shouted and watched as some women grimaced and didn't reply.

'If you are going to return and you want to be part of the team, give me your shirts. I'll take them home and make sure you get a white Yorkshire rose sewn on them so that we can be distinguished from any other Bradford club that we might play. But you'll have to wash and alter them for size yourselves,' Anne announced, and noticed that some, especially the ones from the weaving rooms, were leaving their shirts and shorts on the benches and exiting quietly without acknowledgement.

'We are going to be lucky to be left with a team at this rate,' Maggie sighed. 'They like the idea of playing but aren't willing to commit. That's not good.'

Anne smiled and said thank you as two women from the carding room came forward and handed her their shirts. 'It was hard, but to be expected. We'll be back next week,' Rosie Maddocks said. 'You can't have a team without working at it.'

'Thank you,' Anne said and all four women smiled at the two hardy women from the carding room and knew that they would return. They needed just another five for it to be a team. Preferably six, just in case of illness, but five would do, they all thought, as they watched some leave without a word and others give Anne their shirts with a thank you.

Maggie put her arm through Anne's as the four walked back and worried about her friend taking the football shirts home to be dealt with. 'Will you be all right with them?'

'I'll say that they have been dropped off at my sewing group to be changed. My mother doesn't have a clue about any sport, and I'm not going to attempt to wash and dry them, not in this weather, we struggle to dry our own.' Anne hugged the bag of shirts and smiled. 'She'll no doubt question me when I get home. Thank heavens she can't see my dirty knees.'

'It'll be more than dirty knees in a while. I don't know how you are going to get away with her not knowing,' Maggie said with concern in her voice.

'I'll sort it somehow,' Anne replied quietly.

'I'd just tell her. You are allowed a life of your own,' Lorna said sharply. 'I hope my girls don't hide stuff from me. It's enough that the fecking husband did. Although he never did a good job of it. He thinks I don't know where he's gone, but I'd bet my last bob that he's with his brother in Dublin. Two eejits together.' Lorna sighed.

'So, he's not back then?' Maggie asked, and instead of a straight answer, just got a string of expletives. 'And I thought I could swear,' she laughed and climbed onto the busy Saturday-packed tram where everybody was looking at the random bunch of women that edged their way onto seats, smelling of sweat and with flushed cheeks. Ordinary women had been window-shopping and taking tea, but not her and her new-found friends. They had a plan and they were going to put it into action if it killed them, she thought, as she watched the gas lights being lit along Bradford's streets and shop workers lock their doors after a hard day's work. Another few weeks and their names would be on everybody's lips as The Yorkshire Roses, and with a following that would cheer them on through thick and thin, hopefully.

Tom Maley sat down and took out a packet of cigarettes and lit one. He lay back and thought about his practice as he gazed across his beloved football field, the day's light slipping away. What had he gone and got himself into? Some of the women couldn't run, let alone play for ninety minutes in a gruelling football match. He took a drag from his cigarette and closed his eyes, looking heavenwards. Had his life come to this? He was once the manager of Celtic, and now he managed a load of unfit women. Bloody war, bloody FA, but he would show both if he had his way. It would be one hell of a football team.

17

'I can't understand why a football team would come into your sewing group and ask you to make and sew thirteen white roses? The shirts aren't even clean; they smell of sweat and grass. They are quite disgusting.' Cynthia Birtwistle pulled a face as she watched her daughter Anne tack another white rose made from a piece of white cotton onto the grubby back of a twill football shirt. 'What has your sewing group got to do with football, and why didn't you do all this in your group? It seems unfair to me that you have been given all the work and have to do it at home.' She took off her reading glasses and folded her newspaper in agitation as Anne put her foot down on the Singer treadle sewing machine for the fifth time that morning. 'Really, Anne, it's Sunday, a day of rest, and hopefully peace if that exists in your world.'

'Sorry, Mother, but I want to get them done before I start work again in the morning. They need them finished and done by next Saturday, when they will collect them from our sewing group. Isn't it exciting that women are playing football? I couldn't believe it when their top player walked into our group, looking for help in putting their strip together. I could hardly refuse now, could I?' Anne felt guilty at lying to her mother, but it was easier for her to do that than have an almighty row.

'A women's football club! How ridiculous, you didn't say it was for a women's club. Women aren't built for suchlike. Besides, we have to keep a certain demure look, not become common ruffians.' Cynthia tutted and then stood up. 'I'll go and have a quick lie down on my bed and close my bedroom door, and then I will be going out for afternoon tea as usual. A welcome break from the noise of that infernal machine.'

Anne watched her mother leave the room and then continued with her task. Why her mother had airs and graces, she had no idea. They were, after all, only from a working-class background and had inherited the house that they lived in from some distant relation, and although large, it needed a lot of repair. She smiled as she moved on to the next shirt. 'Women aren't built for suchlike,' she mused as her foot went down hard upon the treadle. 'Oh, Mother, if you did but know!' she whispered as she thought about the previous day.

Hattie watched as Maggie pulled on her shawl and tied her boots.

'Are you going to see Anne? You usually do on a Sunday,' Hattie said as she cleared the dinner table and looked up at Maggie.

'No, not today. After all, we saw one another yesterday. Her mother will only get suspicious if she starts nearly pushing her out of the house to see me privately, and besides, I bet her mother has had something to say about all the shirts she took home with her yesterday.' Maggie grinned. 'I'm going to do a bit of spying.'

'Spying! Who are you going to be spying on in this weather?' Hattie asked and grinned at her housemate. She was always up to something.

'I'm going to go and sit unnoticed in the seats at Valley Parade and see how Hey's Ladies are shaping up. After all, they are going to be our rivals. I know how to get in without paying. There's a loose board behind the main stand. I'll squeeze through it, like I used to do, and just watch the opposition.'

'You'll get caught, and then what are you going to do?' Hattie stopped with two dinner plates in her hands and couldn't believe what Maggie was going to do.

'Nah, I won't. It's a wet day, they'll be too busy training like we were yesterday. I just thought I could see who our danger would be if we played them; that is, if we do have enough players for a team after yesterday and if we can ever get a match. I'll be back about three, so don't worry, I'm not going for a drink today. Even though I'm tempted to slip into The Diplomat and thank Joshua Swainbank when he's not that formal and away from work.'

'I don't know how you dare talk to him when we are not at work. He's our boss, he has the power to make or break us,' Hattie said and reflected on her good-looking boss, who had always been kind to her family.

'He's just a fella, like any other, but I'm careful what I say to him, although I'll never bow and scrape like my father and mother do. Right, wish me luck and I'll tell you all when I get back.' Maggie wrapped her shawl around her and walked out into the rain that was coming down and was part snow, showing that winter was on its way as she hurried down the street.

Hattie pulled the lace curtain back and watched

Maggie walk down the street. If Hey's Brewery Ladies were playing in this, they were truly devoted, she thought, as she ignored the dirty plates and went to sit in the chair next to the fire, enjoying her time alone in the house and thinking that Maggie was totally obsessed with football.

Maggie pulled the worn wooden board to one side and squeezed through the fence and hid in the darkest corner of the ground, hoping that she wouldn't be seen. She pulled her shawl around her. It was freezing, the sleety rain was filled with ice, and across the valley the hills above Bradford were starting to look white. She blew on her hands and peeked over the edge of the stand at the group of footballers on the field with Peter O'Rourke shouting at them as they practised, aiming at the goals.

'You are going to have to do better than this if we are to have a match against Lister Mills or even them from Swainbank's Mill, although they haven't even got a team yet.'

Maggie watched as woman after woman aimed and shot at the goals and missed. She smiled. If there was one thing she was good at, it was scoring, unlike half of the Hey's team.

'Bloody hell, Mabel, show the rest of them how it's done, will you?' Arthur Hey, dressed in a full-length camel coat, walked onto the field and prompted a petite woman dressed in Bradford colours and with a woollen hat to walk up to the goals as he stood with Peter O'Rourke and gave him his advice.

Maggie watched as Mabel positioned the ball, then took a short run-up and kicked it with her left foot hard and firm into the back of the net.

'That lady is how you do it, and that is why Mabel Brennan will be your captain, and if all of you end up scoring goals like her, then we will have a team and a half.' Arthur Hey stood back and took a cigar out of his pocket and lit it with pride. 'Never mind playing Lister Mills or them other lot, Swainbank's. With goals like that, we are good enough to take on Dick Kerr's Ladies from Preston. Now, I hear that they have a team and a half. Fix a game with them, O'Rourke, see to it, good man.' Arthur Hey patted Peter on his back and continued to watch as his team took shot after shot, missing most of the time. Peter O'Rourke watched and wished that he could just be left to his training. Playing Dick Kerr's Ladies was not likely yet; a local derby perhaps, just to bring in the crowds and give a bit of support and confidence for his team, but not taking on a team that had been practising and playing longer than them and already were getting a reputation down in their own county of Lancashire.

Maggie smiled. So Mabel Brennan was a left-footed goal scorer who favoured kicking the ball to the right-hand top corner. It had been worth her sneaking in just to find that out. She would tell Lorna, just in case they did get to play against Hey's Ladies. She blew on her hands and shivered as she heard Arthur Hey demanding more from his team and watched as a frustrated Peter O'Rourke tried to explain it was not all about scoring, but team spirit. Making Maggie truly thankful, as she sneaked out the same way as she had got in, that Joshua Swainbank did not interfere with their game. She could match Mabel Brennan with her scoring, she thought, as she started whistling and walked back down the street, thinking about Dick Kerr's Ladies that Arthur Hey had mentioned. He was right, they were the team to take on, but not yet, not until her team had bonded and knew exactly how everyone played on the field together. So, Lister Mills, the largest mill in Bradford, had a ladies' team forming; times were going to be interesting indeed.

*

Hattie woke up from her snooze in the kitchen chair and knew instantly that somebody was in the room with her. There was a smell in the air that she recognised, the smell of tobacco mixed with carbolic. It was the smell of her father, the smell that put all her senses on guard as soon as she opened her eyes and saw the man that had always been in her life, but had always made her feel small and useless. Today was not going to be an exception as he watched her stir and rifled through the kitchen drawers looking for his only pair of cufflinks and collar stud which he had forgotten to take with him when he had left in a hurry.

'You lazy bitch, the whole street could hear you snoring. I could have helped myself to anything in this house if I had a mind to,' Burt Gilbert swore as he rummaged in the kitchen drawer that held a mixture of odd things that people had put in it, and where he thought he had left his little-used links and stud.

'I never heard you come in. Did you knock? I'd have woken up if you had knocked,' Hattie said and watched as her father, in his haste and temper, pulled papers and keys out of the drawer onto the stone kitchen floor.

'I don't need to knock in my own house. Where are these blasted things? I'm not about to buy a new set when these will do.' Burt swore again and kicked the kitchen table and stared at his daughter.

'It's not your house, though, is it, Father? I pay the rent now. You've no right to be in here,' Hattie answered back, now fully awake and determined to stand her ground. 'What are you looking for? Perhaps I can help.'

'My bloody cufflinks and collar stud, they are usually in here. What have you done, pawned them? I wouldn't put it past you.'

'You'll find them in the box under the mirror next to the door. Where they properly belong, along with gloves and a clothes brush. You can take your good gloves as well, you've left them behind.' Hattie stood up and watched her father open the small wooden box and swear when at last he found what he had been looking for and put the silver and garnet links into his pocket and put his gloves on.

'They never used to be kept there! No wonder I couldn't find them. Anyway, it'll be the last time I'll be visiting you. I'm getting married to Betty Booth on Boxing Day. We have just set the date. Now, she knows how to look after a man, good meals, clothes washed and ironed and never a bad word from her.' Burt looked at the two unwashed dishes in the sink.

'Had company this dinner time? A fella, perhaps? Wouldn't put it past you now he's away fighting.'

'Just get out, Father, it's nothing to do with you. In the past I have had to tolerate you because you are my father, but that doesn't mean I have to like you.' Hattie could feel tears rising in her eyes. 'I wish you all the best on your wedding day, but I won't be attending.'

'That's a good job, because I wasn't thinking of asking you.' Burt stood with his hand on the door handle, with it slightly ajar, letting the cold air into the warm kitchen. 'Your heart is as cold as that biting wind that's blowing down these streets. I don't know what I ever did to deserve you. You'll not be seeing me again.' He stood and stared at his daughter as she crumpled into a heap in the fireside chair. His job was done; he'd told her what he thought of her, and now he was to make a new life without his family from the past. She could go to hell for all he cared. He had always doubted that Hattie was his true daughter.

Hattie's day had been ruined as she sobbed and

held herself in the chair next to the fire. Her father always knew how to hurt her. In truth, she didn't think that he had ever loved her, even when she was young. Good luck to Betty Booth. She'd soon find out what he was like. He couldn't keep a pleasant face on him for ever, she thought as she sobbed, lifting her head up as Maggie entered the kitchen.

'I was right, Hattie, they were playing. I watched them for about half an hour, taking shots and Arthur Hey dictating to Peter O'Rourke. He won't put up with that for long.' Maggie hadn't noticed the state Hattie was in as she took her shawl off and hung it up, and kicked her clogs from off her feet.

'Good, I'm glad.' Hattie snuffled and blew her nose and tried not to look upset.

'What's up? What's happened while I've been away? You haven't received a telegram? Bruce and Oliver are all right, aren't they?' Maggie walked to Hattie's side and crouched down by her, and took her hand.

'They are fine, as far as I know. It's my father. He came into the house when I was dozing and took me by surprise when I woke up. He had just walked in and was rifling through the drawers looking for something of his. He was just so rude. He hates me,

I know he does.' Hattie sobbed and clung to Maggie.

'Shh. He's gone now. I wish I'd have been here. I can go round to where he lives, if you want me to, and tell him not to bother you again.' Maggie cradled Hattie and felt her upset.

Hattie raised her head and wiped her eyes. 'No, there's no need. He'll not be coming here again. He's getting married on Boxing Day to Betty Booth. That poor woman doesn't know what she's marrying.'

'Do you think we should warn her?' Maggie replied and stood up from her haunches.

'No, leave them to it. He'd only land back here if she threw him out. She will have to take her chance, like my mother did.' Hattie blew her nose and watched as Maggie stirred the dying coals and put the kettle on to boil. 'So your spying mission was a success, you'll have to tell me all about it. I'm just glad that you didn't get caught.' Hattie gave a weak smile and watched as Maggie warmed the teapot, and knew she couldn't hold back with her news of what she had seen.

'Let's put it this way, Hattie, they are just the same as us, learning. They have a scorer, a Mabel Brennan, but they haven't got four like us who love the game. When we have all trained together, we will knock them for six, just like I'd like to knock your father's head from off his shoulders. Families, you couldn't make it up!'

18

The Battle of the Somme, November 1916

The cold, and the never-ending rain had been coming down in sheets over the battlefields. Trenches were filled with stagnant water, rats and disenchanted soldiers, sick of the squalor and conditions of fighting the Germans. Artillery, horses and men were bogged down in fields of mud, with rows of barbed wire stretched out and dead and dying soldiers upon them.

'A living hell,' Bruce commented as he lit a cigarette and passed it to Oliver. 'That might have been the village of Serre, but all that's left of it now are two stumps of trees that used to stand on the high street. The poor buggers that used to live there have no homes to return to.' Bruce sighed as he lit a fag for himself after looking over the trench walls at what used to be a quaint French village occupied by those who wanted nothing more than to live in peace. He slapped his neck and swore.

'Bloody little bastards, these lice are driving me mad. If it isn't them crawling on you, it's the rats looking at you and wondering when you are going to be their next meal.' Bruce put his head down with his cigarette drooping in his mouth. He'd have liked to have slept, but the sound of the never-ending artillery rounds prevented anybody from getting any peace.

'At least you haven't got trench foot. My feet stink and are rotting from not being kept dry. Hopefully, the Aussie Anzacs are going to make life a little better. They are laying wooden roadways for easier movement. Bloody brave, they are. Gerry could pop them off at any moment.' Oliver looked up as a messenger ran towards them, keeping his head down as shells flew over above. They recognised him as Tommy Brewster from their division, and he looked as if he had something important to tell them.

'What's up, Tommy? Have we got new orders?' Bruce looked at the young lad, who must have lied about his age to go and fight the Hun.

'No, not yet, but I hear on the grapevine that we will be moving out of here sometime tonight. General Plumer and Haig are in a meeting now, setting our next assault for us. Not that they will be leading the charge.' Tommy looked at Bruce. 'Give us a drag of your fag, mine are all wet. I dropped the bloody things in the trench.'

Bruce passed him his fag and looked at the young lad. 'Tha looks as if tha's got something more to say. It must be something important if you've risked your life running along this trench to tell us.' Bruce took his fag back off the lad and looked quizzically at him.

'I have, because I know that you are both Bradford City fans.' He nodded at Oliver and pinched a drag off him, breathing out the smoke before sitting back on his haunches to tell his tale. 'They've been picking up the dead from the ground we have won back, and you'll never guess who they found, once they had dug him out of this black soup?'

'Go on, don't give us half a tale!' Oliver looked at the young lad and wondered what he was going to say.

'Only Jimmy Speirs, the striker for Bradford City, who scored the winning goal in the FA Cup final against Newcastle United. He'd been shot in the leg and left in a shell hole by his mate, but he hadn't been able to go back and get him.' Tommy shook his head sadly. 'Jimmy Speirs! Can you bloody believe it? He played for Glasgow Rangers before he came to Bradford.'

'Aye, and a brief time for Leeds, the poor bugger. One minute you are the hero of Bradford and the next you are lying dead in a bloody shell hole in France. He shouldn't have gone that way; he was a true sportsman.' The three men looked at one another and all thought, there but by the grace of God go I.

'Here, I've something that will make you laugh. My Hattie has got herself a football team. She and some of the lasses from Swainbank's Mill have got a team together. Sounds a bit ramshackle, but Hattie could always play football. They are even playing on Bradford Park Avenue's ground.'

'Women playing football? Now what I'd do to see that. Do they wear shorts or bloomers?' Tommy asked, and Bruce knocked his cap off his head with a laugh.

'You go and watch their skills, not the colour of their bloomers and how much leg you can see; and this is my wife you are talking about.' Bruce grinned.

'Aye, and my sister. She told me the same, and that the lodger she's taken in is a dab hand at scoring goals. I'd give anything to go home and watch them.' Oliver shook his head. 'Jimmy Speirs dead! Now that I'll have to remember next time one of these bloody Germans shows his head. We had only just got a decent team together.'

All three had not long to wait as Haig and his generals decided that the Germans had suffered severe losses and that it was time to advance and take the next ridge, take the French and English line forward with a creeping barrage. At two thirty in the morning, all the troops were ready to advance at five twenty, and they finally got the order to go and fight one of the most bloody battles of the First World War. Shells fell around the attacking troops, mustard gas was thrown, and German machine guns pinned down British soldiers by embedded bunkers at Believe, causing huge losses. On the first day of the Somme nearly two thousand soldiers of the West Yorkshire Regiment had died and the numbers of casualties kept on building with every day and month. The German forces had been totally underestimated, and soldiers had just become cannon fodder, for a few yards of land. Bruce and Oliver were lucky that day. They lived to tell the tale. The war was only going to get worse.

19

There was an excited buzz around Swainbank's Mill. Women could be heard discussing tactics and commenting on footballers' skills as they weaved, carded and fulfilled the mill's orders.

'Bloody hell, what have you started? I can't get an inch of sense out of anybody in the carding room,' Len sighed as he came back with a huge empty basket that he had taken full of fleeces to the carding room. 'Sara Turner is pulling her hair out. She says it's all yours and Hattie's fault. She'll be complaining to them upstairs if you are not careful.'

'She can complain all she likes, the boss knows what we are doing and it's not interfering with our work. Our lunchtime is our own, and he doesn't own us over the weekend. Besides, he wouldn't be paying for our boots if he wasn't all for it.' Maggie started to pull wraps of sheep wool into the empty basket and looked at Len, and then at Bob who still vowed not to get involved in just a game. 'Anyway, where were you last Saturday? I thought you were going to be our linesman?'

'I'm not being your linesman. Other men will laugh at me. Even Bob here thinks it's a mad idea.' Len pulled another empty basket over and started to fill it up with the grease-filled fleeces.

'I didn't say mad, I just said not ladylike. I wouldn't want to marry a woman who played football. Women should be petite and demure, not act like clumsy workhorses,' Bob said quietly. He'd never made his feelings known before, but he had done so now and hoped that he'd not live to regret it. He labelled up a batch of ready-woven material to be delivered to Higher Mill and got on with his job.

Maggie, with a wicked grin on her face, stood on her tiptoes with the basket next to her and winked at Len. 'Oh, Bob, dear. Could you lift me this fleece? It seems rather heavy to me. It must have been a good sheep this one, worth a shilling or two of anybody's money.'

'I'm just labelling this delivery. Len, you are nearer, you help.'

'Sorry, Bob, my basket is full again. They are yelling for fleece this morning. They might be doing some yacking, but they are working hard in the carding department.' Len winked and suddenly disappeared, pushing a half-empty basket through the warehouse doors.

'Oh, you see, I rest my case. You are of the fairer sex. You shouldn't be playing football if you can't even pull that fleece down from its pile.' Bob left his job and stood on his toes. 'Why don't you get the ones lower down and then it will fall in place?' He shook his head and balanced precariously. Just enough for Maggie to knock him off balance and push him into her huge, nearly empty basket and laugh as he wriggled about trying to right himself at the bottom to climb out.

'Clumsy workhorses, are we? Not petite and demure perhaps, but let's give you a quick ride around the warehouse, so that you can change your mind.' Maggie laughed as Bob tried his best to climb out of the basket as she pushed it on its wheels with all her might around the warehouse. Bob shouted and screamed. 'Stop it, you'll tip me over, I'll hit my head, you are going to kill me!' As she turned the corners of the stacking bays and headed for the warehouse doors, Bob held on for dear life, thinking that he was going to be thrown out into the yard. 'Stop it,

Maggie. I take it all back. You are all very capable. I didn't mean it, let me out!'

'Em, yes, Miss Fleming, I do suggest that you come to a halt, whatever this is about.' Joshua Swainbank himself stood at the bottom of the stairs and looked sternly at the wild woman running riot in his warehouse with a screaming warehouse worker looking as white as a sheet in the basket.

'Mr Swainbank, sir. I'm sorry, it was only a joke I was playing on Bob.' Maggie, for once in her life, blushed and looked shame-faced. 'I'm sorry, I was just teaching him a lesson.'

'You weren't, you were trying to kill me, you mad woman. That's what you were trying to do.' Bob stood up and put his leg over the basket edge, and brushed himself down as he stood shakily on the warehouse floor. 'That just proves my point. You are all blinking clumsy workhorses, rough ones at that.'

'Perhaps, Miss Fleming, we had better have a word in my office. Now, right away!' Joshua Swainbank said in a grim voice and pointed for Maggie to climb the stairs to his office.

'Yes, sir, straight away, sir.' Maggie, for once, was subservient. If she still had a job after that episode, she would think herself more than lucky, she thought, as she climbed the stairs and saw all the carding room workers were following her with their eyes as Joshua Swainbank walked behind her with a dark look on his face.

The whole of the upstairs office turned and watched as Joshua Swainbank marched Maggie across the upper floor and into his office, closing the door behind him firmly.

'Now, what exactly was that all about? You know I should sack you here and now.' Joshua stood behind his desk and looked down upon the repentant Maggie.

'I'm sorry. He called us women footballers clumsy workhorses and said we should be all demure. I only meant to frighten him,' Maggie replied, avoiding Joshua's gaze.

'Football! I should have known it would involve football somewhere along the line. As it is, Bob Briggs should be careful what he says. He should not be throwing stones at anybody, with him being a conscientious objector. He should keep his views to himself if he knows what's good for him,' Joshua growled and sat down in his chair. 'That doesn't mean that I can ignore your behaviour. I think an apology is in order, when you go back down, whether he deserves it or not.'

Maggie raised her head and was relieved that was all she was expected to do. Maybe she had got off lightly because nobody liked a conscientious objector. They should be fighting for their country, regardless of their views on the carnage that was taking place.

'Thank you, sir. I'm truly sorry, he just riled me.' Maggie thought she caught the flicker of a smile on Joshua's face. 'I'll apologise.'

'You were unlucky that I caught you. I was just on my way to ask you if Tom Maley had ordered your boots and what time you practise. I thought I might have a wander down to Park Avenue and watch one Saturday, when I have the time. If Miss Braithwaite had not been talking to Sara Turner, I would have asked her. However, I hear Mrs Turner is not altogether happy with her workers being footballers.' Joshua looked at Maggie. 'You do realise just how much controversy this football team is causing?'

'I do, sir, but it can't just be at this mill. Lister Mills have an up-and-coming team, and you already know Hey's Brewery are playing. It can only do good for every mill, especially if all teams play for charity.' Maggie looked with interest at Joshua.

'It will give us all hope and a feeling of slight relief from the terrible news that we read every day. I wasn't sure what to think at first, but I can see no harm in it. If Lister Mills has a team, then it is only right that we have one. I will sponsor you when you are in need of new boots, or perhaps even transport, if you get that big that you have to travel. Although I think it will be a while till you play at Wembley Stadium.' Joshua smirked.

'Oh, thank you, sir. That is far more than we deserve, or should I say I deserve, seeing that I was being a little tempestuous in my treatment of Bob.' Maggie smiled.

'Nothing more than what he deserved. Now, when is your next match or training? I will try and come down to watch you all,' Joshua asked eagerly.

'It's this Saturday, sir. We gather for one o'clock and go home when the light begins to dim. But I think you would be better waiting a week or two before you come down and watch, just until most of us get used to how one another plays and gain confidence.' Maggie hesitated. 'With no disrespect, sir, you are our boss; our livelihoods depend on you. We would hate to make fools of ourselves until we have mastered most of the skills.'

'I can understand that, and I probably wouldn't be able to keep my mouth shut if I knew a move was wrong. I'll give you a month then, before I come and watch. I'm sure by then a team will have been formed and that you should be near to having a proper match.' Joshua noticed that Mary Mason was watching what was happening in his office with Maggie Fleming, whom she had taken an instant dislike to. 'Now, back to work, no more fooling about, else I will have to fine you for wasting time. I really should do now, but perhaps Bob deserved what he got, although don't quote me.' Joshua stood up and indicated the door, and spoke loudly as Maggie walked towards it.

'I'm sure you will make Swainbank's proud when you play your first match. I hope that it is against Lister Mills. They always overshadow us, with being more prosperous.'

Maggie couldn't help but notice Mary Mason's face as she walked out of the main office past her desk. She looked as if she had just swallowed a wasp. Another reason to show what the team and the girls were capable of, she thought, as she went back to her work and to apologise to Bob. Although she didn't see why she should, now she knew that he wasn't even prepared to fight for his country. He deserved a white feather of cowardice more than an apology.

Nobody dared to gather outside the warehouse

for a practice. Word had gone around the mill that Maggie had been reprimanded heavily and that a lot of higher positions were starting to complain about the wave of football mania that was taking over the firm. Nobody wanted to lose their jobs, so until they knew the lay of the land, they weren't going to take any chances.

Len went back and forward with wool fleeces to the carding room and whispered to Anne and Hattie that Maggie was none the worse for her reprimand and not to take any notice of what people were saying. However, he didn't dare stay too long, knowing that both the top office and Sara Turner were watching his every move.

Maggie got back on with her job and ignored Bob until she thought the silence between them had been long enough.

'Bob, I want to apologise. I don't know what got into me.' Maggie stood across from him as he ate his brawn sandwiches, which he brought with him every day for his dinner. He was sitting as usual on a bale of wool and just ignored her.

'I thought that you'd be sacked, thrown out, which in my eyes you should be, carrying on like you do. You do know you shook my nerves to pieces.' Bob ate his sandwich and couldn't look at the woman who was causing him concern in his pristine warehouse.

'No, I wasn't sacked, just told not to be so stupid, especially with you, as you must be of a nervous disposition,' Maggie replied and eyeballed the bitter little man who had not liked her since the day she had started.

'What do you mean by that? Who says I'm bad with my nerves?' Bob snapped.

'I just gathered that you were, when you were squealing like a stuck pig as I tore around the warehouse with you. It's a good job that you are not on the front line, fighting for our country. You'd be asked to do more than have a ride in a wool basket,' Maggie snidely replied.

'Well, I'm not, I'm stuck here with you, and the reason I'm not fighting for my country is that I'm a Quaker, I don't believe in war. Not that I have to explain myself to you.' Bob wrapped up what was left of the sandwiches and put them in his rucksack. 'We all have our secrets, some more dark than others. I've seen you, Maggie Fleming, you and that Anne. You do not need to criticise me. You too have a splinter in your eye, as the good Bible tells us.'

'Then we will judge one another and leave it at

that.' Maggie held her head high. 'And as for football, Joshua Swainbank is only too willing to back us. In fact, he's coming to watch us once we have a team. How about we live and let live, Bob? You can't help being what you are, and I can't help being what I am.'

'Huh! You are asking a lot of me, but I have to work with you. I'm more likely to lose my job through my beliefs than you through your secret lifestyle. I suppose we had better be civil with one another if nothing else.' Bob turned his back on her and walked away, leaving Maggie feeling a little shaken. Bob was a dark one. He noticed everything, and she was going to have to be more careful around him. He was not to be fooled with.

Anne, Hattie and Lorna all waited outside the warehouse for Maggie when at last she appeared at the end of the day.

'We were bothered about you, we thought that you'd be sacked. The rumours are flying around the mill about you and Bob Briggs.' Hattie scanned her friend's face and wondered if she had been crying, as she knew she would have been doing if she had been ordered to the mill owner's office.

'Ahh, it was nowt, the two-faced little rat. I was only having fun. Trouble is Joshua Swainbank just happened to be on his way down to see me and caught me just when I was going to tip him out into the street. He deserved all he got, comparing us to workhorses.'

'Oh, Lord, Maggie. Joshua Swainbank must have been hard with you. He won't be happy that you did that with his warehouse man. Bob Briggs is nothing but a worm, but he's a worker.' Lorna folded her arms and shook her head.

'No, he wasn't at all. He gave me a good dressing down, told me a few things that I should have known, and then I promised him not to act like an idiot again. In fact, he is going to get even more involved with our team. Although he says some of the overseers are frightened it will interfere with our work.'

Maggie's three friends looked at her. It would seem she was afraid of nothing and that Joshua Swainbank was as big a football fan as they were. Now they just had to prove that they were worthy of his time and support.

'I thought you were going to be sacked for sure.' Anne looked up at her love. 'And instead you have come away with even more support for us all.'

'I can't believe it either. Now all we have to do is

play and play well. Let's hope that everybody turns up this Saturday and Tom gives us something a little less taxing.' Maggie felt a glow of pride. She might not be popular with some of the overseers, but the mill owner had faith in her and the team, and that was all that mattered.

20

'Please don't let Tom make us run that many times around the pitch,' Hattie said as she stripped off in the changing room and looked at the newly embellished tops that Anne was giving out. 'They look better, a bit more feminine.' Hattie pulled her shirt over her head and watched as the other players smiled and pulled them on. They truly did feel in a club now.

'He's only doing it to get us fit. Not that we aren't anyway. You have to be to do the work we do.' Lorna pulled up her socks and put her everyday boots back on. 'It's a pity our boots weren't here waiting for us, but never mind. I suppose we have a shortage of cobblers, there's a shortage of everything at the moment.'

'Clumsy workhorses, that's what Bob Briggs called us. Perhaps he was right.' Maggie sighed. 'Right, we look more like it this Saturday, girls, let's see what Tom has got lined up for us today.' Maggie opened the changing hut's door and let in the sharp air. Autumn was nearly over, and winter was on its way. It was truly the football season, and most men who weren't at war must be missing their Saturday afternoon sport, she thought, as she ventured out onto the pitch in front of her team.

'Good afternoon, ladies. How are we today? Ready for another session? You know the drill. Like last week, laps around the pitch to warm up, and then I have a new skill for you to learn. Two laps will be enough, and then come and line up next to me at the far end of the pitch.' Tom heard the moans and grinned. 'It's for your own good. Go, go on. The quicker you get the laps done, the quicker you can start learning skills.'

'Come on, we will all jog around together. You will easily keep up with me. There's no need to set off like a whippet out of its box. We will take it more easily today.' Maggie picked her feet up and started around the pitch, and everybody else followed, their breath coming fast as they steadily jogged.

'Keep going another time around and then come over to me.' Tom watched as he walked down the centre of the pitch and placed stakes at equal distances all down the field in a long line before walking back to the pitch edge.

The team came back, panting and catching their breath as they stood in front of him.

'I need you to do that every time you come to warm up and get flexible. Right, today, we won't be doing squats. We'll see how good you all are at controlling a ball. Hattie, there's a sack of balls over there. Bring them here, and I'll show you what I want you all to do, and then we will practise passing.'

Hattie ran for the sack of heavy leather balls from off the touchline and put it down at Tom's feet.

'I'll show you how it's done. I might be too old to play, but I can still handle a football. It's a skill you never lose, and I can thank my days at Celtic for that.' Tom walked up to the start of the poles and placed a ball firmly down on the ground, and then kicked and dribbled it with skill in and out of the poles, weaving without ever losing control of the ball. He grinned. 'It's as simple as that. Now, Maggie, you go first. I've heard you can play football. Let's see if this is a skill you possess.'

Maggie took a ball out of the sack and felt her heart pounding. She might have played football a time or two, but never in front of a professional footballer.

'Remember, it's control of the ball, not always

speed.' Tom turned and addressed everybody. 'It's no good running with it just for you to lose control of it. Go on, Maggie, let's see what you can do.'

Maggie kicked it gently in front of her, trying to guide it with both feet in between the poles. She had never concentrated so hard and was doing well until she got to the end of the line and kicked the ball too far, losing control and having to run for it before repeating the act to get back to her team. She shook her head and bent down with her hands on her knees. She was disappointed.

'That wasn't too bad, but you saw the end of the line and rushed it. Hattie, you next.'

Hattie stood and looked at the course of poles, imagining them to be players, just like Bruce and Oliver, and that they were trying to get the ball off her. She'd played this game before, and just as Maggie was good at getting goals, she was good at dribbling. She was nimble and quick on her feet. She placed the ball down and kicked off slowly and steadily, picking up pace as she gained confidence, turning on her heels at the end of the run and returning without ever losing control of the ball. She beamed and smiled as the rest of the women clapped. She was good at dribbling thanks to days playing in the alleyway behind the house. Oliver's many kicks of her shins had taught her to be nimble and concentrate.

'Well, that's shown me. Well done. Next!' Tom urged Anne forward and watched as she completed the drill before overseeing everyone having a turn. He then put up another row of poles and split the group into two and watched as he made them practise and practise again, shouting encouragement or giving advice when they needed it.

'This is more like it, we are learning skills,' Lorna said. 'And look, everyone is enjoying it. They are even laughing at one another and cursing when they lose the ball.' Lorna leaned on Hattie's shoulder and caught her breath. 'Now you know why I played in goal, not that good with my feet, but with my hand-eye combination, I can't be beaten.'

'You are not that bad. Some have never done anything like this before in their lives, and they are improving every time they have another go. Imagine what we'll be like in a few weeks if we keep this up!'

'Better than bloody Hey's Brewery and hopefully Lister Mills, if we can do this with our ordinary boots on. There will be no stopping us when we get our new ones.' Maggie caught her breath and watched as Anne weaved in and out of the poles, sometimes losing the ball but quickly recovering it. Competition was building between them, and the determination to prove that they could do it and would.

'Good passing is making sure your fellow teammate gets the ball at his feet, not a million miles away at the other side of the field and given to the opponent. You have to be accurate with your kick, so this afternoon, split up into twos. One of you will have to play with me, and the rest just kick the ball back and forward to one another. You need to focus it to land at your partner's feet. Don't drop-kick it or kick it too high today, just back and forward; but don't make it too predictable, you've got to keep your wits about you.' Tom watched the women separate into twos and looked at Rosie, who smiled up at him. 'Got the short straw, eh, Rosie? Well, we will show them how it's done,' he said as they both walked down the pitch together.

'I don't mind, Mr Maley. I know I'm being taught by the best.' Rosie smiled as he took his thick winter coat off.

'Aye, well, that's not what the FA thinks, but we will show them, lass, we will bloody well show them.'

*

Hattie and Maggie had little to say to one another as they sat together in the flickering light of the fire after returning from their practice. Muscles they hadn't known they had before ached. But they were content; they had proved a point that they could play football and that they could build a good team with the help of Tom Maley.

Hattie stood up and reached for the letter that had arrived in the late afternoon post. It was from the front, from Bruce, and she lovingly fingered it before opening it. Her heart ached for her husband. She missed him so much, she thought, as she read the loving words within. Some had been crossed out, censored by the army, but she got the feeling that things were not as rosy as Bruce was trying to make out. You had only to read the daily papers to realise that. She folded it and thought that she would read it again once in her bed and on her own.

'Is he all right? Are he and Oliver still holding their ground and keeping Gerry from ruling us?' Maggie yawned and noticed Hattie wipe away a tear.

'They are. Oliver is asking for me to send him some new socks, it seems his feet are always wet; and Bruce just says it's getting colder and everyone is fed up of fighting for a foot or two of land, although where he is he's not been able to say.' Hattie's cries turned to sobs. 'I wish he were home, I wish both of them were home. It isn't fair that we had only been married for a short while before he left.' Hattie put her letter in her apron pocket and wiped her eyes.

'I'm sorry, Hattie. I truly am. There's me, full of hope for this brilliant idea of a football team, and there's you feeling heartbroken every day, along with the rest of this country's mothers, wives and sisters. The only way we can help is to raise funds for the lads that are fighting our corner and make their lives a little better. At least they will know that we support them as well as we can.' Maggie gently reached forward to take Hattie's hand. 'I can't mend a broken heart, though I would if I could.' She grimaced. 'I'm sorry, hopefully the war will soon be over.'

'I don't think it will be by the sounds of it. But I'm not on my own. Nearly every house on this street has someone fighting for our country. Sorry, I didn't mean to cry in front of you, I'm just tired.' Hattie sighed and pulled her hand out of Maggie's.

'I know, and I hope that you know I'm here if you need to talk. I've not always got my head in the clouds and thinking of football, contrary to what some folk think. I know what it's like to love someone so much that it hurts.' Maggie smiled slightly and thought of Anne. They could never be together, while her mother was alive, but one day . . . perhaps they would be.

21

The newspaper sellers were yelling out the latest news from the front, none of it sounding good, and everybody was shaking their heads as they picked up a paper and took it home to read after their evening meal. Battles might be raging, but the news that caught most men's eyes was the picture of notorious temptress and spy Mata Hari. A seductive picture on the front of the *Bradford Mercury* was making everybody buy a copy and read about Margaretha Zelle from Holland, who had been given freedom to roam between lines and officers on both sides of the war. The headline 'A Harlot, but is she a traitoress?' had everyone reading about the glamorous model and wondering how she was adored by both sides of the war.

'She's nothing more than a floozie. How can she fraternise with the enemy?' Hattie said as she paid for her paper and then hurried to keep up with Maggie.

'Don't believe everything you read. Women are always made out to be evil, ever since Eve had a bite of that apple. They never treat men like they do women,' Maggie growled. Her day had not been a good one working with Bob Briggs, who still hadn't forgiven her; and Len had been shifty all day after she had asked him again why he hadn't shown up for training the previous Saturday, despite them not needing a linesman, but she had asked out of friendship.

'Well, I'm going to read all about her when I get back home. I can't wait to sit down to my supper and take my shoes off. My feet ache, and every muscle in my body does too.' Hattie nearly had to run to keep up with Maggie. 'Thank heavens we just have to fry some potatoes and cabbage left over from yesterday with a bit of bacon for supper. I don't want to cook much tonight.'

'Don't even bother doing that. Look, the pie shop is still open. I'll pop in and get us a pie and some pease pudding. I don't fancy having warmed-up potatoes tonight. I'm tired and I know I sound right bad-tempered. It's that bloody Bob Briggs, he's watched me all day.' Maggie, without waiting for Hattie to answer, turned into the pie shop on the corner of the street while Hattie waited outside for her. By the dim lights of the shop, she started reading her paper, leaving the main headlines and turning towards the back pages where all the sports news was usually displayed. Her mouth fell open as she read one of the headlines.

> HEY'S BREWERY LADIES TO PLAY THE FIRST ALL-WOMEN FOOTBALL MATCH AGAINST DICK KERR'S LADIES FROM PRESTON AT VALLEY PARADE.

She read it again and then closed the newspaper quickly as Maggie came out of the shop, carrying steaming hot pie and pease pudding in a dish that would have to be returned the following day to the bakery.

'There, that will fill us. I needed something comforting to make me feel better. Let's get home quickly, put the kettle on and enjoy our supper in peace.' Maggie strode off, and Hattie followed, wondering if she dared tell Maggie the news or if she should wait until they had eaten and Maggie had calmed herself.

Later that evening, the house smelled of tattie hash pie and pease pudding, and two empty unwashed plates sat on the kitchen table as Maggie added coal to the fire and watched Hattie read her paper.

'Any news other than her?' Maggie asked and looked across at Hattie as she started to fold the newspaper to the back pages after reading what she had wanted about Mata Hari.

'There is. I don't know if you'll want to read it though. It's just under the advert for Mrs Codswallop's ankle strain cure lozenges. I can't believe that they will work for one minute. Here, read it yourself, and then I won't get shouted at.'

Maggie took the folded paper and read the headline stating Hey's Brewery's intentions.

'What, they are nowhere near being able to play a decent game against Dick Kerr's Ladies. I think Dick Kerr must have been training for weeks. I keep hearing they are really good. There's always something about them in the newspapers, and the Hey's team can hardly pass a ball straight; they are worse than us!' Maggie swore and looked down at the paper.

'They say it's going to be played on Boxing Day at Valley Parade. But nothing is definite yet. They are still waiting to hear confirmation from Dick Kerr.'

'I bet that it's Hey himself who has given this report. Peter O'Rourke wouldn't until he's certain that he's got a winning team. I'm sure he won't have yet, the way he's told what to do. The poor devil has his hands tied.' Maggie looked at the report again. 'Bugger, I wanted our team to be one of the first to play in Bradford. Not these!'

'Don't get worried. It might not ever happen. If Hey's Brewery Ladies aren't ready for playing, then they will get slaughtered, so it might be in our favour. We can show them how it's really played,' Hattie said quietly and could almost hear Maggie's brain ticking while she thought of ways to interfere with the match.

'It should be a local derby, especially on Boxing Day. It would get half of Bradford watching them. I bet Tom has seen it and is cursing too. We'll have to talk to him on Saturday at our next practice. That match should be ours!'

Peter O'Rourke and Tom Maley sat in the snug area of Peter's favourite pub on Manningham Lane. They were enjoying a pint of Hey's Bitter and sat back and viewed one another with an unspoken curiosity.

'Well, bloody Hey can brew bitter, but he's no football coach. I wish he'd leave me to my job, and I'll leave him to his.' Peter O'Rourke wiped the froth from around his mouth and looked at his friend, who was however an enemy when it came to football teams.

'Nay, his team must be good. He's making enough noise about playing Dick Kerr's Ladies on Boxing Day at your ground.' Tom couldn't help but snigger.

'He's put that in the paper without even telling me. Just because he's a director, he thinks he can do anything he likes. The lasses will get there eventually, but I need longer to train them. He just wants to get the publicity for his brewery, whereas I want the lasses to shine. Women's football is taking off all around the country, and it's going to be as popular as men's by the time this war is out.'

'Well, you turned down two women who could really play and their mate, the Irish goalie. Not that I'm complaining because you sent them my way, and we have the makings of a damn good team. They are determined and are quick learners. Maggie Fleming could score a goal with her eyes shut; she just has the knack.' Tom sat back and looked at Peter as he shook his head.

'I caught a glimpse of her as she was leaving my ground the other day. She'd been spying on the team – she's a determined one, is that lass. She used to come and have a play with her cousin Fred Howell on the pitch after he'd done training. There's not much she won't know about football. I could do with her in my team.'

'Well, you said no to her, so it's your loss.' Tom grinned. 'Do you really think this women's football is going to prove to be popular? I'm hoping it will, just to spite the FA. They should have supported them last time when there was that little spat about them playing.'

'I can see it running wild through the country, especially if they play for charity. After all, they'll not be offered payment from the FA. They have made that abundantly plain in a letter they wrote to me and all the clubs. You'll have had one, surely?' Peter looked at Tom and put down his pint.

'I probably have. It'll be in a pile of letters they keep sending me. I tend not to read everything they send me. Half the time it's a load of rubbish, and with no games being played, they should have nothing to say.' Tom sat back and looked at Peter, and decided to ask him what had been on his mind since he had read the newspaper with news of the match.

'If you don't want your lasses to play Dick Kerr's team, or if they decline, why don't our teams play one another? My lasses would love that. I also hear

Lister Mills has a team, and that the cotton mill at Skipton might have one in the making, but it would be good if we could fix one between us. Half of Bradford would turn out to watch, if not for the football, for the curiosity of seeing women play; although my lasses will be true professionals by then.' Tom took a long sip.

'Careful what you say, it's not that far away, is Christmas. It'll depend on whether Kerr's gets back to Arthur Hey and if he agrees to their demands. But aye, I think it would be a good game for both our teams. They are more suited for one another, and they would play to win, and the game would be played in the true nature of the game, sportsmanship.' Peter nodded his head and winked. He'd rather play Tom's team than have them shown up by Dick Kerr's team, who had the pick of his huge munition plant and who he had heard were as sharp as a knife.

'Right, let's hope that Dick Kerr turns your boss down. It will be a cracking game if we can organise it. It will raise some funds if folk are willing to put their hands in their pockets. What about if they both play for the Soldiers and Sailors Rehabilitation Homes? They need every penny of support. But that will be up to you to organise if we are to play at your ground.' Tom had been thinking about his suggestion ever since he had heard the news.

'Aye, that would be right with me. It would be a good test for both our teams. I bloody hope Kerr's going to turn him down flat. Hopefully, we can play them too when both our teams are more proficient.'

'Aye, by then we should be able to go all over the country. Or at least you can; my lot have a lukewarm boss behind them as a backer. Once he's seen them play a match, he might change his mind. If he doesn't, I'll have to put my hand in my pocket. After all, I haven't much else in my life, other than the love of the game, since I lost my lad to this war and my missis.'

'I'm sorry you lost your lad. It came so early in the war. It must have broken your heart.'

'It did, but I'm not alone, and no amount of tears is going to bring him or my wife back. You've just got to get on with your life.' Tom spoke quietly and looked around the nearly empty pub. In days gone by, the pub would have been filled with young men drinking and laughing, but now it was almost dead, just a handful of men like Peter and him trying to put the world to rights. It made them both feel old and worthless, unable to serve because of their age and ailments.

‘Aye, well, perhaps our teams of ladies will bring us all some pride and purpose in life. We can but try.’ Peter finished his pint and stood up to go.

‘That we will, it’ll be a good match, if we can pull it off. Keep in touch, Peter. Keep that director of yours in his place.’ Tom grinned.

‘I’ll try, but I can’t guarantee it. He holds the purse strings, him and the FA.’

‘Aye, well, you know what I think of them. Night, Peter, here’s to our ladies.’ Tom sipped the last of his pint and watched as Peter left the pub and prayed that he would be successful with his suggestion to Arthur Hey.

‘Bugger.’ Arthur Hey sat at his desk and looked at the letter that had arrived from the secretary of Kerr’s munitions. It was a curt letter saying that their ladies’ football team would not be prepared to play Hey’s Brewery Ladies, due to an alternative fixture to be played with a Sheffield club on Boxing Day. However, they would consider dates for further matches.

‘Damn, damn, and I announced it in the *Mercury*, everybody will be expecting a match,’ he grumbled to his secretary, who just shook her head.

‘Perhaps another team? Surely, there’s another

somewhere? Lister Mills and I hear Swainbank's have a sort of a team,' his secretary replied as she wished he would concentrate on the business letters that needed signing.

'Lister's, they get enough publicity, and they are the wealthiest mill in Bradford. It would grab the headlines, but I don't want my team to lose to them. I would never hear the last of it, everywhere I showed my face in Bradford,' Arthur growled. 'I'll see if O'Rourke knows anything about this team from Swainbank's. At least there would be a match to go to and raise money.'

'Yes, Mr Hey. That sounds like a good solution, at least you wouldn't be losing face by promising something you shouldn't have. Now perhaps you could sign me those letters, please?' his secretary pleaded.

'Aye, and then I'm going out, I've football plans to sort.'

22

It was Friday evening, and Hattie was sitting at the kitchen table writing to Bruce and Oliver. Thanking them for the payment she had collected from the Post Office that day and assuring them both that it had been put to good use. Her letters were filled with love and news of what was going on in Bradford, as well as an update on how the Yorkshire Ladies' Football Club was performing. She tried to keep the letter full of cheer, anything to stop her boys from worrying, she thought, as she licked both envelopes down and sealed them with a kiss, and then left them on the table ready to be posted along with a parcel containing socks for both of them before she took the tram to the next day's match.

'I never see you writing home, and you've never been back to see your parents since you moved in. Do you not think they will be worrying about you?' Hattie asked Maggie as she sat and gazed into the fire.

'I'll perhaps go and see them before Christmas. They won't be bothered, they'll know I can look after myself. They don't even know where I live, just that I'm renting with you,' Maggie replied. She had been thinking a lot about her upbringing at Esholt and had come to realise that she had never really been close to her parents.

'It won't be long till Christmas. Once Bonfire Night has been and gone, it will soon be with us. Not that anybody will be celebrating Bonfire Night this year.' Hattie sighed.

'No, the Government have put an end to that with their Defence of the Realm Act. I don't think anybody would want to be signalling to the enemy or encouraging any Zeppelins to bomb here, but you never know. Poor old Guy Fawkes. He gets a year or two off and then we will be back at it.' Maggie watched Hattie as she took her hair down and started brushing it, ready for bed. 'Football training tomorrow. I wonder if our boots will have come, and I wonder what Tom Maley will be having us doing. More training, I expect. That is all we will be doing until we have a game to play. One of us will have to mention the piece in the *Mercury*, if he hasn't already seen it.' Maggie sighed. She had so wanted her team to be the first one in Bradford to play a game.

'We can both talk to Tom, if you want, just see what he says.' Hattie yawned.

'You will be more reserved than me. I'd probably come out with it like a bull in a china shop.' Maggie smiled. 'Are you going to bed?'

'Yes, I'm tired. I know it's only nine, but it's been a long week. We are so busy at the mill.' Hattie lit a candle and stood next to Maggie. 'Don't stay up too long. We need our goal-maker fresh in the morning.'

'I won't. I'll just sit here for a while. I've not had the best of weeks at work and being beaten to a match has just put the lid on it,' Maggie replied and smiled at Hattie as she left her sitting. She wished she could properly be with Anne and that she could tell her all her worries, but that was highly unlikely while her mother was still alive. Instead, she would keep her thoughts to herself and try not to dwell on them.

'Oh, my Lord, Joshua Swainbank is talking to Tom. What's he doing here?' Lorna said as the four women walked into the grounds of Bradford Park Avenue. All four looked at the two men who were deep in conversation on the sidelines of the pitch.

'He never said anything about being here today. Oh, heavens. He's going to see us in our shorts. I'm going to be showing my boss my legs!' Hattie exclaimed.

'We all will, but we will have to get used to that. Everybody will be watching our legs before long,' Anne said quietly and looked up at Maggie.

'Oh look, they've got a load of football boots lined up behind them on the bench. They've come.' Maggie smiled as she walked towards both men and watched as some of the other players took their new boots and sat on the bench to try them on.

'Ah, the four reprobates. Ladies, we were waiting for you to join us.' Tom grinned at the four he knew were the force behind the team. 'Your new boots have arrived, and Mr Swainbank has come to watch your progress. I sent him a note last night, just after the mill closed, in the hope I'd catch him still in his office.'

'Ladies.' Joshua lifted his top hat and noted the blushes on his workers' faces. 'I'll not stop long, and I will not interfere in the tutoring of Mr Maley. I might know how to run a woollen mill, and I might like to watch a game of football, but I am no coach.'

'I'm sure Peter O'Rourke would welcome those

words from Arthur Hey when he comes to watch his girls. Thank you, Mr Swainbank, we are more than grateful for the gift of the boots and your support,' Tom replied and smiled.

'Yes, thank you, Mr Swainbank, the boots are wonderful,' Hattie exclaimed and then walked to get her pair and change into her shirt and shorts, which she was going to be embarrassed to wear in front of her boss.

Maggie watched Anne, Lorna and Hattie get their boots and then go and change, but she hung back a while before she collected hers. She touched Tom Maley's arm as he turned to walk away with Joshua. 'Can I speak to you after the training session?'

'Indeed. I need to talk to all of you. But for now, let's show your employer just what you all can do. You are going to need him.' Tom winked. 'Tell the girls to give their best today while he is here. Especially Lorna; tell her there's going to be shooting practice this session, and I need her to prove her worth.'

Maggie looked at Tom. He was planning something. But she couldn't ask, as he quickly walked to catch up with Joshua and to make sure that he was happy in his seat.

'Joshua Swainbank is here for more than just to see

the boots he's paid for have arrived.' Maggie looked around at the thirteen women who had been faithful to the training days since they had started. 'Lorna, Tom says to be on your best form today. He's going to be putting you in the goal, and we are all going to practise scoring. He's up to something, I can tell, by the way he's acting.' Maggie tied her shorts tight and looked at her group of like-minded sports friends.

'We all need to play well today, because I don't know what Tom is about, but I do know that Hey's Brewery are to play Dick Kerr's Ladies at Valley Parade on Boxing Day and that first match should have been ours.'

'Yes, we've all seen. We are all annoyed and Hattie has just told us that they are not even good players,' Rosie said and looked at the group of dejected women.

'They were hopeless, although I shouldn't judge. Now, don't let the game that's booked dishearten you. Let's go out there and show Tom that we have spirit, and even though we may be the underdogs, we still mean business. You especially, Lorna. Without a good goalie, we are lost, but equally, everybody do your best to put that ball in the back of that net and listen to Tom's advice. Joshua Swainbank will be watching our every move, and we need to prove that we have earned our boots.'

The team walked out onto the pitch and was greeted by Tom with his usual sack of footballs.

'Right, ladies, let's see who has a good eye for striking and who hasn't. Sometimes known as penalty taking. A lot of it is about which way the goalie favours and how much force you can put behind the ball. Try not to aim straight at the goalie, who will be Lorna; that's too easy for the goalie to save. Maggie, you show them how it's done, followed by Hattie, and then line up and keep going until I say stop.' Tom watched Maggie walk up to the penalty spot and Lorna stand in the goal with her arms ready to catch or block whatever came her way, dressed in a warm jumper and a hand-knit hat. As she shouted, 'Go on, I bet you can't get past me,' Maggie took three steps back and then ran up, kicking the ball hard, focusing on putting it in the right corner.

Everybody held their breath as Lorna reached up like a coiled spring and saved the ball from going into the net, much to Maggie's disgust. She shook her head and swore under her breath as she went and joined the back of the queue. Lorna rolled the ball back to Hattie, who felt her legs were made of jelly as she placed it firmly on the penalty spot and looked at Tom to blow his whistle.

'Hard luck, Miss Fleming. I know that you usually would have made a goal out of that if it had been in the mill yard,' Joshua Swainbank yelled encouragingly and then watched Hattie, holding his breath.

Hattie stared at Lorna. She was determined to get past the hard-talking woman. If she saved from the right corner before, perhaps she wouldn't expect it at that angle again, or should she go for the left corner? Tom blew his whistle. Hattie took a short run-up to the ball and aimed with all her might, into the same corner as Maggie had. The ball seemed to move in slow motion, and Lorna leaped again, but this time she had judged it wrong and just missed the ball as it hit the string netting of the back of the goal, to the cheers of the rest of the team.

Lorna shook her head and rolled the ball back after bending over and feeling that she had let herself down, as a jubilant Hattie returned to her team with a smile on her face.

'Excellent goal! Well done!' cried Joshua as he jumped up from his bench on the touchline.

Hattie smiled and looked at her boss. He really did enjoy his football, and she was so glad that she had not let her team down. Anne took her place and had a go at scoring, but failed miserably before the next player took their turn.

Penalty kicks were taken for the next hour. Maggie took over the whistle after nailing a few goals herself, as Tom Maley walked over to the bench that Joshua Swainbank was on. She watched as Tom and Joshua shook hands, and then Joshua Swainbank put his hand in the air to signal his departure to them all.

After showing Joshua out, Tom then walked over to Maggie and took the whistle from her and smiled. 'He was pleased with you all. It's been a good day. Aye, I can say it's been a good day and nobody has let me down.' He summoned all the team to gather around him and could tell Maggie was itching to tell him something. However, his news had to come first, he decided, as he looked at all their expectant faces and hoped what he was going to say would make their day.

'I know it's cold and you need to all get changed, but I want to tell you a bit of good news. I sent for Joshua Swainbank to join us today because I needed his support for you, or at least his partial support. After all, we are going to need some money behind us.' Tom stopped and watched his girls look at one another and wonder what he was going to come out with next.

'You will all probably have heard that Hey's Brewery Ladies were going to play Dick Kerr's Ladies on Boxing Day.' Tom looked at Maggie. 'Aye, I saw it, lass, so there's no need to worry.' He took a deep breath. 'You'll notice I said were, because they aren't any longer. Arthur Hey had taken it into his head that they wouldn't be turned down. But Dick Kerr's Ladies already have a game booked. Now, I don't know if you are going to like me for this, but Peter O'Rourke at Valley Parade and I had an informal meeting and we agreed for both our teams to play against one another at Valley Parade on Boxing Day.'

The whole of the team beamed and laughed, and hugged one another. Maggie just stood in delighted shock and looked at Tom, and Anne hugged her as Lorna and Hattie grinned at one another.

'I can't believe you've done that! We are going to be playing Hey's Brewery on Boxing Day. That is absolutely wonderful,' Maggie yelled and nearly wanted to kiss Tom.

'Well, it's not cut and dried yet. Arthur Hey is not that happy. He was wanting to play a team from out of Lancashire, but Peter has tried to convince him that a local derby will be better. Besides, Maggie Fleming, I think you were wanting to also tell me that Hey's team is not that accomplished. They will improve before we play them, so don't take anything for granted.' Tom smiled at Maggie.

'How do you know that I have seen them playing?' Maggie looked aghast.

'Because Peter saw you as you left after hiding in the stands. You need to be more careful. Even he says they're not doing that well at the moment, but he is going to speak to Arthur Hey and ask him not to attend their training sessions, as he interferes and puts his workers off playing.'

'That will not be an easy thing to do. Arthur Hey is always in authority over everything at Bradford City with being a director.' Maggie dropped her head and then lifted it. 'And our boss, Joshua Swainbank, he's not going to be here every training day, is he? He's not going to want to change our team name? We are all proud of being from Yorkshire. I think our name is perfect, despite us all working at Swainbank's. But if we have to change our name to Swainbank's we will have to be satisfied.' Maggie looked around at the group and saw a few of the workers who had worked there for a long time nod their heads.

'No, like I told you earlier, Maggie, I initially sent him a note to thank him for the boots and to see if he wanted to watch you play. However, we have since talked for a while and have had a good chinwag. It turns out he's part Scottish, and his father was a big Celtic fan when it was first formed. We got on so well and he's proud of what you women are doing. In fact, so proud that he has offered to back you once more if there is anything that you desperately need. He's going to be more than useful, especially if you start visiting other clubs for matches.' Tom noticed the look on all his players' faces. Everything had fallen into place for the Yorkshire Ladies, but they were going to have to work for it before their match and keep their skills sharp. Once Peter had got his way and got Arthur Hey to stay away from training, things would be run differently there. The game at Valley Parade would be no pushover, he thought, as he watched the excitement on his team's faces. There was a lot to be done at both clubs, and dedication and skills would have to be crafted quickly.

'Swainbank's Mill? Is that the best we can do? I think I'd rather play Lister's. At least they have the name, even though I don't like them,' Arthur Hey said from behind his desk, with Peter O'Rourke sitting at the other side.

'Their name is The Yorkshire Roses, even though they are all workers from Swainbank's Mill, and perhaps should play under the mill name. Especially as Joshua is taking an interest in them now that they have a team. They practise at Bradford Park Avenue, so it will be a real Bradford derby.' Peter looked at Arthur as he sat back in his chair and weighed up whether the match would suit him or not.

'If they have Tom Maley as their manager, we'll beat them easily. He never does as he's told. He's a right loose cannon. It's a wonder he's still in a job with the FA. It might be a good one to show my team off at. We won't have a seat free, two Bradford teams, and half of them will be coming to watch just for the novelty of it. We'll have to do some promotions, the newspaper and the like. Posters are what we need, and I'll have to come and stir them lasses on, O'Rourke. Shout at them a bit, that's where you are going wrong.' Arthur Hey's mind was running ahead of itself as he sat back and thought about the day. 'Proceeds to a deserving charity, which will bring folk in and do our fighting lads good as well. After all, these women can't expect pay. They are women, for heaven's sake, running around in bloomers.'

'Mr Hey, they could be professional and will be, if I could ask one more thing of you, and that is you leave me to the training. The women see you as their boss to be feared, and are acting reserved when you tell them what to do. Leave them with me for the next month, and then before the match, do come and watch them. I swear you will see a change in them.' Peter had not relished saying it as it was, but it was in the team's interest.

'What are you trying to say to me? That they're frightened of me, man?'

'Just that I'm sure they respect you for giving them employment, but when it comes to football, they need to have clear minds, not be wondering if they will be keeping their jobs the following week if they miss the ball.' Peter watched as Arthur looked darkly at him and then leaned forward so close that he could smell his breath over the desk.

'You can do what you want with them, O'Rourke; but we win that match, do you hear?'

'I hear, and we will try our best.'

23

The weeks were flying by, and work at the mill was becoming busier, while football training grew more intense each Saturday. The team was determined to win and chuckled and laughed when they saw the match advertised in the *Bradford Mercury*. A photographer had come and taken pictures of the team during practice, giving pride of place to Lorna, dressed in her goalie's kit, wearing her knitted hat and her ginger hair hanging loose, giving it the main coverage on the back page. They also mentioned Maggie's cousin, Fred Howell, who used to play for City, to prove the love of football was bred within the team and quoted a few lines about her thoughts on women's football. Ordinary people on the street began to notice them all. Women nudged and smiled, while men nodded and wondered what the women's team would be playing in. Crowds gathered around the open railings of Park Avenue, and Len from the warehouse was asked to go around collecting contributions from the spectators for the Red Cross Hospital funds. He felt quite proud that he was part of a new era in the game of football. Even Bob Briggs seemed to have softened towards Maggie when she said goodnight to him on leaving the warehouse and stepping out into the cold December night air. It was a fortnight before Christmas, and the bell ringers of St Mark's church could be heard practising, the bells ringing out in the crisp winter air as the mill workers made their way home. Maggie looked around for Hattie before starting to walk home alone. She was late leaving work. The warehouse had been busy ensuring the supply of woven cloth to Higher Mill as more uniforms were needed. She walked to the end of the street and noticed a woman standing under the gas street light, and watched as she walked towards her.

'Maggie, I knew if I waited long enough for you, I'd catch you. I can't stay long, my train leaves in an hour.' Maude Fleming, Maggie's mother, gently smiled at her daughter.

'Mother, what are you doing here and at this time of day?' Maggie was taken aback; the last person she had expected to see was her mother.

'I've come into Bradford for a few pieces for Christmas, and I hoped that I'd get to see you. This was the only place I knew you'd be at because you never sent us your address.' Maude looked at her daughter in the street's light and hoped that she was well; she missed her company.

'No, I'm sorry, I needed to make a clean break from Esholt and home. I'm happy here, Mother. Nobody looks twice at me and I've got a good job, so there is no need for you to worry about me.' Maggie smiled at her mother. She looked to have aged, even though she hadn't been that long apart from her daughter. 'How are you both? Father still working at Nanson's? You should both be all right now I've left home. You have only yourselves to feed.'

'Aye, he's still working for his beloved car firm, driving me mad with just sitting there and having nothing to say of the evening. I could do with your coming home. The evenings are long without your company.' Maggie's mother gently touched her arm. 'Will you not come home, not even for Christmas?'

Maggie sighed. 'No, Mother, I'm living with Hattie, and she's without her husband and family. I'm not leaving her on her own. You and Father will be all right on your own. Besides, I'm playing in a football match on Boxing Day at the Bradford City ground.' Maggie shook her head. She had always spent Christmas with her parents, where the day was quiet and where her father complained about almost everything that was put in front of him and her mother got stressed over his comments. She would prefer Christmas with Hattie this year, and besides, her mind would be full of the thoughts of the coming match.

'Football, that's all that you ever have in your head. I should have known. I read the article in the newspaper and wondered if you would be part of the sham. Your parents should come first, never mind anything else,' Maude replied and shook her head.

'Mother, you know I love you, but I need my own life now. Besides, my father will be glad to see the back of me. I always got the feeling he was ashamed of me.' Maggie looked at her mother, who she had never understood .

'No wonder, we both know about your other love in your life, that . . . that Anne. I don't suppose the so-called secret affair has ended. You do realise just how scandalous it is?' Maude had come to ask her daughter to return home. For all her flaws, she missed her, but it was obvious that she had made a new life for herself in Bradford and it left little time for her or her father in her life.

'That's my business. I'm sorry, Mother, but I'll not be coming home. My home is now here in Bradford. I have good friends here.'

'Friends that are all like you, I bet. We are ashamed of you, Maggie Fleming,' her mother couldn't stop herself from saying. Although in her heart she still loved her.

'Then go back to my father and Esholt and leave me be,' Maggie said, and with hurt in her eyes, walked away from her mother, leaving her standing under the gas light. She couldn't alter, and she wouldn't, not for anybody.

'What's up, Maggie?' Hattie stood in front of her quiet friend as she cleared the supper table. 'You have hardly said a word all evening.'

Maggie bowed her head. 'My mother was waiting for me outside work this evening. She came to ask me to go home and have Christmas with them, but I can't. I don't want to. Then, before I knew it, we had broken out into an argument, and things were said between us that both of us will regret. She actually said that they were ashamed of me.'

'Oh, Maggie, she wouldn't mean it. She'd say it in the heat of the moment. I think you should go and have Christmas with your parents. You don't have to worry about me being on my own. It doesn't feel like Christmas with Bruce and Oliver away fighting, anyway,' Hattie gently replied and saw that Maggie was close to tears as she lifted her head.

'No, I'm not going home. This is more like home. You have accepted me for what I am, and I'm living the life I have always dreamed of, even though Anne and I can't be together, because of her interfering mother.' Maggie blew her nose on her handkerchief and smiled. 'They will be singing a different tune when we are a famous football club and everyone is saying our names. Thank you, Hattie, for being my friend. You have changed my life. I promise I will leave when Bruce and Oliver return, I won't be lodging with you for ever.'

'You can stay as long as you need to, Maggie, and we will try to enjoy Christmas together. Anne will be more than welcome to come and join us, but I don't know how we can ask her without her mother being upset,' Hattie replied and wished she could do more.

'It's all right, I always spend an hour or two with her on Christmas Eve, while her mother is in bed.

We should keep it that way,' Maggie whispered and held back the tears.

'Well, perhaps things will change in another few years. I know that both of you are good people who just love one another.' Hattie still couldn't understand the attraction between them both, but she did realise that they loved one another. It was obvious to everyone who saw them together.

'One day, just like we have had to wait for the day football is played by women.' Maggie smiled and squeezed Hattie's hand. 'Thank you for understanding.'

Hattie returned the smile. She didn't fully understand, but she would never say so.

'I've sent Bruce and Oliver their Christmas presents, another pair of socks for them both and some chocolate and ciggies, just something to make them know they are loved and missed. The Post Office is inundated with gifts and presents to be sent to loved ones. I only hope that they receive them in time.' Hattie changed the subject as she washed up. 'Perhaps you could send something to your mother and father. You needn't visit, just something to show that you are sorry for the misunderstanding and to wish them a happy Christmas.'

'It's more than a misunderstanding. I'm not sure they deserve anything, but I'll see,' Maggie moaned. Her heart was hurt. She loved her parents even though they might not love her. She would think about it.

Hattie remembered buying her gifts for Bruce and wrapping them with love and hope for better times, adding a photograph of herself with her love expressed on the back. Perhaps Maggie would feel better if she did that as well.

24

'A training day on Christmas Eve, now that is dedication.' Lorna pulled her goalie's jumper on and shivered. It was cold in the changing room, and she had things to do at home. The busiest day for any woman, and she was playing football in the freezing weather when she should have been keeping an eye on the plum pudding that was gently simmering in a pan of water on the fireside. She only hoped that one of her daughters would keep their eye on it for her. She had left enough instructions to do so.

'Yes, and I'm supposed to be out buying my mother a Christmas present. I only hope she doesn't notice if I go back with mud on my face or knees. It's getting harder to come and play here every day. My Boxing Day excuse is that I'm helping out at the orphanage. I'll never get to heaven,' Anne sighed as everyone stood together before going out onto the still frost-covered pitch.

'Right, ladies, five-a-side today. Don't hold back, play like it is a proper match and mind what you are doing on this rock-hard pitch. We'll play for just an hour, because I know you'll all have better things to do today. Then I'll show you your positions for Boxing Day.' Tom Maley noted the smiles as he said 'just an hour'. There were other things more important than kicking a football about today. There was stuffing and sauces to make, not to mention presents to wrap up. There might be a war on, but people still liked to celebrate Christmas. But a warm-up before the big match was needed.

'Oh, it's bloody freezing. My legs have never felt so cold,' Maggie said as she jogged onto the pitch and took her position as striker with Hattie in attack and Anne in midfield. 'The sooner we get this training match over, the better. My stomach is already churning with the thought of the Boxing Day match. I swear, I'll not eat any of that duck that you've bought. It will be completely wasted,' Maggie said as she jumped up and down and spread her arms and legs out.

'Right, let's see what you are made of. Rosie, you kick off today and choose which end is yours, not that there's anything to be gained in either end.' Tom threw the ball into the centre and watched as Rosie pointed to the goal she was choosing for her side to score in, the one at the top of the field next to the stands, and then placed the ball down in the centre. Tom blew long and hard and watched as his team, which he had spent so much time and energy on, passed the ball to one another with skill and ease. Not quite as fast as his male team did, but they were still good, he thought, as he watched Hattie run rings around Rosie and pass the ball to Maggie, who wasted no time in lining it up to take a shot, booting it with ease past poor Florrie Middleton, who had been put in goal unwillingly. The air was filled with frosted breath and shouts of encouragement as both sides played on and soon got warm despite the cold winter weather. Nobody was watching on the sidelines today. It was too cold, and people were too busy with Christmas preparations to come and watch the latest novelty at Park Avenue. Tom only hoped that they would have more support on Boxing Day as he blew the full-time whistle and watched his team walk off, patting one another on the back and smiling.

'Ladies, go and change and then come and see me in the clubhouse. I have a plan of play for you to study which will show where I think you will be strongest. It won't take long.' Tom walked off and left the team, all hoping that they had managed to keep the shorts and shirts clean enough to play in on Boxing Day. The last thing they wanted was washing hanging around the fire on Christmas Day.

'I already feel sick to my stomach,' Anne said as she pulled on her skirts and buttoned her blouse. 'It's all right for you lot, you can go and play and not have to explain your every movement. My mother's bound to find out. These shorts could really do with a wash, but she'll find them no matter where I dry them.'

'Give them to me and I'll wash them for you. There's only Maggie and me at home. I'll put them on the drying rack and bring them with us on Boxing Day.' Hattie took them off Anne and smiled.

'I could bring them back later tonight when I call around after your mother's gone to bed.' Maggie looked at Anne. 'I thought that I'd come and see Christmas Day in with you. Your mother always goes to bed early, and I'll not make any noise,' she whispered in Anne's ear.

'Oh, could you? What if my mother hears you? I don't know if I dare,' Anne whispered back and gave her a wicked look.

'I'll be quiet, and Hattie won't mind having an hour on her own.' Maggie winked.

'All right, I'll leave the back door open. Mother is usually in bed by ten thirty. She goes a little later on Christmas Eve, though. I'll put the oil lamp in the front window to let you know it's all clear.' Anne looked with love at Maggie. It would be wonderful to have a little time with her on Christmas Eve, with her mother hopefully upstairs fast asleep.

'I'll be there,' Maggie whispered and then turned to talk to Lorna.

'What sort of a Christmas are you going to have without your fella? Have you been able to buy yourselves a goose or some sort of a bird? And presents?' Maggie couldn't help but notice the look on Lorna's face as she pulled her shawl around her and slipped into her clogs.

'Ha! Don't you talk to me about the eejit. He's only back home with us. Came trailing home with his tail between his legs last night, although he's out and about in Bradford now. Probably in some godforsaken pub with his cronies. I told him, I'm not putting up with his comings and goings, and I know what he's all about.' Lorna breathed in and looked fierce. 'He'd better not have anything to say about me playing on Boxing Day, else it will be the worse for him.'

Maggie and Hannah looked at one another. It seemed that Christmas was going to be eventful if nothing else.

The dressing-room door opened.

'Are you all decent? Come on, get a move on. I need to get home as well. My sister and her family are coming to have Christmas with me, and I want everything just right. I haven't seen her for years.' Tom looked at all his team, and knew that everyone wanted to be home with their families. 'I'll only be a second, just come and look at where you are all playing, and then you can be on your way.'

The team gathered around the blackboard, which Tom had drawn all their names on inside the outline of a football pitch.

'This is called the Pyramid, and this is the way both teams will be playing. At least I've found this out from Peter, if nothing else. Five near the opposition's goal, three midfield, two in defence and, Lorna, you in goal. Number 1. Tess, left wing, number 11; Rosie, number 10, inside left; Maggie, centre forward, number 9; inside right for you, Hattie, number

8; right wing, Anne, number 7; left half, Maureen, number 6; centre half, Winnie, number 5; Brenda, right half, number 4. In defence, Pat, number 3, you'd better fell them; and Florrie, number 2, we will be counting on you. Don't let all these positions worry you; it will be pretty flexible, and the referee is a man of my own heart, a Scotsman who manages Shipley United when they are not at war. Just play as you usually do with courage and determination.' Tom stood back and listened to the chatter. They would not let him down; he knew they wouldn't. 'Oh, and ladies, Mr Swainbank and I have a little present for you all before you go home.' Tom pointed to a table with thirteen brand-new football shirts, pairs of shorts and stockings laid out upon it. 'There's your number on the backs of them. There are thirteen shirts, two have no numbers on them, but I thought you all deserved one, even if you are not playing on Boxing Day. One day they will see the sense to have backup players on the bench in case of injuries, but until that day we will have to play with a man down if an accident happens. Or should I say a woman.' Tom smiled as all the women rushed and picked up their brand-new clothes. 'Sorry, Bridget and Molly, next match you will be included.' Tom looked at the two women that he had dropped out of the team, but they weren't quite fit enough.

'Mr Swainbank hopes you don't mind, but on the back of all your shirts, he has had stitched SWAINBANK'S MILL. THE YORKSHIRE ROSES. I must say, they are a lot better than the old shirts that you've been playing in. They are a bonny colour of burgundy that shows up that white rose that's embroidered upon them. They'll have cost Joshua Swainbank a pretty penny.'

'Oh, they are wonderful. We will feel like proper players.' Maggie held her shirt close to her and could nearly have cried.

'Oh, I wish my Bruce and Oliver could see these, they would never believe it.' Hattie grinned.

'Aye, well, Happy Christmas, ladies. Now play like your lives depend on it come Boxing Day. Make sure you thank Joshua Swainbank when he comes to watch you play. He's investing a lot in you all.'

Hattie sat in her favourite chair in the kitchen. The fire was dwindling, and the grandfather clock was striking midnight. It was the first Christmas Eve that she had been on her own, but she felt strangely calm as she thought about Christmas past, when her father had always moaned about the waste of money on just one day. Maggie had brought the smallest, scraggiest tree left on Bradford's main market on her way back home from the practice, and both had decorated it with paper doilies and chains. And now the kitchen smelled of pine. The duck was cooking in the side oven, slow and tender, and would be ready by the morning, for them both to share. But right now, Maggie would be whispering sweet nothings to Anne and hoping not to be caught by her mother. It was a strange life she lived, Hattie thought, and sighed.

Would Father Christmas be calling in at the O'Donnells', or were Lorna's children too old for Saint Nick? At least their father had returned, wanted or not, but all families should be together at Christmas, she thought, as she looked at the two Christmas cards sent from the front line with so much love written in them. A tear ran down her cheek as she thought of the two men she loved most in the world. 'I have a Christmas wish, Father Christmas, and that is to keep Oliver and Bruce safe this Christmas and have them know that I love them. That is all I wish for, if you can do that, please.'

*

In the trenches of the Somme, a strange silence had fallen, and as if from heaven itself, the sound of 'Silent Night' could be heard coming from the German trenches.

Oliver and Bruce looked at one another and their comrades. The Germans were celebrating Christmas with a carol that they knew. Everyone was listening, and despite the cold and the squalor, they started to sing along with their enemy. Smiles appeared on drawn faces for the first time in a long time, as for a second time and a third time it was sung. It ended with a voice shouting, 'Happy Christmas, Tommy.'

'Happy Christmas, Fritz,' Bruce shouted back.

'Football in the morning, Tommy. We play, yah?' came an enquiring German voice.

Bruce looked around at the group of men who were all nodding.

'Tell him yes, just as long as it isn't a trap. I don't know if we should trust them or not,' said one of the more senior officers.

'You'll shoot us, Fritz,' Bruce shouted back.

'Nein, it is Christmas Day, Tommy. We will play football and share schnapps. No guns, Tommy.'

All the men in the trench smiled and nodded their heads.

'A game we will have, Fritz. Just for one day, we will have peace.' Bruce closed his eyes and thought of his loving Hattie. He wished that he were with her instead of the hellhole that he was in. He took the picture of her, that she had sent him, out of his pocket and kissed it. 'Happy Christmas, Hattie. Next year we will celebrate together.'

25

'I hope you like it? It was such a lovely little needlework case, and I don't think you have one.' Maggie smiled at Hattie as she wished her Happy Christmas and exchanged presents.

'Yes, thank you, I love it. And yours? Is your shawl the right colour? I spotted it on the market on my way back from the Post Office,' Hattie said anxiously.

'It's wonderful. Oh, that duck and roast potatoes smell so good. Isn't it lovely to be able to sit down together at dinner time and enjoy the feast of Christmas Dinner? Especially without my father sneering at me and my mother getting all flustered about the cooking, just you and me.' Maggie sat back in her chair and looked at the table laid with cutlery and condiments, and enjoyed the peace.

'I suppose it is, but I'm used to a little rowdiness. Oliver is always playing jokes, and Bruce used to come around with gifts and food. Even my father would give a smile on Christmas Day, a true miracle in itself.' Hattie mused over years past and couldn't help but think about how her family used to celebrate, especially when she was small and her mother was still alive. Her thoughts, however, were with her two menfolk, hundreds of miles away in the trenches, and she wondered what they would be eating for their Christmas dinner as she watched Maggie trying her shawl on.

'Did Anne's mother not catch you last night? You must have been late back. I never heard you come home.'

'No, once she's asleep, she's dead to the world. She takes some sort of sleeping draught to help with her aches and pains. The world could come to an end, and she still wouldn't wake up.' Maggie gazed into space. 'It was nice to have some time together, completely on our own. A lovely Christmas present for both of us.'

Hattie didn't quite know what to say to Maggie, but if she loved Anne as much as she loved Bruce, then she felt sorry that they couldn't be together properly, whether it was right or wrong in people's eyes.

*

Cynthia Birtwistle looked at her daughter, Anne, who sat at the other side of the dinner table. She couldn't keep her thoughts to herself any longer as she noticed Anne smile and touch the brooch that had appeared on her blouse like magic.

'This goose is exceptionally tender this year. I nearly bought a turkey, but I prefer the darker, stronger meat of a goose.' She smiled across at Anne, who didn't reply. 'I heard the back door being closed at around two, when nature called me.' Cynthia quietly laughed. 'I thought it must be Father Christmas leaving us our presents, but being exceptionally noisy with it. Imagine my surprise when I saw in the shadow of the street light a young woman going out of the garden gate, who looked remarkably like the woman whom I know you have feelings for and who I forbade you from seeing.' Cynthia stared across at her daughter and folded her napkin. 'I presume that trinket that is on your blouse is a present from her, seeing as you have done nothing but look at it this dinner time. My slippers have hardly been looked at.'

Anne stopped fingering her brooch and looked with shock at her mother. She didn't know what to say. She and Maggie had been caught.

'I blame your father. His side of the family never

knew what exactly they were, when it came to liking men or women. His aunt Charlotte got taken away, never to be seen again outside the walls of the lunatic asylum. She was the same as you, would rather have a woman servicing her than a man.' Cynthia looked disgusted at Anne and shook her head.

'Mother, it isn't like that. We are just good friends. You aren't thinking of putting me into an asylum, are you?' Anne pushed her dinner plate away and suddenly felt sick.

'Lord, no, but a week in one might do you good, put a bit of sense in your head.' Cynthia shook her head. 'I might if you don't stop lying to me, though. You'll never know how embarrassed I was when I was telling the vicar that you were going to help out at the orphanage tomorrow. Only for him to say how disappointed he would be if you weren't playing in this so-called football match on Manningham Lane.' Cynthia stared at Anne. 'I felt such a fool! And the sewing classes, I suppose you were playing football, not doing anything ladylike at all? That would account for that pile of football shirts that you were sewing and the secret washes out in the backyard that you thought I'd not seen.'

'Sorry, Mother, I did mean to tell you. I thought

you would be so angry with me. After all, you said that you would report us both to the police if Maggie didn't stop calling for me. And when she started a football team at Swainbank's, how could I say no? Father and I used to always go to a match when he was alive.' Anne was near to tears as she looked at the anger on her mother's face.

'That man has a lot to answer for. You are the image of him, sneaking around behind my back. I could be furious with you and not let you out of the house tomorrow.' Cynthia sat back and looked at her daughter's crumpling face. 'Oh, stop it, the vicar has saved your skin. He was singing both teams' praises, in playing for charity. He even said he was going to look forward to seeing you all playing in bloomers. I couldn't believe it, and he is a man of the cloth!'

Anne put her head down and couldn't help but smile as she wiped the tears away. 'He's going to be disappointed. We all have brand-new pairs of shorts and shirts, and stockings, thanks to Joshua Swainbank.'

'It's not like him to put his hand in his pocket. He must think you can all play. I take it this Maggie is in the team, along with other workers. I can't say I'm happy about it, but I understand it is hoped to raise much-needed funds for our brave lads.'

'Yes, it is, and we are playing a ladies' team from Hey's Brewery. We are hoping that they are not that good. And all takings on the day will be given to The Soldiers' Welcome Home Fund,' Anne replied and looked across at her mother, unable to believe that she was taking it all in her stride.

'Never underestimate the enemy, Anne, that's how games are lost. Now, can I get a ticket on the day, and are there seats? I'm not going to stand. After all, my daughter is a player.' Cynthia tried to keep her face straight as her daughter walked around and hugged her.

'Thank you, Mother. This has made my Christmas. I hate lying to you. I'll make sure that you get a good seat near the halfway line. Sorry if I make you worry,' Anne whispered as she kissed her mother.

'Yes, well, I'm not going to change you know, am I? This Maggie, whom I really don't care for, had better come and visit at a decent hour. Perhaps on a Sunday, when I will partake in having tea with a friend. That would be better for you both than sneaking around in the witching hours. All I ask is that you behave yourselves in public. We have our reputations to protect.' Cynthia looked down at her dinner plate. 'Now, let's eat up, else the plum pudding will be boiling dry, and it costs far too much to have it spoil.'

Anne felt as if a weight had been lifted from her shoulders. Tomorrow, she would give everything she had to give without the threat of her mother's wrath; and Maggie was free to visit! What a Christmas present!

26

The day was crisp and dry, and the ground at Valley Parade looked green and fresh as the linesmen and referee walked around the pitch before both teams played, and the crowds gathered excitedly outside the gates.

'Well, this is a first, a load of women running around half-dressed thinking they can play football,' one of the linesmen said with a grin.

'You'll treat them with respect, lad, like you would any other players. I know the Swainbank team will have worked hard to get here,' Jock McIntyre, the referee for the day, replied as he walked the length of the pitch and inspected it for play.

'I didn't mean anything wrong. I just think football's a man's game. Women aren't built for it,' the linesman replied.

'You've been reading too much rubbish from the critics in the papers. I'm sure they'll prove to you today that they are just as competent as any man. Them out there behind the gates must think so, else they wouldn't be lining up to get in and watch. There must be over a thousand folk queuing up to see them, nearly as much as a Bradford City home match, and every penny going to charity. These women are to be applauded,' Jock replied and looked towards the benches at Arthur Hey, Peter O'Rourke and Tom Maley, giving a thumbs up for the match to proceed. Peter O'Rourke looked up to the men on the gates and gave them the signal to open them and let the crowds into the ground. All three men looked at one another as folk from all of society came and bustled their way into the stands and seats. Everyone wrapped up against the cold and wondering what sort of match they were about to watch and just how daringly the women would be dressed.

'Right, may the best women win,' Tom Maley said and shook Peter's hand as he walked down onto the pitch and stood outside the entrance to The Yorkshire Roses' changing room. He didn't know who was going to win, but he would have liked to have placed a bet on his team.

'Oh, Lord, I feel sick,' said Anne. 'Look at the people out there and listen to the noise, and to make things worse, my mother is sitting next to Joshua Swainbank. She must have wormed her way into one of the best seats. She shouldn't be sitting there at all.'

'Don't you worry, Anne, she will be all right there. He must have been told that she is your mother. You must feel relieved that there's no more sneaking about between us, although I'll still be dreading meeting her.' Maggie tied her boots and looked at the metal spikes on the bottom of them. They were lethal if you scraped your leg by accident with them, and she hoped that Hey's team would not resort to dirty tactics.

'My old fella is here and my two lasses.' Lorna smiled as she pulled her knitted hat over her hair. 'We've had a right good Christmas, to my surprise. He's hardly drunk. He's a different man when sober.'

Hattie looked around at the team and caught her breath. The big day was here, now they had to prove a point, she thought, as she shrugged her shoulders and tried to relax. Not only was it match day, but somewhere in Bradford, her father was getting married to his new bride and, in honesty, it hurt when she thought about it. She buried her feelings and looked at the team. Maggie was a good captain, Lorna could catch anything that came her way, and they all knew their roles and where they were best at playing. The horde of supporters on Manningham Lane as she and Maggie had walked together to the club had made her jittery. There were even metal badges with Hey's Brewery Ladies and Yorkshire Roses being sold outside the ground by the pedlars. It would seem everybody in Bradford knew about the match. If Anne had wanted to keep it from her mother, she would have had no chance.

The sound of the crowd singing 'Pack Up Your Troubles in Your Old Kit Bag' reverberated around the ground, and the women looked at one another as Tom put his head around the door and nodded.

'Are you ready, ladies? Listen, they are waiting for you. Keep your heads, take control from the start and remember you are better than Hey's any day.' Tom opened the door of the dressing room at the same time as Peter O'Rourke, who led his team out across the other side of the pitch.

The crowd erupted and whistles could be heard and then constant clapping until both teams stood in their positions, all eyeing one another over and wondering how each other played once on the field. Maggie stood in the centre and shook the captain of Hey's Brewery's hand as the referee flipped a coin and asked Hey's heads or tails?

'Heads,' the tall, thin, dark-haired woman said and smiled when the coin landed in her favour, enabling them to take the kick-off.

Jock patted both captains on the back. 'Let's have a good game, ladies, no fouling, biting or kicking when a man is down.'

Then, in the blink of an eye, they were off. Hey's captain passed to her left half, and Anne intercepted it, running and dribbling the ball with all her might, ready to pass to Maggie or Hattie. But a leg came out from Hey's defence, and she tripped, landing face down on the field, while the ball was still kept in play, and the crowd surged as Hey's captain and main striker ran towards Lorna and the goal.

'No, you don't, you bitch.' Lorna stood and watched like a hawk as the striker weighed up which was her weakest side and then kicked the ball hard and straight at her.

'You'll not get goals doing that, not with me. You eejit,' Lorna shouted and then kicked the ball as far as she could back down to the other end of the pitch. 'Rosie, where were you? Guard her and tackle her,' Lorna shouted above the crowd, her cheeks nearly as red as her hair, as she concentrated on watching where the ball was going. Anne had picked herself up from off the ground, and she pushed the woman who had tripped her. 'We can play that way or we can play decent,' she said to the blonde-haired, angelic-faced woman, who looked like butter wouldn't melt in her mouth. She just shrugged her shoulders and jostled her as Maggie came running towards them, dribbling and controlling the ball.

'Over there, Hattie, then pass it back to me,' Maggie shouted, as she passed the ball a few feet in front of Hattie, who caught it, steadied herself and then passed to Maggie, who had found a gap in front of the opposing team's goal, and then, with the quickness of a striking snake, lifted her left foot and slammed the ball into the back of the net.

The crowd went mad, and cheers echoed around the ground in excitement. Maggie put her head down and just smiled. She had been born to do this, she thought, as her teammates patted her on the back and the scoreboard went up to 1–0 in favour of The Yorkshire Roses.

At half-time, it was still 1–0 to The Yorkshire Roses. Both teams of ladies were exhausted. The Yorkshire Ladies had never played so hard in their lives, their shirts were wet with sweat, and as they got instructions from Tom, they just wished they could get on with it and go to the warmth and comfort of their homes. But at the same time, their pulses were pounding, they were beating Hey's Brewery and the crowds were yelling for more.

'Listen to them, they are backing every one of you. Those cheers are for you, ladies. Now, Rosie, be a bit tighter on defence. Maureen, watch that blonde-haired player, number 5; she's a devil for tackling dirty. Maggie, Hattie, another one of those in the second half and we are smiling. And for God's sake, Lorna, stop your swearing, especially if you talk to the men from the newspapers after the match.'

'They deserve all the swearing they are getting from me. Their defence plays dirty,' Lorna replied, bending down and saying under her breath that she was fecked.

'Right, come on, let's get back out there.' Tom clapped his hands and urged his team back out. He knew they were tired, that the second half would tell on them, that ninety minutes on a full-length pitch was asking a lot of them.

'Aye, let's show the feckers,' Lorna shouted and grinned as she noticed the reporter from the *Bradford Mercury*.

*

Peter O'Rourke stood on the other side of the ground and watched as his team played to the best of their ability. Tom's team was more organised, whereas Arthur Hey had encouraged his team to turn to dirty tactics if they had to. It wasn't about the sport; it was about winning, in Arthur's eyes. He watched as Jean Munroe, number 5, tackled her opposite number, the spikes on her boots running down the side of her opponent's leg, making her pull up and wince with pain. That was not to be proud of, Peter thought, as he watched Maggie fight for the ball. Now, if he only had her in Hey's team, she was the best player on the pitch. Peter stood up in excitement as his team's best striker won the ball from Maggie and went chasing up the field. Nobody could catch her. Legs were heavy, bodies were moving slowly as Trudy Fletcher hesitated for a moment outside the goal box and, with a steady eye fixed, aimed her kick at the left-hand corner of the net.

Lorna stretched as far as she could, her woollen hat falling off her head as she caught it on the goal post. She felt like she was in slow motion as the ball slipped past her hands and went into the back of the net. A wave of despair came over her. She'd let her team down, she thought, as she saw some of her team members shake their heads while Hey's Ladies celebrated along with the crowd. She picked her hat up and put it back on, and watched as the scoreboard showed 1–1 and the referee looked at his pocket watch to see how much time was left to play.

Jock signalled to Tom and Peter that there were another ten minutes of play left as he blew his whistle and watched both teams battle it out in front of him.

Hattie looked at the usually lethal Jean Munroe, who had lost control of the ball as she tried to show off skills that she didn't possess, and knew it was her time. She found an extra spurt of energy, looked for Maggie to pass to, but couldn't see her. She weaved past one defender, then another, and then patted the ball between her feet, running rings around the remaining defender, looked at the goal and took a chance! She closed her eyes, hardly daring to look as the ball just skimmed under the bar, making the goalie fall to her knees.

Hattie did the same. She had scored a goal for her team, and every bone in her body ached, but hopefully that would be the winning goal.

Joshua Swainbank leaped from his seat and shouted with joy as the final whistle blew. His team had won, and he had players to be proud of, as Arthur Hey graciously approached and shook his hand, acknowledging that his had been beaten by the better team.

'There are three players that I wouldn't mind having in my team, if we ever get to the point where we can swap or even buy,' Arthur said as he patted his shoulder. 'Those two that scored and the blonde-haired one that's being hugged now.'

Arthur, Joshua and Anne's mother looked at the celebrating team as they hugged one another, Maggie and Anne embracing before turning to wave at the horde of fans cheering them.

Lorna blew a kiss to her husband up in the crowd and gasped as she realised that he was dressed in uniform. He had joined up! Then she waved at her children. Maggie and Hattie shook their heads.

'Oh, he might be an eejit, but I must love him.' Lorna grinned as she put her arms around her best friends and felt her heart could burst.

'Aye, and my mother being here watching, this game is changing everything,' Anne said as they gave a final wave to the crowd and went into the changing room to get warm and celebrate.

Joshua Swainbank turned and replied to Arthur Hey. 'Sorry, they work for me and are loyal to the team they play for. I don't think even if you paid them they would leave.' Joshua smiled down at Cynthia. 'Isn't that right, Mrs Birtwistle? Your Anne is a loyal soul.'

'She is indeed, and I'm proud that she's my daughter even though she has been telling me for weeks that she's been going to a sewing club when it's been football she's been playing,' Cynthia said with pride and smiled as she saw Maggie look across at her. She would have to turn a blind eye to her daughter's loves. All she wanted was for Anne to be happy; life was too short.

'We did it, we blinking well did it. We've won our first match!' Maggie shouted and laughed. 'They might have played a few dirty tricks, but we won!' The noise in their changing hut was so loud it could be heard in the opposition's, making Hey's women bow their heads and feel defeated. They had tried their best, but Arthur Hey wouldn't think so.

Tom leaned on the changing-room door and smiled. 'Aye, you've won lasses. Well done, and I can tell you that today's game has raised over £300 for The Soldiers' Welcome Home Fund. The newspapers are going to be covered with you lasses. They want a photograph before you all change. Come on, line up on the seats and smile for the camera.' Tom watched as his women's team filed out and posed for the many cameras. They beamed and laughed. They had won their first game and were pioneers in the field of football.

The changing room was quiet. Everyone had gone home except Maggie and Hattie, who were tidying the Yorkshire Ladies' Football Club colours away.

They sat together on the bench and looked around them at the dirty shirts and shorts, which they had volunteered to take home and wash in the excitement of winning the match.

Hattie's face was flushed, not just from winning but from the look she had seen on Joshua Swainbank's face as he had shaken her hand. Maggie perhaps had been right in her observations.

'Well, we've done it, Hattie. We have bloody well done it! Did you see Joshua Swainbank's face? I swear he was wondering if he dared kiss you.' Maggie leaned back and drew a deep breath.

'Yes, we have done it.' Hattie smiled and felt warm and content. 'I'll write to my Bruce and tell him. He will have missed his Boxing Day match.' She smiled. She had indeed noticed the look on Joshua Swainbank's face and had seen him hesitate before congratulating her. But he was a gentleman and she was married and very much in love with her husband.

'Don't talk so silly, Joshua Swainbank was the same with everyone. He's even offered to buy all our players a drink at The Diplomat on Friday night after work, which is good of him.'

'Aye, it is. We will be famous before we know it.' Maggie grinned.

Both knew it was the start of something big, and the small derby match would just be the beginning for the Yorkshire Ladies' Football Club. Football was back. It was a reawakening of women's football after a brief spell that came to nothing. This time, they were more prepared and meant business in order to support their men at war.

The First Goal: A brief story about the start of the Football Association and Women's Football

Autumn 1863

Ebenezer Morley folded his arms and looked around at his fellow like-minded men sitting around the table at The Freemasons' Tavern, which stood at 61–65 Great Queen Street in the middle of London's Freemason District. It was the first meeting of what would become the Football Association. He had just been voted in as the secretary to the new association, and he felt proud of his position as he faced the representatives of various football teams that had evolved out of public school sports and were now proving to be popular.

'We need rules and organisation, no more

hacking,' he said to the members of the ten football clubs that sat around the table. 'It becomes a brutal game when it gets to the point where people make every attempt to break another man's legs or do as much damage to their shins as possible. It isn't then a game, it's a battle.' Ebenezer shook his head and looked at his colleagues.

Francis Campbell, a well-to-do man, but ruthless in business and in sport, from Blackheath FC, shook his head.

'It's the hacking that makes the game. It is what masculine toughness and true football mean. My club will take no further part in this discussion. You are going to ruin the game of football as played on the public fields.' And saying that, he rose and left the table, much to everybody else's dismay.

'If that is how you feel, Francis, then you indeed leave, and we will continue to discuss the new rules we have in mind.' Ebenezer looked at the man who had been to a good public school, as opposed to some of his other colleagues who had been brought up with a good education, but had not had the same experiences as the ex-public school boy who stood in front of him. Campbell had no idea how the other half lived and that the working classes had embraced the game of football. He saw the remaining members shake their heads. They knew they were up against it in their attempts to put rules to the game, especially where public schools had their say.

'Never mind, gentlemen, we will continue with our discussions over values for the game and hope that other teams will realise that our desire to put rules in place will enhance the game. I'll be calling another meeting next week, so let's use this time to think and see what can be done to make the game a little more civilised.'

Ebenezer Morley felt deflated but was not about to give in. He was determined to work hard in his quest to change football's rules and by the spring of 1867 he had the backing and the strength of the northern mill towns behind him, with working-class men playing for their towns with pride, and soon becoming local celebrities. They were playing games all over England, while Ebenezer watched with pride at his achievement.

Nettie Honeyball, a strong-minded woman with a strong Yorkshire accent and whose past was virtually unknown, but who had influence in high places, was holding court in her office. She was a determined woman, a staunch supporter of women having more rights and not being owned by the men in their lives. Her good friend Lady Florence Dixie sat across from her and smiled as a reporter sat and read an article that had been drafted by both women with a request that he print it in his paper.

> A LADIES' FOOTBALL CLUB
>
> Several sturdy young ladies have recently banded themselves together for the purpose of building a football club exclusively for the fairer sex. One of the leading spirits of this new and unexpected venture is Lady Florence Dixie, who is president of the club, but as her ladyship does not contemplate competing . . . Active participation in the game will be represented by Miss Nettie Honeyball, the originator and the secretary, who does play. Please contact the *Westminster Gazette* for further particulars.

Nettie smiled a smile that she knew the reporter could not ignore. She had already replied to the reporter's concerns, stating the game would be played, as it was by the men, in sixty minutes and to the FA rules and that they hoped to play some weaker men's teams shortly. The young reporter looked at her with disbelief at the idea of women playing men in the rough game of football.

'Miss Honeyball, with no disrespect to the fairer sex, I'd be interested to know if you will be taking any precautions to protect yourselves from hard knocks and tumbles?' the reporter asked candidly.

Nettie scowled and replied, 'No, why should we, young man? We used to wear heeled pointed boots, but these have now been abandoned, and we wear proper football boots with corrugated padding in the toes and heels. We wear ankle pads, shin pads and blue knickerbockers. We also wear a knitted cap to protect our hair, which is held in place by hairpins.' Nettie looked at the young man and smirked. 'We are not as delicate as you men would like to think, perhaps?'

'And are the club and supporters growing?' the reporter asked as he wrote down her reply, hoping to add to the advertisement for players. He was also quite unable to believe the outspoken Miss Honeyball and the mention of knickerbockers.

'We have twenty-two members, the oldest woman being twenty-eight and the youngest fourteen, and most are from the middle classes. There are also four or five married ladies,' Nettie said and looked at the disgust on the reporter's face.

'Do their husbands not complain? Surely they should not be allowed?' the reporter replied and sat open-mouthed at the forthright woman who he seemed to think had no morals.

'Surely, sir, women have the right to play football just as any man? We are homely girls, not too la-di-da, and we play our game with spirit. We allow charging, but no insulting words will ever pass our lips. Now, my dear sir, do place the article and the ad in the *Gazette* and please stop looking at me as if I have two heads. You will see my girls will be just as popular as the men are, mark my words.' Nettie stood up and dismissed the young reporter by opening her office door and showing him his way back to the busy London street. She stopped in her tracks for a short moment, scowling at the departing reporter.

He turned before leaving. 'I sincerely hope that you are successful, Miss Honeyball, but I can't see women playing the game ever being popular; even the men's teams struggle sometimes. Good evening, Miss Honeyball. It will be published in tomorrow's edition of the *Gazette*.

Nettie closed the door behind him and leaned against it. She would eventually have a first-class team of women players. 'I will have a team of women and we will play better than any man,' she said and clenched her fists in determination and went back to discuss the interview with Lady Dixie.

'Don't worry, my dear. Unbeknownst to the man from the press, we have persuaded plenty of people in the right places. Let's face it, we have the Tottenham Hotspur centre-half J. W. Julian to be their coach, and not only that, they had contacted Charles Alcock, a member of the Football Association, to apply for them to play their first game at The Oval, home of the Surrey County Cricket Club. I'd say we are well organised.' Lady Dixie sat back and sipped her tea gracefully.

'Yes, you are right. It is only a matter of time before we do get our first game and are taken seriously,' Nettie replied and watched as Lady Dixie reached for her cloak to leave. After she had left she would write more determined letters to all the mainstream press, inviting them to show interest in the club's activities, hoping that not all of them would ridicule her.

A fortnight later, Charles Alcock looked at Nettie with bad news.

'You can play at Crouch End's field. You can be the opening match before Crouch End and the 3rd Grenadier Guards on 23 March. The Board of Surrey County Cricket has washed their hands of you. They are not quite ready for women running around in knickerbockers at their ground,' Charles Alcock said and sniggered as he sat back in his chair in the room that Nettie called her office. 'That's the best I can do for you.'

'That's not good enough,' Nettie replied and stared at Charles. 'Can you do no better?' She would have liked to have wiped the smirk from his face.

'I can't do any better. Before you know it, you women will be wanting the vote, and then where will we be? I ask you, women playing football, we will be the laughing stock of the world, it's unbelievable. The world is not yet ready for women football players, Nettie.' Charles shrugged and looked at the young, wiry woman with strength of character that he had never seen in a woman before.

Nettie sighed but looked determined. 'Then, Crouch End it will be, Charles. My girls will not be worried about where we play, just as long as we can show our skills and prove that we are as good as any man. I must admit I'm a little disappointed. I had set my heart on The Oval, but Crouch End will do. I have made us all new costumes, a shirt of dark and light blue, or one of red and white, depending on which team my girls are playing for. The knickerbockers I've made of blue serge are tied up at the waist, with an elastic band, and we all have black ribbed stockings. We will look the part and we will play the part.' Nettie finished her speech as she looked at Charles with a hint of discontent. 'Could we not play one of the men's teams, Charles? Would they not even think of letting us do that?'

'No, Nettie, I have really pushed my luck to have got you your first public game at Crouch End. Now be content with that.' Charles held his hat in his hands and looked down at the rug on the wooden floor. Neither Lady Dixie nor Nettie Honeyball realised just how much their women's team of footballers were being ridiculed by the FA. There would be crowds there to witness the first women's football match, but only to laugh at them. Women in knickerbockers would be a novelty for the men and an embarrassment for some women. How little she knew of the real world, he thought, as she stared at him with a look that made him know his place in the eyes of Nettie Honeyball without a doubt.

'Very well, we will make the best of it and put on a good show. It will not be our last or only one. We will be setting a trend, Mr Alcock, you mark my words,' Nettie replied, knowing that her girls would put on a good show, play fair and hard and look more professional than any male player.

It was Saturday afternoon at Nightingale Lane End Ground at Crouch End. Nettie stood with her two teams of defiant women, ready to show the crowds that women could play football, no matter what was said or thought of them. They had certainly drawn the crowds with cabs, carriages and other vehicles bringing people to watch the first British Ladies' Football team play. Nettie, for once in her life, felt quite faint as she realised that there were near enough ten thousand people gathered to watch her and her team.

The crowds shouted abuse and cheers as the women's teams ran out onto the pitch. Everyone scrutinised the women players, especially young Daisy Allen, who looked remarkably like a boy, or so the crowds thought as they watched her run and dribble the ball.

It was only a matter of minutes into the game

when despair came over both sides. The ball was smaller than usual, and even the strongest of the women could only kick it a matter of a few yards. But still Nettie persisted and encouraged her teams on. Passes were missed, legs ached, and the knickerbockers' elastic worked its way loose.

Referee Mr C. Squires looked as if he wished he had never volunteered to referee the match, as time and time again the rules had to be explained to the novices. The game was a disaster.

With just one goal scored between both the women's teams, Nettie came off the pitch with her head still held high. They had played their first game and brought in the crowds, which was what mattered. They would get better with every match played, regardless of the shouts and comments being made by the crowd and reporters. However, there was one worry that she could not escape as she hurried Daisy Allen, who had scored the only goal in the match, to the changing rooms. She had to hide Daisy from the press, and leave the press to their own conclusions. She was not going to admit or deny anything. She also worried that if anybody looked into her own past, they would realise that her name was not Nettie Honeyball at all and it was fictitious. In fact, she was starting to rue the day when she had even thought about women's football. Her real name was Phoebe Wainwright, and along with her brother Alfred, it had started as a ruse. She sighed and put on a brave face while thinking of her next move. She would gather her ladies together to tour the grounds that had hosted them, and then hand the reins over to another who was also devoted to making the women's game as good as the men's. After all, she was promised to be married. It was perhaps time for her to disappear and lead a normal, respectful life, up north. However, she had proved her point that women could and would play football.

On a station platform, with nothing to read,
and a four-hour train journey stretching ahead of him...

That's where the story began for Penguin founder Allen Lane. With only 'shabby reprints of shoddy novels' on offer, he resolved to make better books for readers everywhere.

By the time his train pulled into London, the idea was formed. He would bring the best writing, in stylish and affordable formats, to everyone. His books would be sold in bookstores, stationers and tobacconists, for no more than the price of a ten-pack of cigarettes.

And on every book would be a Penguin, a bird with a certain 'dignified flippancy', and a friendly invitation to anyone who wished to spend their time reading.

In 1935, the first ten Penguin paperbacks were published. Just a year later, three million Penguins had made their way onto our shelves.

Reading was changed forever.

—

A lot has changed since 1935, including Penguin, but in the most important ways we're still the same. We still believe that books and reading are for everyone. And we still believe that whether you're seeking an afternoon's escape, a vigorous debate or a soothing bedtime story, all possibilities open with a book.

Whoever you are, whatever you're looking for,
you can find it with Penguin.